Touch of Music

by Dorothy Clarke

New Victoria Publishers Inc.

Published by New Victoria Publishers Inc., a feminist literary and cultural organizaton, P.O. Box 27 Norwich, Vermont.

ACKNOWLEDGEMENTS: My love and thanks to Valarie, Penny, Chantal, the Xantippe Women, Roderick F. Blom, Phd. Thank you Susie for Northampton. My love and thank you for your vote, ReBecca. And thank you Maria José for your patient ear—these lines are for you: For ten years my heart lay still; then it met you. Perhaps in another life, yours will meet mine too.

Library of Congress Cataloging-in-Publication Data

Clarke, Dorothy, 1953-
    Touch of music / by Dorothy Clarke.
        p.   cm.
    ISBN 0-934678-31-6 : $8.95
    I. Title.
PR9130.9.C48T68   1991
823'.914--dc20   90-24052
                                                       CIP

Printed on recycled paper

To Mieke Hemmekam;
you were always there when I needed you.

To my brother Michael who has always believed in me.

Chapter 1

Tossing back her jet black hair, Roxanna jammed on the brakes of her stalwart, but over-heating Chevy. She was lost in heavy traffic—utterly lost. The long highway had been easy, but this city driving was a nightmare. There was Zoe's map, of course, and her own vague recollections of the place.

Roxanna had been born here, in this overdeveloped town of Straker thirty-four years ago. She recognized some familiar sights remembered from photographs her mother (who had never really forgiven her husband for dragging the family away) always carried around with her. But all those dog-eared photographs had been of the old part of town.

The color rose to her cheeks in frustration. Straker had grown too much in the last twenty or so years. Zoe's crudely drawn map, meant to guide her through the new parts of town, looked like the hidden paths to the wrong side of the moon.

A week before she had left Colorado for sunny California, she had been on the phone with Zoe who had advised her: "Don't get a map at a gas station, you'll only get lost. Use the one I sent you."

And she had. Zoe had said, "You'll have to find Atlas Crossing, as long as you find Atlas Crossing...." And she had. Only, nobody better ask her how.

After she had found it, she had began a series of lefts and rights, ups and downs, and once again left and right. *Then you will notice*, said Zoe's scribble, *that everything will be greener, perhaps greener than Van Buren Street, which, after you turn right....*

Now Roxanna realized the hopelessness of both the scribbles, and the map. What on earth was she doing on a boulevard all of a sudden? Lined with—why for Godsake hadn't Zoe mentioned palm trees? Or a boulevard for that matter? Roxanna's tired

1

hands gripped the steering wheel, and then suddenly her left hand banged down on the turn signal. She was going to park the minute she found a place.

As if she smelled the palm trees, Melissa, her six year old daughter, woke up, sat up weakly from the back seat made cozy with a sleeping bag and blankets, to look at these strange, tall trees topped with a crown of torn fans. Melissa had never seen palm trees before.

Roxanna parked, deciding not to let the difficult beginning of this new life venture work on her nerves any more than it already was doing. But she had wanted to be at Van Buren Street before Melissa really woke up.

She turned, leaned with forearm and chin on the back of the seat and tried to hide her annoyance. "Hi, honey," she said, sighing. "How'd you sleep? Is your tummy okay?"

"Mommy, it smells funny." Melissa crawled halfway out the window. Roxanna's left arm shot out to keep Melissa from falling out. "Melissa, get back in here." She couldn't help but grin. The kid couldn't be that sick if her curiosity was going full tilt. "Listen, why don't you check all this out—stay in the car. I'm going to ask somebody where the hell we are. Okay? How're you feeling?"

"Hungry, I'm tired." Melissa sank back into the back seat and sighed.

Roxanna reached out, tapped Melissa's knee. "I'm not going far. Just out the door to stop the first person who walks by. You wanna know something?"

"What?"

"I'm tired too." Roxanna ripped off a banana from the cluster of four beside her on the front seat and held it out to Melissa.

"Nah, I don't want a banana," Melissa muttered, ill-tempered suddenly. "When're we going to get there?"

"I thought you said you were hungry, baby. If you change your mind about the banana...." Roxanna dropped it near Melissa's pillow. She opened the car door. "Be right back."

"Where are you going?" Melissa blurted, panic in her voice.

"I just told you—out the door." She left the car hurriedly and looked up and down the wide, empty sidewalk. I am going to kill Zoe Breckner the minute I see her, she thought. I can take get-

2

ting hopelessly lost, but not with Melissa this worn out. Here you have the most gorgeous climate and everybody's inside glued to the air-conditioning, or else out of contact in their cars. It wasn't that she had never heard of Van Buren Street before. It was simply impossible to find it after all the rearrangements in Straker. She remembered the boulevard, but these hotels? Standing like sentries on the other side, chic buildings rose out of well-tended greenery, their balconies hidden behind arches keeping the harsh sunlight out. I'll say they are beautiful buildings the minute I get us out of here. But where are the guests? Someone ought to be out on the terraces.

A swishing, grating sound caught her attention and she looked along the pavement where, to her relief, a young man on roller-skates was approaching. She waved him to a stop, flapping the map at him, and after a short study of it, he told her where she was, and how to find Van Buren Street.

It took her a few more wrong turns, all in unforgiving traffic, and waving down two other people before she *finally* saw the blue-on-white Van Buren Street sign gleefully displaying itself. By that time Melissa was asleep again.

Good Goddess—were the houses here really this big and fancy? When Zoe had said 'a really nice house,' how could Roxanna have imagined mansion? One doesn't live in mansions if one is an editor of a feminist periodical. No way—unless of course, one is Zoe. Only Zoe could have the connections.

Now what number was that one—that ostentatious brownstone? She actually heard Zoe's scream of delight, (or was it relief?) before she saw her dancing in the middle of the broad, sunscorched street like an ant on a heating-pad.

Zoe's scream brought her son, Bobby, and her lover, Joan, out of the house to her aid as though she were in mortal danger. Zoe waved the car to the driveway, and as the car died, Zoe opened the driver's door and was embracing Roxanna, who was still trying to get her backside unstuck from the vinyl seat. As a joyful Zoe took her off dancing, right there in the middle of Van Buren Street, thoughts of homicide left Roxanna. They chatted about the last time they had seen each other three years before, was it that long ago? —at that conference, what was it called? *Let The Women Go* or something.

3

Then Zoe proudly introduced Joan; the tall, lanky woman was a complete surprise to Roxanna. Zoe had never, ever written or said in her phone calls that Joan was a beautiful Latina. (In truth, Roxanna had always envisioned her as a California blond.)

And then there was Bobby, a Zoe duplicate with chestnut-colored hair hanging in his eyes, still a bit chubby with baby-fat; he was initially shy, but a little person in his own right already. He peered into the back seat, wanting Melissa awake and admiring his toys, but she was a girl, so he wondered if was she really going to appreciate his transformer.

"How did she hold up on the trip out?" Zoe whispered, opening the back door. "God, but she looks like you, Rox!"

"Yeech, look at the banana." Bobby made a face. "Gross. It's all black."

"She doesn't complain, but she just has no stamina. And when she sleeps like this—Zoe, I've got to put her to...."

"I know. Everything's ready upstairs. Need any help?"

Roxanna strained over the back seat, lifting her frail, rag doll of a daughter into her arms. "Bring that blue bag. Can the car stay here for a while?"

Joan said, "I'll see if I can get it into the garage, okay?"

Roxanna followed Zoe down a gravel path, bordered by an assortment of blooming flowers. They entered the house by a side door into a hall, walked briskly on though a wide living room, and went up an imposing stairway with deep off-white carpeting. Reaching the airy landing of the next floor, they stepped directly into a small suite where Zoe pointed to yet another door. "In there. The window is open because this part of the house has been shut for some time. Want me to close it?"

"Just a little." Roxanna placed Melissa gently on the bed, pulled out the sheet from under the limp body and covered her. Blowing wispy dark hair off the pale face, Roxanna rose stiffly, a kink in her lower back. "She'll sleep on for a while." She kept her voice at a low level. "You wouldn't happen to have a cold, cold beer for a very weary driver, would you?"

"Sure. Let's go downstairs and relax. Joan said she'll fix an early dinner. How's that?"

"Fine with me. What about your errant landlady. Is she

4

around?" Roxanna left the bedroom door ajar and followed Zoe back the way they came.

"Remember I told you she was going on tour? Well, she's not back yet. She still has performances to do in the Bay Area and at a music festival." They were clattering down the steps, and at the bottom Zoe pointed Roxanna into the living room. "Or would you prefer going out on the porch?"

"If there's air out there, yes."

"Through the sliding doors. I'll go get your beer."

Roxanna sat down in an iron garden chair, one of four around a wide garden table with a closed sun umbrella jutting into the air. Her eyes swept the thirsty back garden—crisp, leafless bushes crouched in the middle of a surprisingly green hedge which crawled along the fence, almost hiding it. There was grass, freshly green in the shade of the hedge, yellowish, dead beyond the shade, bordering the red concrete porch which held at least three basketballs and a battered, blue Schwinn bike.

Presently Zoe joined her. As she greedily sucked at the beer Zoe handed her, the weariness which had settled into prickles behind her eyeballs, began to lift. The cold liquid hit her overworked brain and her empty, dried-up stomach like a bomb. But already she began to feel a bit like her old self—could relax—let the exhaustion flow through her body. Behind her, she heard voices coming out of the kitchen; pots and pans rattled, glassware clinked. Joan was instructing Bobby where and how to put things. "It sure has changed around here," Roxanna said. I mean, Straker. Gone all touristy. I expected development but...."

"That's a part of Straker we don't notice much, the beach is a bit away from here. Mercifully."

"Yes, Van Buren Street is quite the hideaway. How did your landlady come by this anyway? How did you come by it? I mean, does she leave it to you often?"

"We're the solid tenants, yes." Zoe nodded. "Always here when she leaves, always here when she comes back."

"She leaves everything in your hands?"

"Yes and no. She has three brothers to contact should there be an emergency—it still is a family homestead. But all is going smoothly. And quietly."

"What did she say about Melissa? I know you wrote me

everything was all right, but tell me—how did she react?" Roxanna tried to ask this casually but inside she was anxious.

"About Melissa?"

"Yes, about her being...sick and everything. It didn't bother her?"

Zoe finished her beer and crumpled the can between strong, able fingers, then let it clatter on the table. "Your stalling didn't help, you know," Zoe said accusingly.

Roxanna lifted her left eyebrow, a sign Zoe knew well, so Zoe clarified. "About what ailed Melissa."

"Jeez, Zoe, I had to get used to the idea that I might lose my daughter. Then I get your job offer. I refused at least twice, and you wanted to know why, so I told you why. I mean how did I know, really know, you'd still want to offer it to me, knowing I'd be terribly preoccupied?"

"Okay, okay." Zoe held out a hand. "I got your letter about your accepting the job and coming, two days before Rebecca left on tour. It takes a while for her to react to a summons for a house meeting, it took her two days to show up, half an hour before she was leaving."

"Oh, great, Zoe. What did she say about Melissa?"

"Hold it a sec. It gets better. As long as she doesn't have to burp Melissa, she is welcome. She also doesn't want to baby-sit her. But she's glad the apartment is rented—helps take care of the taxes, see. I don't think she ever minded you coming with Melissa. It's...well...."

Roxanna's voice was dangerously flat. "What?"

"I...don't think she understands the severity of Melissa's illness. To tell the truth, neither did I. As you know, Joan is an RN and she has worked in the children's cancer wing at the Straker clinic. She told me all about Ewing Tumors. More detailed than you...." Zoe's voice dropped a notch. "I'm sorry, Rox. I can't imagine what you're going through."

Roxanna sighed and looked up at the vast, cloudless blue sky above them. "So what about this landlady? She thinks Melissa has a cold or something?"

"Oh, no," Zoe said hastily. "She knows it's cancer. She knows it's serious, but it only dawned on me how serious after Joan explained the nature of this...Ewing Tumor thing. So I called

Becky...."

"You called her—and she's on tour? Zoe, that's how you broke it to her? Zoe...." Roxanna took a deep breath, combed her left hand through her dark hair in sudden frustration.

Zoe went on, unperturbed it seemed. "You're right. I didn't reach her. The band, the whole damn entourage had already left that hotel, but I got an address." Zoe sighed the world off her shoulders. "So I wrote her a letter."

"And you're sure she got it?" Roxanna said with a hint of resignation in her voice. "Zoe, do you realize this is all I needed?"

"No, I don't, Roxanna." Zoe took a deep breath: "You're welcome here. I wouldn't have invited you if you weren't, you know that. Joan and Bobby are delighted you're here to help me out with the editorial work. I'm more than thrilled, actually, I'm ecstatic. So why don't we drop the landlady and get down to business. Do you need help unpacking your car? Or would you prefer we just wait for dinner?"

Roxanna opened her mouth, wanting to pursue the matter of a letter written to a landlady on tour, when exhaustion flooded her already battered physique. She said she'd prefer a bed first, and Zoe understood, told her there was a connecting door to her own bedroom through Melissa's. "The one that has the balcony!" Zoe promised to keep her dinner under wraps should she want to sleep the rest of the day away.

Before Roxanna went to lie down, she gently sat down on Melissa's bed and watched her closely through the grayness of the room. The child was deeply asleep and did not stir when Roxanna kissed her slack lips, and, for a second, put her cheek against the softness of Melissa's. I love you, kid, she thought; whatever happens.

Chapter 2

It was a hot Friday afternoon. Roxanna, in shorts and T-shirt, dozed in the dust flecked rays of the sun caressing her balcony. Her body was suspended in rest; her brain activity for once switched to its lowest level, nearing point zero as it were. Only her sense of hearing was tuned in to pick up the sounds Melissa was making on the porch below. After the past hectic week, she needed this repose. All through unpacking their things, working together with Melissa to give the apartment their personal touch, two appointments with Melissa's new pediatrician, haggling about the admittance date for Melissa at the clinic, one other thing had been preying on her mind: the return of the absent house member. The landlady. Was Zoe telling the truth when she said not to worry? Rebecca Morgan was a highly successful singer locally and according to Joan she, Roxanna, needed a crash-course in How To Live With The Artistically Gifted. Zoe denied the landlady was such a difficult person, but rather, was shy and often went to extreme lengths to prove this was not so.

Great, Roxanna had thought more then once, suspecting Zoe was trying to soften the blow. What kind of woman was this Rebecca Morgan?

"Mommy? Mommy can I go over to Freddie's house?"

The tiny voice cut through her ruminations. Christ, she knew Melissa was going to ask to see those wriggling newborn puppies sooner or later. They had been yelping very loudly and Melissa had wanted to see them despite her mother's refusal, her explanations of why she couldn't. Melissa seemed to be very forgetful on this matter.

Roxanna straightened in the deck chair so she could see her daughter standing below on the parched lawn. Melissa was looking up at the balcony, her dark eyes squeezed nearly shut against the glare of the sun, her shoulder-length, silken hair was uncombed and her scanty clothes were full of grassy things, showing she had been rolling around. Melissa had inherited her mother's Latina side. Because of this, Roxanna noted with pleasure, the sun was quickly bringing a healthy color back to her skin. Right now, the scrawny all-legs child was obviously waiting for an answer, and even though Roxanna would allow her all the wonders in the world, she had to deny her this one.

"Freddie isn't home, Mel. He's with Bobby at the swimming pool, remember?"

"But Mom, I'm bored. Can't I go play with the puppies?"

"No, you can't, Melissa. Listen to me. The mother dog is very protective of her litter right now and I m afraid she'll hurt you if you come too close, especially when Freddie and Bobby aren't around. Aren't you afraid of that great, big dog?"

"Why? Mom, what's a litter?"

"All the puppies put together...."

"Well, I'll just go over and take a look at her litter, okay?"

Roxanna decided not to blow her top at this attempt to be cute, instead kept her voice light. "Hon, let's wait for Freddie to come home, and then—maybe—you can go. All right?" Knowing damn well Freddie and Bobby wouldn't be home early on a Friday afternoon; knowing damn well Melissa would be too tired when the boys did show up.

"Oh, all right." Melissa pouted, and hung her head down to her bare toes.

"Do you want us to play a game?" Roxanna offered, her heart aching.

"Nah," Melissa answered impolitely and dragged her feet towards a dried up patch of bushes where she had left Bobby's fierce red fire-engine, along with a doll perched on top. She took it's stuffed arm and pulled it off the fire-engine. The doll trailed behind her as she zig-zagged towards the meager shade of a bush. She left the doll just outside the range of the shade, pretending this was all the poor thing's fault. Oh, for a distraction! —but surely, her inventive daughter could come up with something that made perfect sense soon, like, "Bobby always goes, why can't I?"

Roxanna leaned back into the canvas of the chair. She tried

9

to take her mind off Melissa and pets, but she could as well have pretended the sun wasn't there. Melissa and pets were proving to become a problem: Melissa wasn't allowed near them— Melissa was crazy about them. Melissa agreed to and seemed to understand everything else the nice doctor had told her, why couldn't she understand this?

Because, stupid, she's a six year old child. How much more do you want her to take? To agree to? To understand?

When the breeze coming in from the valley became cooler, Roxanna moved back into her room, where the sun could still reach her bronzing legs. She had just settled back into the chair when she heard the sound of a dying car engine; the sudden sound of voices shattered her feeling of timelessness.

"Cindy, Michael will hang you if you drop that case—watch those wires. Jeez, am I glad to be back home."

"Hey, who's this?" said another voice. "You're going to get yourself all wet like that. What's your name?"

"Melissa," Roxanna heard her daughter answer in a timid voice.

"What's she doing, playing with the water hose? Okay, little neighborhood delinquent, drop that." The first voice commanded.

"Melissa? That's a pretty name. I'm Cindy, Becky's piano player, and see the one over there who's trying not to carry anything? That's her—Becky."

Roxanna straightened to peer through the balcony railing and catch a glimpse of the owners' of the voices, but all she saw was the dark-blue hood of a Ford Mustang parked half-way on the lawn. Instead of acknowledging her presence—even help Melissa out—she sat back again—no, not to eavesdrop, but (yes) to eavesdrop. Besides, the landlady—the one who wasn't carrying anything—needed to acclimatize while she, herself, could get a lay of the land.

The one who called herself Cindy was gasping, lugging something heavy, at the same time, trying to talk, "Hey, Becky? Do you remember...remember the line 'be not like those bitter widows whose tongues are frozen?' "

"I remember. Didn't I write that?"

"Well, I was wondering if you shouldn't change the bitter widows into something else."

10

"Why? Let's dump this stuff right here and have a drink. How about it?"

Cindy let out an exaggerated sound of relief. "One of your better ideas. Beer—all right?"

Garden chairs scraped on the small patch of red concrete outside the kitchen door and for a while the only sounds were ohs and ahs, and one loud burp.

"So. What was it you were wondering about, oh, aspiring poet?" Rebecca asked then.

"Widows need not necessarily be bitter," Cindy stated. "And their tongues need not be frozen."

"Oh, hell, there I was, thinking I was on my way to immortality, or at least to page six of the Book of Quotations, side by side with Shakespeare...."

"All right, all right," Cindy moaned. "I had to ask."

"How about..." Rebecca paused, and on the second floor Roxanna cocked an ear.

"Scorned lovers? Nah, too lyrical, huh? Cheated—cheating lovers? Be not like dead lovers?" Rebecca went on like this for a while until Cindy asked her to please shut up.

There was a small pause in the conversation downstairs on the porch. Roxanna thought of making her presence known, when suddenly Cindy said, "Pat called, said she saw us on Channel Seven, Eyewitness News. The tour was a hit, huh?"

"Yeah. But I hate cameras in my face. Or anywhere else, you know that."

"That's why you kept your foot in front of the lens! Listen, I've got to go call Pat, tell her I'm back." A chair scraped and Cindy seemed to rise to her feet, but was held back by a sudden thought. "Melissa, it's getting late. Don't you have to go home? Do you live far from here?"

"No."

"So? Where do you live?"

"Here. So does my Mommy now."

A noise came out of Rebecca like beer being spit out. "Oh, wait a sec...."

"She was a reporta first," Melissa babbled proudly. "She's a writer now."

"Her mother," Becky groaned, and Cindy said, with more em-

11

phasis in her voice then was necessary, "A reporta? Oh, great. That's all you need, Becky. A live-in rep. Maybe she'll do a story on you. Don't they all...."

"Cut it out, Cindy...."

Breathlessly, Melissa said, "Mommy works for Aunt Zoe now."

"I see." Becky's voice was definitely cool, and once again Roxanna thought of helping Melissa out. Not that her daughter seemed to be in need of any help.

"Cindy'll get you a soda, won't you, Cindy?"

"I can't have a soda," Melissa chirped. "Don't you like reportas? Don't you like writers too? I like singers."

"Melissa...," Becky began rather loudly, "Don't you have something else to do than bother us?"

Melissa eyed Rebecca Morgan for a blank, touchy moment, then rose to her feet. "I don't like you," she said in a still, strangely dangerous tone of voice. "I'm going away."

Melissa disappeared, probably to play with the water hose again.

Rebecca huffed, "Jeez, snotty little brat."

Rebecca's friend was not amused. "She's just a kid. You didn't have to behave so high and mighty."

"What did I say? Okay, cut! Dear sister in travel and drink, let us toast to the end of another crazy tour; may there be no more for many, many moons."

Rebecca took a hearty slug of beer, slammed both her blue-jeaned, booted legs on an empty chair, swung her sandy colored, bleach-streaked hair behind her shoulders and looked up into the vast, cloudless blue sky above her. She blinked, needed to blink again, before something up there registered. When it did, Rebecca took a deep breath. The apparition, standing immobile at the railing of the balcony wore little, but the eyes—the darkest eyes she had ever seen—told her plenty. The breeze stirred the blue-black hair, lifting it away from her face, accentuating high cheekbones. The tanned face was cool, tight, the corners of the mouth angry, the nose flared slightly and the look in those eyes licked at Rebecca's all too sensitive, but rusty heart-strings. The impact of this unexpected gift left Rebecca hot, flustered.

"There was no need to yell at my snotty little brat," said the apparition.

Rebecca blushed to her roots. Cindy produced a strangled sound and turned her head; looking upwards and without missing a beat, she said, "Hi. Becky didn't mean anything. She gets...gruff when she's tired, yells a lot, mopes, you understand. We just got back from a long trip."

"I see." Roxanna smiled at Cindy showing she bore her no grudge. "A long trip can be very trying, yes."

Cindy looked like her voice, sweet, absent-minded; she had almost colorless eyes with blonde, nearly white hair which was pasted to her forehead and cheeks by the heat. Then Roxanna's eyes travelled slowly, deliberately so, back to the other woman. "She yelled at the wrong person this time," Roxanna remarked, never taking her eyes away from Rebecca Morgan.

And Cindy, intermediary whether she wanted to be or not, proposed, "Why don't you have a drink with us. What's your pleasure?"

"I'll take a cold, cold beer—if I'm not intruding?"

Just then, Melissa, anything but shy, danced back into view, singing clear as a bell: "Mommy, what's a neighborhood delinquent?"

"Something I hope you aren't. Stay there. Could you bring Melissa an orange juice? I'll be right down." Roxanna turned her back.

"I didn't yell at the kid," Rebecca mumbled under her breath, eyeing Melissa who had spied her black guitar case leaning against the garden table.

"Sure, you didn't. I'll go get...."

"What's in there?" Melissa asked politely.

"My guitar," Rebecca answered, promising little. Cindy, just knowing Melissa was going to ask to see it, took Becky's attention away. "I've known you for at least five years, Morgan, and I have never ever seen you blush."

"Oh? Are you going somewhere? Start thinking about it or shut up." Becky took her eyes off Melissa, glanced up at the balcony. "So she's the new tenant Zoe mentioned. Christ, I had forgotten all about...."

She was interrupted, this time by a loud "Hi, I'm home!" honk coming from behind Becky's Mustang. Without a second thought, she leaped to her feet, ran towards the side of the house, into Zoe's arms. The twosome embraced, Zoe squealing with delight, Rebecca holding on as if she was drowning.

"Cindy," Zoe squealed again, hugging the piano player, "have you been home long? How was the trip back?"

Cindy mumbled loud enough for all to hear, "Let's not talk about the color of her face," and speaking louder, "I'll go get what I was supposed to get half an hour ago."

As Cindy disappeared into the house, Rebecca took Zoe's upper arm and shook it. "Who's that?"

Zoe followed Becky's scathing look. "Oh, that's.... Becky, don't you remember? That's Melissa; her mother's around somewhere. Let's go find her." But Rebecca held an already suspicious Zoe back. "We've met, thank you. I had no idea they'd already be here. I thought...."

"Becky, didn't you get my letter?" Zoe asked in a quiet voice.

Rebecca growled, "What letter?"

"Oh, great!" Zoe exclaimed. "Listen, Joan's on a late shift and she'll scream if there's nothing to eat when she gets home. Let's go get some Take-out...."

"I'll go," Becky volunteered quickly, and when Zoe looked like she was about to object, she continued, "I've got to drop Cindy off anyway. What shall I get?"

"Chinese sounds fine. Some spare-ribs for Joan. Listen, I'll tell you...."

"Don't bother. Cindy! Say, I'm broke though...."

"I'll get some money. Hold it a sec."

Zoe was in the kitchen rummaging through a dark-green tin box when Roxanna walked in, shrugging into a short, blue robe. Zoe looked up and saw her closed, lackluster face. Zoe sighed. "She put her foot in it?" Roxanna only made a sound in the back of her throat and continued on her way out. Zoe held her back. "She's not in a very good mood, my dear friend."

"Neither am I." The screen door slapped shut. Zoe let her breath out in a careful whoosh, shut the tin box with a slam, counting the money slowly. Satisfied, she left the kitchen. She came out of the house just in time to see both women withdrawing their hands after their introduction. Then Melissa started on her mother. She wanted to go with Becky and Cindy, do *something* exciting to get rid of her boredom.

14

"This is Cindy Phillips, my piano player," Becky was saying formally.

"Can I go with her, Mom? I'm not upset anymore."

"Were you upset, honey?"

"Not really," Melissa corrected, realizing her mistake. "She asked me." Melissa's eyes were eager, as if being asked by Becky to go anywhere with her was the ultimate pleasure.

"How are you feeling? Be honest now."

"I'm all right, Mom. Can I?" Roxanna nodded, unable to resist the plea. She avoided looking straight into Becky's eyes. If this was Becky's 'making-up' gesture, it was working.

After they left, Zoe said, "Becky's such a pain sometimes."

"Is that what she does when she's shy?" Roxanna took a healthy gulp of her ice-cold beer.

Zoe had to laugh, and suddenly Roxanna snickered too—offering Zoe the easy companionship they had always shared since, oh so long ago. Zoe sputtered, "She's an obnoxious, self-centered little twerp, that's what she is. Thing is, I like her, especially when she makes up for what she has done wrong—then it's sky-rockets and balloons. And she pours it out on stage when she sings, believe me."

"Melissa seems to think so," Roxanna said. "Or she hasn't heard what the landlady thinks of her. You said 'entourage' the other night—does she have a band?"

Zoe shook her head. "She has a back-up singer sometimes. Becky doesn't go on tour that often. When she does, it's shortly before she starts new sessions at the Blue Notes. That's her home base. It's a small, but highly successful club near Pavilion. I'll take you there sometime." Zoe reflected a moment, "She used to sing at folk festivals—a lot. She doesn't anymore—just women's festivals."

"Oh?" Roxanna sounded far-away.

"There was a lousy incident some years ago at a festival she was appearing at. Fighting broke out in the audience and someone broke an arm. The person went to court to get compensation. Becky also had to show her face, but you know, things like that often happen—even to movie stars. Thing is, that scandal sheet, *The Evening News,* picked it up and the article they did on her bordered on slander. Becky nearly dragged them to court, but I

15

convinced her to ignore it. It would just have become worse.

"It didn't sit well with Becky that—and I quote, 'her dear departed mother' unquote—was mentioned, and her father for that matter; the man turned into a recluse at the ranch they have on Canyon Ridge ever since the mother died about four years ago.

"To understand the smear campaign you must know that Becky is not an unknown in this hick town. Her father is-or rather, was—an important man. I mean, this neighborhood, this house..... Becky doesn't really care about her background, she goes around singing what she wants. But don't touch her parents. Anyway, they're food for scandal...."

"I wouldn't mind some food myself right now." Roxanna crumpled the empty can and tossed it into the recycling bin. She was interested in the mention of the smear campaign, but hunger was making her interest wane.

"So, because Becky does nothing but with a lick and a promise, she decided to despise everything that spelled media. She's backed down a bit, thinks the phenomenon a necessary evil—my influence undoubtedly."

It's getting better all the time, Roxanna thought with fatalistic certainty. Thank you, Zoe.

And, as if Zoe could read her mind, she said, "Don't worry about it, Rox. Like I said, she's got a big mouth, but she listens to reason. When she feels like it, anyway."

"Why didn't you tell me about this before, Zoe? I can fight this all out on my own, but I've got Melissa to contend with. I don't want her hurt."

"Rox, you're exaggerating, okay? And this is all coming out now because you have been very busy, I've been busy, and Joan probably thinks this is my business. And all my doing too. Don't worry. Okay?"

Roxanna looked into Zoe's pleading eyes and she found herself nodding. She not only wanted to believe her friend, she needed to, especially now, after the long awaited meeting with the landlady, a grown woman, who as Zoe had just said, had a big mouth, but listened to reason. When she felt like it.

Suddenly Zoe said, "By the way, you withdrew your article on lesbian mothers from *The Evening News*, didn't you? They had contacted me initially wanting me to provide them with

16

more writers on the subject. I was about to tell them to screw off when they mentioned your name."

"Thank God you let me know, Zoe. I told my agent to inform me where he was sending my articles, even though I encouraged him to sell in California. He was all adamant about me going more mainstream. Later I got a woman agent."

"We sang your praises, you know," Zoe commented with a wistful 'oh well' look on her face. *The Evening News* ran another article instead. Among other things, how lesbian households are seen as a threat to the all-round supposedly successful nuclear family....You know, Rox, my kid doesn't seem to mind. I don't believe love hurts. Do you?"

Roxanna shook her head. "Of course not. Hey, why didn't you give me a call from work? I could have fixed dinner."

"Be glad I didn't. First of all, the roster says it's my turn, second of all, we've got Becky to contend with now. And Joan loves Chinese Take-out, especially spareribs." And in the same breath Zoe said, "Unanswered love hurts. So I give my loved ones all I've got."

"So do I," Roxanna said emphatically, thinking just as emphatically, even if it kills me.

Chapter 3

In the living room time ticked by. Roxanna began to imagine herself on stage—the set, the players, in place. On the couch the main character—herself—nursed a drink and turned over glossy pages of a magazine lying on her lap. Across the elegant living room—all furnished in sedate, over-stuffed, brown leather—sprawled supporting actress, Becky, sulking in an armchair. They even had an audience—Zoe and Joan murmured occasionally in the background just outside.

After a few moments of morose silence, Becky, the supporting actress remembered she wasn't alone and said suddenly and dramatically, "One of the great mysteries in life—how to keep a relationship going. Don't you think so? I always wind up reading the telephone book. You know, the heavy, romantic, total commitment kind of relationship? Like whats-their-faces...." Becky motioned absent-mindedly, her voice dropping. "Like Zoe and Joan?" Then she rolled her eyes, sighing. "I don't think the one has ever cheated on the other. Brother. Do you have them? I mean, relationships?"

Outside, the audience mumbled on showing it wasn't paying much attention to the play. Roxanna shook her head almost imperceptibly as if trying to wake herself up. She did not speak, doubting Becky wanted an answer.

Rebecca suddenly catapulted herself out of the wing-back chair and walked to a well-supplied, built-in bar occupying one corner of the living room. Flanking the bar on one side was a stereo and a long line of Long Play records, CDs, tapes and on the other side, a big screen color TV.

"Do you want any more of Zoe's drug?"

"A refill? Yes. Please. Thank you."

"There's no need to grovel," Becky mumbled loud enough for everybody present to hear. Roxanna raised her eyes from the

18

magazine and watched Rebecca fix her a drink. She reminded herself of a brave initiative—the handling of Rebecca Morgan who now approached the couch to hand her the drink. Roxanna tried hard to hold on to that newly-found credo—I can handle little Ms. Bad Temper. I can handle all the Rebecca Morgans of the world. Or I lie a lot.

She took a hearty sip from the surprisingly tasty drink. Her eyes never left Rebecca's back as the latter sauntered away—thinking of more cleverness to say, no doubt.

"I know how," Becky said reflectively, swirling the ice around in her drink. "Have plenty or have none. Whaddayasay?"

"Pardon? I don't...." Roxanna really didn't.

"To keep relationships going. Oh, never mind, I'm babbling." Becky sighed, perhaps realizing she was being a pest. The first signs of exhaustion seemed to enter her sagging frame as she rubbed her eyes with one hand. She hoisted one hip on the bar, placed her drink delicately beside her and then forgetting she was perhaps being a pest, she said into Roxanna's general direction, "Didn't I hear that you write for *The Evening News?*"

"Excuse me?" The question genuinely startled Roxanna.

"If I was paranoid, I'd suspect they planted you here."

"I can't be planted. I'm a human being," Roxanna deadpanned.

Rebecca worked her most engaging laugh. To Roxanna it seemed as if she was trying to charm her out of her pants. The next thing Becky said put them back on. "Zoe know you're a spy? I guess not, huh? She wouldn't let you near her precious files."

Being too occupied with the harassment campaign, Rebecca didn't notice the frost appearing on every door jamb in sight. "Whoa, you're the strong, silent type, aren't you? What do you think Zoe will say when she finds out about your side-line?"

When Roxanna still refused to answer, Becky bristled. "I hope you don't write like you talk."

Roxanna shut the magazine, planning every move she made. She was thinking that the person sitting there in her place, was surely not Roxanna Gabriella Vaughan. It could not be, no ma'am. Just the other day she believed she had found a haven—peace—for her daughter, for herself. And now something idiotic was happening.

"So how could you know I despise the looks of those jerks they have on their payroll, but hell, didn't you know they're Zoe's best competitor? Especially because Zoe puts sense into her articles?"

"Could you lower your voice? You'll wake up the kids."

"It's soundproof upstairs. Or else I couldn't practice. There's cork under the linoleum."

"Soundproof?"

"Look, all I mean to say is this. If you are Zoe's long lost pal and if you have been reading her letters for the past three years—I mean, don't you check the premises before you apply for a job?"

The sound of the magazine clapping on the table was like a gunshot, and Becky jumped. She stared as Roxanna rose to her feet; she saw that Roxanna was aroused, good and angry, and her eyes widened.

"I think you've harassed me enough for one day," Roxanna said in a controlled voice. "If you don't want me in this house, well, just say so. If—I said if—I've done Zoe some wrong, I owe the explanation to Zoe and to Zoe alone, to no one else, least of all, to you. Besides, I withdrew my article. It was never published. I don't write for said paper. And another thing—as much as you'd like my daughter and me to genuflect each time you dance by...."

"Aw, come on...."

"Now that we're on the subject, the only person to put my daughter and me out of this house is the person who invited us in in the first place. Got that?"

Rebecca, pretending she still had the whole situation under control, changed her weight from one foot to the other. About to put her hands on her hips, she said, "May I remind you that this is my house?"

"You may. And may I remind you that I have signed an official lease? That promises have been made to me? That you will need a lawyer and a pretty damn good cause to throw me out of here? However, I'm not willing to subject both myself or my child to this shit, so it's settled." Roxanna picked up the magazine and squeezed the poor thing dry. God, she hadn't been this angry since she could not remember when. "Do forgive our pagan feet on your spotless tiled floor. We'll get out of here the minute we're packed."

The magazine clapped on the glass top or the coffee table. Roxanna made about-face and strode out of the living room. At the threshold she remembered a remark, and paused to ask, "If it's soundproof up there, does that mean we can't hear what's going on up there?"

"Why? Are you going to blow up the place?"

But Roxanna was gone, leaving Becky with the echo of a row she had not expected, and with three facts a good and able landlady ought to know about tenants.

"That'll teach you not to mess with her," a soft voice said through the kitchen hatch. It was Zoe. Wryly she continued, "Guess I've lost a delegate, haven't I?"

"Will you lock up? I'm going to play in traffic. Maybe there's a dump-truck on the way. Good-night and good-bye, Zoe. Give Joan my love. And Bobby."

"Hold it, hold it. Becky, I knew she sold an article to *The Evening News*—her agent did. I knew the staff writer who accepted it, and who got fired for the changes he was trying to make there. As soon as I called her up, she took care of it. Anyway, that's when I decided I wanted her on my staff. She has a year's contract. Now, why don't you go upstairs and apologize for throwing all your baggage onto her. She'll hear you out, I'm sure."

Did Becky hear 'I hope' instead?

"Not tonight Zoe. I've had it. Even traffic will have to wait. I'm going to bed where it's *sound* proof."

* * *

I feel good. I feel great. She had it coming. Sure opened those cute eyes wide and bright. How about this for a headline: *A Day in the Life of Queen Sheba*. The day she got back-talk. Granted, the old Queen could not possibly have known that I am my father's daughter—Holy Mother of Christ, could he lose precious patience. *Yes! I do feel good.* Roxanna nearly said out loud, distracted because she was glancing at her watch. It was time for Melissa's medicine, and painkiller.

Entering her dark bedroom, she switched on the light—the

21

bothersome landlady suddenly forgotten—and walked to her bed where she had left Melissa's medication after the last injection. Taking the plastic bag full of small colored boxes which in turn were full of ampules, each containing a carefully measured dose of relief for Melissa's oftentimes excruciating pain, she turned from her bed and nearly screamed with fright at the black figure outlined in her doorway.

"*Jesus!*" Roxanna exclaimed resentfully. "You scared the hell out of me!"

"I...I'm s-sorry," Becky mumbled, stepping aside to let an angry Roxanna pass on her way out of the bedroom. "I only wanted to talk to you...."

"You've done a lot of talking already, thank you." The light in the bathroom snapped on, and Roxanna set out to do what she had come to do. She pulled a plastic cup out of the bag, rinsed it, filled it with water, and put it to one side. She then took out two tiny teardrop vials and started to shake one of them. In the act, her eyes met Rebecca's reflection in the mirror.

She said nothing, but for Becky it was the sign to start rattling on. "I didn't mean what I said downstairs. I'm tired and upset. I'm sorry, you could have been anybody—it's nothing personal." Her arms and hands travelled to her back; she stood there like a naughty eight-year old expecting punishment.

Roxanna didn't care. She said, trying to sound amused, "You meant it, Becky. Don't flatter yourself. I've been in tougher spots and a spoilt little brat like you can never upset me." *Never thought I'd call my landlady a brat either....* She held the ampule she had been shaking up to the light, shook some more, then made it clear she wanted to leave the bathroom. Becky did not budge. "Zoe'll kill me if you leave."

"I know." Roxanna curled her lips into a sweet, never more heartfelt delicate smile. "May I? Or we can spend the night in the bathtub."

Becky, remembering she hadn't budged, stepped aside like a robot, when Roxanna doubled back for the glass of water she had nearly forgotten. She hurried passed Rebecca, through the hall.

After a slight hesitation, Becky followed Roxanna, halting on the threshold of Melissa's small bedroom. She put her arms behind her back again, said nothing. Just stood there.

Roxanna worked like an expert. Waking Melissa up, she murmured encouragement. Then she busied herself uncovering Melissa's thigh, cracked open the ampule she had been shaking without even looking at it, and deftly prepared a syringe. She was in the process of squirting air out of the syringe, when she noticed Becky standing on the threshold, repentant.

Roxanna wasn't someone to rub it in. "There's no need for you to be here, Rebecca. Why don't you...."

"Is she all right?"

"Mommy..." the child's voice was impatient, annoyed even. "...Mommy, it hurts....It's coming."

"It'll go away, sweetheart. Lie still now—that's it. You'll see, it'll go away." Roxanna threw the disposable needle into the medical waste container beside the bed and took Melissa into her arms. "Let's sing it away, baby." She rocked the child gently, and they sang. Melissa's voice was clear and on key, slowly growing sleepier, her voice growing softer, until the mother hummed alone.

"Such a strong little voice.... Where do those songs come from? I don't know them." said Becky awkwardly.

"Raffi—he sings for kids."

When Melissa was sleeping peacefully, Roxanna tucked her in, kissed her and left the bedroom. Leaving the door ajar, she looked at Becky. She knew what the look on Becky's face meant: Becky was beginning to understand about Melissa's illness.

"I propose we start again," said Roxanna, thawing "My name is Roxanna Vaughan. My daughter's name is Melissa."

"I'm Rebecca Morgan but my friends call me Becky."

* * *

The next day Zoe and Roxanna were lunching at Maywood, Zoe's favorite luncheonette which was bursting at the seams this time of day. The waitresses knew all the regulars, knew Zoe, and what she always ordered. Roxanna was the new-comer, so the waitress tossed her a menu.

After Roxanna ordered, the two women went over what Zoe had shown her of operations at the *Point of View* offices in the old Stockholm building, two blocks away. She had met most of the staff, seen where her own smoke-glassed cubicle of an office was, her desk and computer, and the nicety of an in-and-out box.

"And how did you ever get to know Rebecca Morgan, much less rent from her, knowing how she views journalists?" asked Roxanna, sipping soda water.

"Through an ad on the Blue Notes bulletin board, can you believe it? Besides she likes lesbian feminist journalists. It seemed like Joan and I were forever moving in and out of places, either because we were lesbians or had a baby or both. I was so tired, Rox. And then there was this ad. She wanted people in the house, you know, because she isn't. Well, she's in and out. She liked us. She liked Bobby, thought he was cute. Her brothers used to live there but they had gradually moved out, and it was too expensive to look after on her own. She was used to a full rowdy house, though she was the one who never had a guest stay more than forty-eight hours. We got used to seeing the constantly changing guard...."

"Her entourage, you mean."

"You could say that."

So Becky was used to family life, Roxanna thought. She filled up the house because she missed it. Maybe she could cope with another child around, but a sick one? Could she and Melissa live with wild nights upstairs? —ah, soundproofing. No wonder Zoe, Joan and Bobby had taken the downstairs rooms. Somehow, though, she hadn't expected her landlady to be so young.

"...my staff," Zoe was saying.

"Great." Roxanna answered hurriedly. "They seem friendly, open."

"Crazy bunch," Zoe shook her head proudly. "But we have a good time. God, lunch is slow today. When do you have to get back to the clinic?"

"Soon," she said, fumbling with her pocketbook, "Melissa'll be cranky after having those strange people poking at her, but I wasn't allowed to stay. I better be back on time or I'll feel her wrath for the rest of the week."

"And it has just begun." Zoe, not one to beat around the bush, went on, "Are you leaving?"

"Well, yes...." Roxanna sounded and looked mystified. Hadn't Zoe just asked her that? "I said I needed to get back to the clinic.

I don't think I want my daughter who is sick and who is only six...." Suddenly it dawned on Roxanna that this wasn't what Zoe was asking. "Oh. About last night? Jeez, you heard?"

"Well, are you leaving?" Zoe was trying not to laugh. Even though Roxanna didn't know whether to be offended or amused at the memory of the evening before, she had to shake her head. "You know, Joan should have given me the crash-course."

Zoe grinned in a way that made it hard not to join her. Zoe had charm, a charm Roxanna could hardly resist. Her biggest charm lay behind her aviator glasses, the squint in her eye, those hazel-brown eyes which could look oh so innocent and vulnerable. Zoe seldom raised her voice, and at the office where she reigned like an amiable queen, her leadership in times of both prosperity and great panic had earned her the respect of her staff. Roxanna sensed that right away.

She was two or three inches shorter than Roxanna, round in figure and cheerful, all of her that showed golden after various healthy weekends. Subdued in appearance, brown blazer, yellow checkered cotton blouse, dark-brown slacks and shoes, she resembled the copy-editor and not the brains and drive behind *A Differing Point of View*. People were surprised on hearing that this somewhat shy-looking schoolish type kept the whole thing on its feet month after month after month.

—Until the day came when she sent out a cry for help. All the sleepless nights had begun to tell, and both her social life and her love life had begun suffering. Scraping hope and courage together, she wrote to her friend working free-lance at the time, and offered her a steady job:

...If I don't want to become old (and single) before my time, I have to start looking for help. I'm desperately in need of another brain....

Roxanna's long delay in answering, and eventual explanation about Melissa's illness made Zoe do some quick investigations, as was her way. *I have taken the liberty*, she wrote in her next letter, *of getting information from the George Straker Children's Clinic. They have a sophisticated children's cancer ward, and are familiar with cases like Melissa's. They have a summer camp too, but that won't be for this year....*

It had not taken Roxanna long to take on the job after that.

"Listen," Zoe was saying, "I wake up this morning, and who's beside me on the bed—I mean on the other side—asking me to hear her confession when I'm already supposed to be up and stuck in traffic? Look, I told you it is pretty hard for Becky to act like a grown up, but you fell right into it. She gets, uh, she gets...."

"An artistic superiority fit, or is it stardom?"

"Roxy, be serious. Becky...uh...suffers, you understand. I ignore her moods as best I can. Pass them off. Now Joan—you should hear those two tackle each other...."

"She was telling me to get lost, Zoe. How did she even know about my article?" Roxanna's shoulders slumped a little. "Anyway, if I had a choice I guess I would leave, but how can I—Melissa's all settled. She loves the garden. We didn't have a garden where we lived before."

"Thank the goddess you signed a lease! C'mon, here's lunch."

On their way back to the office, Roxanna told Zoe she didn't want the remaining two weeks off until her starting date. "Melissa will be at the clinic for seven weeks, starting tomorrow. She'll come home on Wednesdays and some weekends. Apart from those days I'm going to have an awful lot of time on my hands...."

"You sure? What about arrangements, taking care of insurance and all?"

"Yes well, Melissa's stay at the clinic is covered, but not physical therapy, nor does it cover any possible orthopedic leg—listen, Zoe, I have to work to keep us." I have to work to keep my sanity, she thought.

"But what about the radiologists, the chemotherapy. Isn't that covered?"

"The services, yes. Look. You know, Rick's family has a history of cancer. I never thought it would come out in Melissa, hence the minimum insurance. I bought what I could afford. When she started to complain about a vicious pain in her leg, I knew what was going down. I changed my insurance even before I went to any pediatrician. Still...."

"Why don't you join a support group at the clinic. It would help, you know. I know you—you'll use work as a sedative and use it to death."

"How many lesbian mothers are going to be there ? Who am I going to talk to—I mean really talk to? I don't need the pressure.

"Sooner or later people are going to wonder where Melissa's father is, why isn't he interested. I can lie, of course— Say that I'm divorced, I'm a widow. I don't want to be a burden on you and Joan, if that's why you're proposing a support group."

"You're not. It was a suggestion. We'll talk tonight, okay?" Zoe left Roxanna in the office parking lot. "You'd do the same for me if it was Bobby."

Chapter 4

After the week-end disturbance, the household settled down to an everyday routine. Its members, each on a different schedule, got together around the dinner table. A monthly schedule dictated who was to prepare the evening meal. Joan, who enjoyed running things, sat down at the kitchen table every last Sunday of the month and drew up a new calendar of household chores.

In the five years since she had been doing this, she had learned not to count on Becky, especially in the summer, and to jot Zoe's name down for the week-ends. Although she did assign Zoe to clean Bobby's room at least once a week, help straighten out the house every Sunday, do the laundry room, and the windows when they needed to be done. Joan underlined in glaring red when the books needed to be done, the bills paid, because once the phone was cut off. Needless to say, she took great pains to assign herself the tasks she loved doing which were cooking and gardening. And she tried not to gloat when she succeeded in pinning down wayward house members to pitch in on cleaning toilets and sinks.

But when Joan went on nights at the clinic, the household went through a remarkable transformation for at least nine days. Zoe left her burdened desk at three every afternoon. She'd meet the community school bus which brought Bobby home from elementary school, fix him sandwiches, check the roster, and straighten out what needed tidying, then start supper. (Joan would eat at the clinic cafeteria.) Even Becky would show up, check the roster pinned to the bulletin board on the fridge and stick to it; especially because she didn't other times.

Joan had been right about Roxanna's sense of responsibility, and began counting on her to lighten the daily load. In the early evening after her faithful visit to Melissa at the clinic, she would disappear for a time to her room, and then reappear to help Joan with dinner. It didn't take Roxanna long to realize Joan had charge of things. But Becky's schedule remained a mystery. Urgent business always seemed to keep her away from regular meals, and no one knew how she fed herself.

One Wednesday evening when Melissa was home and Becky was absent as usual, they sat down to a dinner of crisp pork chops, baked potatoes and steamed carrots. Zoe asked for Roxanna's attention by signalling with her fork. "By the way, do all the comings and goings upstairs bother you?"

"You mean the nightly house-guests?"

"She doesn't mean the mice, Roxanna," Joan mumbled with her mouth full.

"We got mice?" Bobby piped, sitting straight.

Joan switched to her story-teller voice, and said, "Our mice walk around on two legs."

"They come out in the mornings...," Roxanna related to a wide-eyed Melissa. "...and most of the time they're wrapped up in a towel. Or less."

Melissa giggled. "Nah, mice don't take showers."

"How come," Zoe began, gazing steadily at Joan, "she knows they're wrapped up in a towel—or less?"

"We have our ways," Joan snickered.

"Where do they come from?" Bobby asked, big brown eyes seeing imaginary mice all over the place.

Zoe reached out to pat the crown of his head, saying, "Joannie and Rox are catching up with the Vaudeville act. Don't you pay them no mind."

"What's a Vaudeville act?"

"What they're doing." Zoe turned to squint at Roxanna. "Are you going to answer me normally or in duet with Ms. RN here?"

"Don't worry about it, Zoe. Remember—soundproofing? It doesn't bother me except up and down the stairs. Otherwise I don't hear a thing."

"Convenient," muttered Joan, then louder, "Zoe's mother instinct is acting up again, although I think it's plain Breckner nosiness, right Breckner Jr.?"

"Yeah, I can jump up and down upstairs, and no one can hear me!" And because he had wanted attention in the first place, he asked innocently, "Do I have to eat these carrots?"

Joan's eyebrows shot up, wise to him, maybe more so than his own mother. "What's the matter with them?" She watched him curl his nose in disgust, saw him glance at Zoe who knew when not to butt in.

Roxanna watched them. How much Bobby looked like Zoe. His eyes changed color in the light just like hers. He even possessed a similar charm.

"Well, there isn't any hair growing on them, is there?" Joan was saying.

"No, but...." Bobby sighed dramatically. In the act his gaze fell accidentally on Melissa's plate. It was rich with vegetables Roxanna had cooked for her; and to Bobby, it must have looked exotic. His eyes shifted back to his bunch of measly carrots, then back to Melissa's plate. Without further ado, he stuck a carrot slice into his mouth.

Joan hiccupped and dove under the table to hide her unpedagogical snicker. She croaked something about having spotted a mouse. Roxanna tried to keep a straight face, because of Zoe's poker one. Roxanna remembered that expression all too well.

After a while of taking Joan and Bobby's hide-and-seek dives, Zoe said sternly, "Are y'all finished hee-hawing down there? Joan, would you act your age? Bobby! Sit straight and eat your desert. Jeez, it's as if I have twins. Joan, please, he has terrible eating habits, and you're not helping any."

Joan tried to be serious, but said, "He's got terrible vegetable eating habits, you mean. Who spoiled him on hamburgers? I'm sure he can find his way to the Pizza Parlor blindfolded."

Joan and Bobby hiccupped with laughter some more. Zoe rolled her eyes and gave up.

Roxanna let the homey argument flow over her. Automatically, she coaxed a distracted Melissa into eating her food. She tried not to dwell on Zoe's question, but couldn't get it out of her mind. It wasn't Becky's house-guests that bothered her. She was wise to Becky's popularity as a singer, both in and out of clothes.

The first time Roxanna met one of Becky's house-guests was early one morning. The woman had been dressed as a stewardess and in an awful hurry, probably missing the plane she thought she could still catch. The others she met roaming the premises were not all there to help Becky practice her do-re-mi. Only once had she seen the same face twice, and anyway, why should she care what Becky did?

No, none of it bothered Roxanna Vaughan, at least, not in the beginning.

* * *

"Had a rough day?"

"It's not over yet," Joan scowled. She padded around the bedroom picking up after Zoe and herself. She had long since given up wishing for a miracle—that Zoe would bother to pick up something behind her and put it back where it belonged. Joan inspected the closet to see if it was time to consult the Maytag. Then she went to the window and rattled its latches; all was properly locked.

"Will you come to bed?" Zoe requested, lying on said piece of furniture. "It won't go away by having it run after you."

"Huh? What won't go away?"

"Whatever it is that's bothering you." Zoe watched Joan climb into bed and punch the pillow into shape with a vengeance she found comical. "Come here," she said gently, "and tell me about it."

"It's nothing Zoe. Honest." Joan snuggled against her, kissing her cheek."Oh, all right. There is something but it'll go away."

"Will this be someday soon? Your clowning around drives me up the wall."

"Oh yeah? And this? This'll drive you up the wall." Before Zoe knew what was happening, Joan attacked her sides.

Zoe leaped, shrieking, "Stop it!"

Joan did. "You're losing weight. Are you going to start that rat-race again? Every summer it's the same old story."

"That's what's on your mind, my coming rat-race? What do you want me to tell you? The same thing I told you last year?"

"Zoe, we're like bats, meeting only at night."

Suddenly Zoe laughed. She hugged Joan and said, "Bats? What's next?"

"I'm serious, Zoe. I'm going on nights next week."

This simple statement made Zoe's jaws shut tight.

"Fourteen nights."

"F-fourteen nights?" It came out of Zoe's mouth in a whisper.

31

"You're doing this to punish me."

"Cynthia took my shift last month, remember? I'm returning the favor."

Zoe fell backwards into her pillow, groaning. "I'll come have a cup of coffee with you once in a while—Will around mid-night suit you? That way you'll recognize me should we ever meet again somewhere."

"Maybe now you know how I feel," said Joan softly.

"Honey, I know how you feel. Dammit."

"I miss you when I don't see you three days in a row."

"I try hard Joan," Zoe said, her voice sincere. "I do. Do you think I don't miss you? I wouldn't be here now if Roxanna wasn't taking over my desk tomorrow morning. I'd be chasing after people. I'd be—I can even make lunch tomorrow. I'll pick you up at the clinic, okay? Hey, look at me."

Joan did, her eyes turning misty, insecure. "I know I should get used to your summer schedule, but I can't. I'm sure we're going away in September again, right? Well, okay, I know you do try. I'm sorry, *Perdoname*."

Zoe passed her fingers through Joan's thick, shiny hair; she loved to feel its texture, loved its scent when she kissed it. "Old bat? Did I ever tell you how much I appreciate the way you manipulate your schedule so we can meet at least a couple of days a week?"

"Yes, you did. You also promised to support me when I get fired for screwing up everybody else's roster."

They looked at each other; two lovers, two old lovers, lovers in love forever....

Zoe said softly, almost absent-mindedly, "Seems I'm going to have to sneak into the house 'round lunchtime for at least two weeks in a row...."

"I'm flattered. All that just to have lunch with me?"

"To go to bed with you, stupid."

"And when do we lunch?"

"Between decks."

They giggled like school-girls who share a secret, drawing together for a gentle, melting kiss; a whisper, a nod and darkness flooded the room. Their bodies met in the most tender motions. In this private embrace existed an understanding of one anoth-

32

er's needs. A fleeting touch, a movement brought forth a sigh; dormant desire ignited as they began the ageless rhythm of making love. The intimate rhythm increased until the pain and enjoyment of desire was released, erupting into their night.

* * *

"Your daughter has a visitor."

Roxanna and Norma Lewis, head nurse of the Children's West Wing, crossed the lawn towards the housing of the youngest patients. "They're with the goldfish, over there." Norma pointed ahead at a cluster of moody willow trees embracing a duck-shaped pond. Roxanna narrowed her eyes against the glare of the sun. She was still too far away to tell who the visitor was, but music floated to her through the silence. Yes, it was a guitar.

"Excuse me, Norma. What did you say?"

"Did you talk with Doctor Henninger?"

"Yes." Roxanna slowed her step. "He's optimistic."

"So should you be. About yourself, Roxanna. I talked to Richard Blumfield, one of our social workers. He's willing to make some time for you, perhaps, if you want to, to introduce you to one of the support groups we've been setting up."

"Thank you, Norma, but I'm fine—no, I'm not neglecting myself."

"You're sure? All right. If you change your mind, you know where to find me. I have to go back to the ward now. Oh yes, Melissa wants to go for a ride. It's all right for her to be out for an hour."

Roxanna waved at Melissa sitting in the shade thrown by the magnificent branches of a large willow. Her visitor was Becky.

"Mom." Melissa rose to meet her mother, and Roxanna could see that her limp was more pronounced. She swallowed away the urge to burst out crying, and knelt in the grass just in time to keep her knees from buckling under her.

Gathering the child into her arms, a vision of Doctor Henninger's scrubbed face frowned at her from behind Melissa's shoulder. And she remembered his words. "Blood count...white cells...invasion, radiation.... We're going in to have a look...

"When?" she had asked.

"Soon as we can...," he had said.

33

"Hi, sweetheart. Was that you singing those lovely notes?"

"I asked her to show me," Melissa said, pointing to the shiny black guitar almost shyly. "She asked me if I wanted to learn how to play it...and she"ll even teach me to sing." Melissa was so happy at this prospect that Roxanna was unable to resist. She tore her eyes away from her daughter's enchanted face to look at Becky and found grey eyes staring at her.

"All for nothing?" Roxanna asked, looking elsewhere quickly, for it seemed those eyes could read the fear, taut in her body.

"All for nothing?" Melissa repeated.

"Well...." Becky plunked her guitar and recited, *"I charge ten bucks an hour, oops, Mom's face turns sour; oh well, I'm a sport rich as hell, (and yeah, I'm the sport who'll teach you well) yeah, yeah, I'm the sport who'll charge you plenny, so how's about a twenny?"*

Melissa laughed and clapped her hands. Roxanna grinned, sending Becky a grateful look. Then she hugged Melissa, not noticing how, all of a sudden, Becky looked all hot and flustered.

Roxanna smacked a kiss on Melissa's cheek, thanking her for laughter. It was the depth of the laugh that had touched her, made her see Becky with different eyes, made her suspect that Becky could do more than entertain house-guests.

Becky said off-handedly, "I promised I'd ask if we could go for a ride."

Roxanna inspected Melissa; she knew how Melissa loved a car ride. "Are you tired?"

"A little. But I can sleep on the way back, can't I, Becky?"

"Your Mom's the boss."

"Okay. The boss gives her permission. On one condition—the boss comes along."

Melissa fell asleep against Roxanna on the back seat, but Roxanna let Becky drive on, out of Straker, past the tourist infested boulevard and up the coast.

Becky stopped her car at the highest point, away from a cluster of unoccupied cars. On this windy spot nature ruled with obstinacy. Its meager trees, sturdy enough to survive the salty air, resembled plucked skeletons. They stood bound to the rock, defying the unceasing winds. High above hung a solitary cloud. Below, mighty waves bashed the frothing rocks, withdrew, only to leap again. The trees, the yellow grass, the naked match stick branches, all existed with sullen perseverance, bloodless but not lifeless, neither ugly nor exciting, silent yet teeming with a thousand vibrations.

Later—on those days when Roxanna felt reality's dry tentacles suck at the blind corners of her sanity—when the word hope became just a word—when she felt the need to run, to scream, to howl—when she needed to dance, to whirl—and when she wanted to be alone together with ghosts, she would take Melissa out to this place. They would listen to the silence, to the roar of these thunderous waves. They'd have their own cozy niche in the rocks and they would sit there looking out across the vast expanse of water. And even though Melissa could not quite understand her mother's unspoken feelings, she'd hold her mother's arms around her and sing, tentatively, children's songs close by her ear.

On that first day, when Becky had showed her the spot, wordlessly telling her that here was an oasis, and that she, Becky, had found it, and that Roxanna also had a right to it—the ride back had been a silent one. While Roxanna carried a sleeping Melissa to her ward, Becky waited in the cool shade of an old, gently rustling elm which guarded the entry of the West Wing. Roxanna returned; they walked down the gravel path leading to the parking lot. Still they did not speak. Just before they parted, each to go to their separate cars, Roxanna said, "Becky?"

Becky turned to her, shading her eyes.

"Thank you."

A shrug. "You're welcome."

Roxanna watched as Becky drove away with her engine roaring. She turned away only when the car disappeared around the bend, and shook her head imperceptibly, an unconscious habit—her Irish Dad's mannerism when it was hard for him to comprehend a certain situation.

Not that this minute motion made her understand Becky.

Chapter 5

After her weekly talk with the Team, Roxanna went for a solitary walk around the grounds of the clinic. The children who could still stand on their feet would soon be allowed out of the wards; Melissa was probably already craning her neck. But Roxanna could not face her, not yet. The medicine folk were going to make her child sicker than she already was, and they were going to do it with her permission.

It hurt. She felt icy pinpoints of pain digging dully and insistently into her temples; she felt a rock of nausea in her stomach, and it had the taste of bile. Her mood was nasty; her thoughts nightmarish.

She thought back over her conversation with the doctor. He had said, "We are going to repeat the whole thing again. For another seven weeks." Jesus, what had she expected? He had gone on, "...And then, to be absolutely sure, we might have to amputate. And you can hope for at least five years; if she passes that milestone we can hope for ten. If the surgeon decides not to amputate—do you understand what this would mean, Ms. Vaughan?"

"Doctor, does this mean she'll be dead within six months? So it's not even worth the trouble?"

"I honestly can't tell you; I honestly can't tell you Ms. Vaughan. We aim not to maim the patient if it is not absolutely necessary—the biopsy...damned if you do, damned if you don't... could have triggered growth—I don't know, we'll have to wait and see, we have to wait and wait and we have to...."

"Dr. Oates, radiologist."

" How do you do?"

"We have agreed to the following treatment—radical high-dose radiation therapy, alternated with chemo-therapy...."

She remembered them all. Dr. Walters, chemotherapist....

36

She had said,"I'm fine, it's my child who's not feeling well."

Dr. Vonstaff, the surgeon...It had been nod, nod, please don't fall asleep, but then again you've heard it all before.

Dr. Sharon McDonnell, pediatrician...Yes, I remember you. I remember your warmth. Hi, Team.

Roxanna strolled on through the meticulously kept gardens, paused beneath a mournful branch of a willow tree. She sat near the pond and watched the goldfish until her sight blurred. She looked up and searched for God's forgiveness. And Melissa's.

* * *

Roxanna began working full-time to get full pay; nearly all her free time she spent with Melissa at the clinic. At the request of the nurses in the children's ward, she and other parents whose children didn't need continuous presence yet, left when it was time for the children to have their evening meal. This old, neglected house rule was put back in effect because of the children's unruliness with the nurses when parents were around.

Roxanna noticed the same behavior in her usually quiet child, but Norma assured her that the restlessness, the tearfulness was natural. Melissa was responding to her surroundings, taking in both the good, and the bad. So, Roxanna had little choice but to go home to the typical suppers already in full swing by the time she walked in.

Zoe was exclaiming, "Me? I trust fish. Hell, when they're six feet under water I trust 'em."

"I like fish," Bobby was informing his mother.

"Whose side are you on? Fish, fish, fish, that's all Joan wants to talk about. She ought to apply to the Zoo."

"The Zoo?" Both Bobby and Joan chorused.

"Caretaker of the aquariums," Zoe recited, one hand cleaving the air. "Ah, there you are, Rox, sit down, sit. Get her a plate, Bobby. Have some fish."

Joan and Bobby laughed. "Zoe respects fish," Joan said to Roxanna. "It's the bones—once one of her fishy friends nearly choked her to death...." Joan's voice abruptly lost its light tone. She stared at Zoe. "God, you nearly croaked. Why am I joking about it?"

Zoe shrugged. "Beats me."

"What happened?" Roxanna asked, inspecting her food.

"Joannie put her finger in Mom's throat..." Bobby began as if Roxanna had appointed him, "...and then she...."

"Bobby..." Zoe tried.

"...puked all over Joannie," Bobby finished, then to rub it in, "and all over the table."

"Bobby," Joan groaned, "your language!"

"Finish up now, Bobby," said Zoe, clearing plates, "you still have some packing to do and I know your father; he'll be here before the chickens are up. Oh the peace and quiet we'll have for the next sixty days or so."

"Poor goats, pigs, chickens, horses and elephants...." Joan clucked.

"Daddy's farm don't have elephants."

"Doesn't have, Bobby," Zoe corrected, absent-mindedly.

"Just all the rest." Bobby grinned at Joan. "Are you coming to help me pack?"

"Yessir. But first...." Joan pointed to the heap of peas on his plate. Bobby began to plough, like always, deeply sorry for having saved his vegetables for the last minute. Zoe watched her son, thinking. You're going away for the summer again. I'm not sending you away, but your father wants a piece of you. I don't mind, not really; your father and I loved each other once. You are the result of that love, so he can have a little of you too. No, I don't mind. There'll come a distant day when you'll call yourself grown-up and your father and I will have to let you go. Who will claim your summers then?

"Bobby, remember I'll be picking you up the last week in August. We'll spend the rest of the summer vacation at the beach house in Little Town, all right? When are you going back to school?" Zoe meant the question more for Joan than for Bobby.

While Bobby looked pensive, trying to figure out if he wouldn't mind trading the farm in for the beach, Joan answered, "The twelfth. September. To tell you the truth, Zoe, this is the first time I'm hearing this. What about my vacation schedule? Are you guys going without me?"

"Can I be excused," Booby squeaked, already of his chair.

38

"Sure," said Joan. "I'll come help you pack your backpack in a minute, okay?"

"Okay." Bobby left the table with the speed of a tornado, nearly colliding with Becky who evaded him like a lithe bull-fighter dodging a charging bull.

"You're excused," She called after him. "Hi folks, I'm off to earn myself a living. Yummie, is that wine I see?" Becky placed her guitar case against the wall and poured herself half a glass. She slugged it down is if it were water, raised her hand in farewell, and was gone.

"Whoever that was," Joan asked her spare-rib, "doesn't she ever eat?"

Roxanna's mind drifted off as she continued eating. She checked the time on her wrist-watch. Her brain rejected what her eyes picked up, and she needed to look twice before the correct time registered.

It wasn't Becky's hurried entrance and exit which had thrown her off slightly, she was sure; after all, she hadn't seen her since Melissa had been re-admitted to the clinic. And while she knew from Norma Lewis that Becky did visit Melissa, toting her guitar, one way or another, these visits did not coincide with her own. Sitting at the dinner table Roxanna admitted to herself, she bothers me. I don't want her to, but she bothers me.

"How old is Becky?" Roxanna heard herself ask, and became acutely aware of having interrupted a conversation. Zoe and Joan looked wonderingly at her. "I'm sorry, I didn't...." She regretted asking such a silly question anyway, and started making leaving signs.

"Becky will be twenty-six next fall," Joan said. "Doesn't look or act a day over sixteen, don't you think?"

"Thank you, Joan." Roxanna said demurely.

Zoe said suddenly, "You haven't seen Becky's performance yet at the club, right?"

"She sings to my daughter...." Roxanna muttered, but Joan heard. Her eyes fell on Roxanna for a silent incomprehensible moment, one eyebrow raised.

Zoe jabbered on, "How about surprising her? Tonight? Come on, you need a break."

Roxanna looked doubtful. "I'll be with Melissa until eight-

39

thirty. I planned on doing some reading afterwards."

"Read tomorrow. Look, Friday night it's sold out, but I'll call one of the waitresses, a friend of mine. I'll ask her for the VIP treatment. Come on, let's have us a night out on the town."

"First let's see if Bobby can stay over at Freddie's." Ever-mindful Joan walked over to the phone. "We can't stay late though."

* * *

The Blue Notes was situated in the very heart of Straker's nightlife district. A simple, blue sign hung vertically above a sculpted wrought-iron gate. It seemed insignificant among the rows of many sparkling red, white and yellow neon, flashing off and on along the avenue. Roxanna knew this was the way the owners wanted it, but had she come alone, it would have taken her a while to find the place. Or maybe she wouldn't have found it at all.

The gate opened into a freshly scrubbed patio the shape and size of a handkerchief. Three widely spaced steps, also rigorously scrubbed and bearing the signs of receding pools of water, led to a battered oaken door. Its only ornament was a small window.

Zoe jabbed at the push-button bell. After a moment the window opened silently. They were aware of a short, but thorough scrutiny of their faces before the door was opened. They entered the club and the door closed behind them, shutting out the sounds of the street. Inside the lights were muted, and the atmosphere was pleasant.

Instantly, Roxanna felt an air of expectancy; the place was packed. Every chair and table and standing space, even strategic points on the floor were occupied. She followed Zoe through the crowd towards the bar situated in the back.

Along the way, they lost Joan who reappeared from an entirely different direction. By jumping up and down, arm raised as if she were at the Stock Exchange, Zoe finally managed to attract her friend's attention.

They were assigned a table just off a tiny raised stage which had enough room for an upright piano, a stool and microphone. This was followed shortly by two waitresses carrying chairs over their heads through the crowd. They plunked down the chairs at an already over-burdened table. This, Roxanna understood, was VIP treatment.

"It isn't always like this," Zoe said as she maneuvered the chairs closer together. "It's worse on Saturday nights."

From where they sat Roxanna had a clear view of a narrow, badly lit passage leading to the back exit. There was another door there; the human traffic going in and out of that particular door was heavy. And it was from this door that Becky emerged, followed by Cindy.

Suddenly a beam of light exploded and the stage came alight. Applause burst forth, whistles shrilled. While this was going on, Roxanna realized that the circle of light also reached the first row of tables, including theirs.

Becky appeared then; tall and handsome in tight blue jeans and a white summer blouse, the sleeves rolled up to her elbows. She stepped into the light as quietly as a ghost. Applause swelled; she bowed and her highlighted hair shifted over her shoulders. She raised her head, let her gaze run over the audience for as far as she could see them. She had a smile for all, blew a kiss here and there, and winked almost imperceptibly at Roxanna.

A muscle jumped in Roxanna's stomach.

Becky picked up her guitar and hooked a black boot into the rail of the stool as she sat. Glaring with one eye into the light, she poked the microphone, "Okay, Laura, we know you don't like competition, but this is ridiculous."

Laughter rippled through the audience. From where the spot-light originated high up in back, a voice shouted, "You got it, honey." The light died abruptly and everything was hurled into a buzzing darkness.

"I told you she doesn't like competition."

The light went back on, the beam searching a wayward path through the audience until it found Becky again.

"She used to work for a circus," Becky said. "But she was fired—she couldn't keep track of the elephant." And she blew a kiss into the air.

"This is her I'm-not-really-nervous routine," Zoe whispered.

"I've never seen her so composed," Roxanna replied, trying to tear her eyes off the woman on stage, but finding she could not.

Feeling her defenses slip, she realized they had been up for a long time, much too long a time. But if the new-born flower of love bloomed in her heart, its smell heady, its honey sweetening her blood, the subtle cruelty of rejection became her merciless shield. Besides, she had other things on her mind.

"Speaking of competition, we have some in tonight. Let's welcome Olivia and Jenney, bar-tenders at the Merry-Go-Round. If there are any other new-comers tonight, I hope you'll enjoy the show. I'll be a regular myself all summer. Every other week we have a real live boogie band in—and one of the members is Cindy, right here. Cindy has been on the road with me for the last few months," Becky tuned her guitar as she spoke. "...we had a blast, played at the Women's Spring Retreat over Memorial Day weekend. (To this came some stomping of feet and whistles.) You were there? Great, great. Didn't we have a good time? Anyway, Cindy will accompany me on the piano. She hopes."

There was a brief round of applause, and Cindy made a face as she sat down at the piano and let her fingers roll softly along the keys. The flowing melody formed a gentle background to Becky's voice. "Tonight I'm going to sing a couple of new songs, try them out on you, a couple of old songs, and some songs I hope will make you stay long after others have gone home to sleep. Maybe this one will make you laugh. It's about a switch-board operator...."

"I got me ten flyin' hands
Hello? Yes, I'm your switchboard operator.
Hello? Yes, a thousand calls from distant lands.
Hello? Yes, sometimes my head's like a broken vibe-rator...."

Roxanna learned how Becky played with the sound of her voice. Laughter from the audience came easily, provoked by the way she carried a line. How she hushed even the restless in the crowd, singing about the joy and pain of love affairs. She moved the audience when she threw the rawness of dreams gone torpid at their feet. She manipulated the feelings of those who clapped for her. That night Roxanna knew why Becky was the sweet-heart of many lonely women.

42

"I'll sing you a song I wrote recently..." Becky gasped a little, took a sip of water from a glass by her stool, "...I really mean recently, so forgive me should anything go wrong. Cindy?"

Cindy nodded, looked neither left nor right, then suddenly started to plink loudly, Oh Suzannah...

"Cindy, please...." Becky tried, but the audience caught on. After the clapping, the stomping and the singing had died down, Becky sent Cindy a 'thank you very much' look before she turned back to the audience. "Now, that's all very well—Cindy, do you mind? Thank you. I wrote the following song for a little girl—she's about this high—who stole my heart. We made it up together and laughed a lot. She has a very clear voice, and I wish she could sing it with me. It'll be a while before she's allowed in here to help out, so tonight..." Becky scanned the audience, her look resting for a tick of time on Roxanna, "tonight I dedicate this song to the woman who is very dear to her, to the woman who loves her, her mother. She's somewhere out there with you all, and I hope..." Becky fumbled with her guitar strings almost shyly, "No, I'm sure this little girl will grow up to teach her generation what she knows—and to sing. Cindy, whenever you're ready...."

> "I know a girl, says she's searching
> for a pony that can fly
> Just like a Queen, she prances,
> leaving magic when she dances.
> I know a girl, says she's searching
> for a rainbow in the sky.
> But for me it's true bliss
> when she searches for a kiss...."

After Becky's sets, the club emptied out noticeably. Still the place remained alive, full of conversation and arguments, cruising, laughter and jostling. Roxanna witnessed how Becky's honey attracted bees, all right. From the moment Becky placed her seat on one of the vacated chairs at their table a continuous flow of admirers visited. Zoe and Joan seemed used to it all; they hardly interrupted their conversation when yet another woman danced by for a hug, a kiss, a date. Roxanna, minding her own

43

business, thought her own thoughts about this phenomenon—It's all very nice but isn't it driving her crazy?

Suddenly Roxanna jumped in her chair, startled by a voice close to her ear. "So you're the one these days?"

Turning she saw a leather-clad woman who gazed intently at her. Conversation at the table had ceased. Zoe was sending Becky an urgent look and Becky opened her mouth to say something to the woman, but did not get further than, "Sss...."

"Yup, I guess you're the one. She goes for brunettes. Is Becky starting her own live-in harem? Good luck. Want some advice? Be good, real good, cause she'll want more and more, and baby, she wants plenty. And then snap, it'll be bye-bye. Well, see ya round Short Story." 'Sss' sent Becky a livid 'so-there' look and swished away with her head held high.

Roxanna was stunned. "Short Story?"

Seconds passed at the table. In that span of time, Joan looked at her fingernails, and Zoe tried hard not to do the whistling.

"I'm a Short Story?" Roxanna repeated, her eyes falling on Becky.

Becky, pretending she had not heard a thing, was looking around the table at the confusion of empty glasses, cigarette packs, and overflowing ashtrays. Ignoring Roxanna's stare, she asked blankly, "How about drinks, anyone? Scotch on the rocks might do, wine, beer? Beer, right?"

Roxanna watched her make her way through the crowd. Then she turned to her companions. "Whatever gave that woman the idea....?"

"Don't you feel a draft all of a sudden?" Joan asked, glancing over her shoulder, up and around the smoke-clogged ceiling.

Zoe leaned towards Roxanna, put a hand on her arm. "Rox, don't get your hackles up over someone who has had too much to drink. Tell me something, Becky didn't try to get fresh with you yet?"

"Zoe!" Joan tugged at Zoe's sleeve. "That's none of your business. Jeez, I definitely feel a draft. Rox, you're making the beer freeze over. Come on, we need to get home soon."

"Anyone can make a mistake," said Zoe soothingly, and although Roxanna's face did thaw, Zoe wasn't convinced the coast was clear.

"Just a minute. You go ahead, I'll be right along."

* * *

Roxanna's first impression of Becky's tiny dressing room was one of chaos— clothes strewn all over the place, mostly shirts and jeans, and a lot of sheet music lying about. Amidst all this jumble sat a green, vinyl couch, stuffing sprouting out where the vinyl had ruptured. Becky was sprawled in her typical Becky-way on it. Her knees were wide apart and her arms and hands dangled between her thighs. When she saw Roxanna she let her tongue hang out in a mock gesture. Then she motioned vaguely towards a wobbly chair in front of the badly battered vanity which bravely sported an old, chipped mirror. "Sit down, won't you?"

Roxanna declined. "Zoe and Joan are waiting for me in the parking lot. Cindy and a couple of others are waiting for you. I came to tell you how much I enjoyed this evening...."

"I'm glad. Did I contribute to that?" Not that Becky sounded interested. In fact, she wasn't even looking at Roxanna; instead she was unbuttoning the first button of her white blouse as she blew a jet stream from her lips. "Jeez, it's hot in here...."

"And I appreciated your gesture, the song you sang for Melissa. I liked it very much."

Becky smiled suddenly, all teeth. "Yeah, so did I. Almost flawless, huh?" She grew more animated. "She's sort of an inspiration to me. I don't know why...." She struggled for words, then dropped whatever she was going to say. Excitedly she continued, "Roxanna, did you ever notice how Melissa goes bonkers when she sees a piano?"

"Uh...no...."

Melissa and pianos? Melissa and tumors had been on her mind. Melissa and life had been on her mind.

"Well?"

"Well what?"

"I can teach her how to play."

Roxanna smiled. "Yes, yes of course."

And the earlier incident was buried.

45

Chapter 6

"Robert was seeing another woman."

"What do you call what you were doing?" Roxanna chuckled.

Zoe snickered as only a conspirator could. They were sitting outside on the porch, discussing the coming special summer edition of *A Differing Point of View*. But the exceptionally cool summer day was distracting, and their conversation kept straying. Two drinks, gin and tonics, and refills helped them to relax some more. Across the lawn in the shade of the hedge, Becky sat strumming her guitar while Joan and Melissa sprawled lazily around her.

"Joan didn't give a hoot that I was six years older."

"Why you lucky old cow, you."

Zoe tried a dirty look which did not have the desired effect. "Do you want to hear the story or not?"

Roxanna refrained from informing Zoe about letters long ago received, knowing Zoe loved to tell the tale. "How about Joan's parents? Didn't they—do they know?"

"Not a thing, and they never will if she can help it. My parents, my family think I'm immorality come to life. Especially after Robert and I divorced. You don't do things like that where I come from."

"Do they know about Joan? All...this?" Roxanna's hand swept the garden.

"I don't think so. They're clear across the country and I don't send Christmas cards. How about your parents? I mean, your mother."

"I told her about two years ago, and it hardly matters to her if I'm unattached. She is very supportive of me and Melissa, especially now. What about custody of Bobby, was that ever a problem?"

"Look, I knew Robert was seeing another woman and if he

46

wouldn't have asked for a divorce, I would have. I knew I could get Bobby because of Robert's adultery. But I was wanting to be with Joan. I didn't dare hasten things or be too conspicuous. What if the judge turned out to be a bigot? Robert didn't mind me keeping the baby. How'd he take care of him up there wherever he was going? But we agreed he's see him once in a while—in the summers when Bobby could walk and he didn't have to wipe ass—I still send Bobby up there reluctantly—Robert is such a scatterbrain. I hear he has a child now with his new woman. Another son."

"I never understood why the hell you got married to him in the first place."

"Oh Rox, think about it. The usual social pressure, my virtuous tradition-ridden upbringing. Last but not least, I loved Robert. I did. He had beautiful long hair—and he still can't keep a job. So now he farms. It took me awhile to realize I loved him like a favorite brother. In the end I think he loved me like a favorite sister...." Zoe's voice faded. "Maybe I thought Bobby could save things," she said as an afterthought. "I don't know. Then I met Joan."

"Yeah—in the delivery room!"

Zoe laughed. "Of all places. There were complications and Robert fainted. The nurses had to carry him out. Poor guy. He wanted so much to be there, you know? So they gave me Joan to hang onto. She stayed with me all those terrible hours. Hours." Zoe sighed, remembering the birth of her big, big baby. "Joan said it was love at first sight for her. Hell of a first sight, let me tell you, but we laughed a lot. It was crazy.... Some time later we met again at the Merry-Go-Round. We became friends and one thing...led to another. I mean, look at her. I couldn't resist her; I still can't.

"Now that I've bored you with the story of my life, tell me what happened between you and Rick."

Zoe's unexpected question startled Roxanna who looked away.

"You ran off with the teacher—Biology, wasn't she?" Suddenly Zoe chuckled and touched Roxanna's arm. "Remember I caught the two of you? Woah, it really opened my eyes to you. Pity I wasn't the only one who caught you with her. Did you see each other again after you were dismissed?"

Roxanna nodded, made as if to speak, but remained silent, and Zoe did not probe. She said, "You and I have always been good friends. Sometimes I wonder why we didn't become lovers."

"You mean, bed and all?"Roxanna seemed relieved to change the subject. "Because I had a crush of Linda for ages. You couldn't have come between us if you had tried."

"Neither could Rick, and he wanted to badly," said Zoe softly.

"Zoe, please." Roxanna sipped her drink, and after a moment's hesitation, began to speak. It didn't take Zoe long to regret her quest to know.

"Rick knew about her from the start. He didn't care, not then. God...we'd fight, Rick and I...about her, about his politics which she didn't like. We'd stay up whole nights, killing each other with words. There was so much hate. Rick always won. Always. I'm great with my pen, you know that, but not with my mouth. So as a perpetual loser I ran away. I ran to her, always. Rick hated it. He began to hate her with a frightening fierceness. The more he hated her, the more I ran to her. I was in an emotional yo-yo, trapped." Roxanna took a sip, another, and an even larger one. She found she was sweating. She didn't want to talk about that confused time in her life, about the two people she had loved. At the same time she couldn't keep her mouth shut. "One morning he woke up and realized he hated himself for not being able to let me go. I finally made up my own mind and told him I wanted to end the whole sordid affair. He was devastated. God, it was six years ago but it's like yesterday."

"Roxanna, I'm sorry. If you don't want to talk about it...."

"Oh, I'm all right, Zoe. Honest." But she didn't look it, and Zoe felt deeply sorry for having brought up ghosts.

"I know a great deal of what was going on," Zoe said quietly. "But I didn't know there was so much hate."

"All three of us were living in a sort of smoky-glass hell. No one else had entrance. I was too in love with Linda to realize how much I was hurting Rick. He wanted us to get married. I was too inexperienced and unsure of myself yet to know that I had a choice.

"Two weeks after I left Rick and moved in with Linda, he came to the house when Linda was at work. He begged me to talk to him. I let him in. He raped me. You know what a lot of guys think: all a lesbo needs is a good fuck and she'll be cured. I cried for days, wouldn't let Linda touch me. And then I was sick, throwing up all the time. I realized I was pregnant. I never told him about Melissa."

"But you kept her...."

"Yes. It was as though she was the small part of myself I found I could love...."

"I'm sorry, I didn't...." Zoe started, bewildered because of Roxanna's factual tone. In the end she kept her mouth shut wondering what had happened to the beautiful day. After a while, breaking her uneasy silence, she asked, "Why didn't you ever tell me?"

Roxanna smiled, showing she was really all right. She said dryly, "You were busy, either organizing demonstrations, speaking out, or getting arrested for civil disobedience, remember? Waiting to get bailed out. What was my saga in comparison? Oh, and the time you spent in the hospital...."

Zoe chuckled; she was more at ease with these recollections though they were just as cruel and frustrating. "The time I got shoved into an oncoming car? I got a good settlement out of it though. How do you think I keep going? Small consolation— there are times my right knee still hurts, especially when there's a change in the weather. I think I'm going to have trouble with it when I'm older—just so I never forget, and can ruminate whether it was worth it...."

"Oh workaholics...." Joan approached them, carrying Melissa who had wrapped her scrawny legs around her waist.

"I think she means us," Zoe said, ignoring Roxanna's look.

"Mel says it's time for her medicine," Joan said as she deposited Melissa on the table. "And she has a teeny weeny headache, nothing Mommy can't take care of."

Roxanna rose immediately and let Melissa's reaching arms encircle her neck as she lifted her. Excusing themselves, she carried Melissa inside.

Joan sat down with a weary sigh.

"What's that mean?" Zoe asked carefully.

"I'm hot," Joan explained, wiping her forehead with a limp wrist, followed by a meaningful look. "Remember last summer when the house was empty?"

Zoe grinned. "You like to claim I was always too busy."

"Except you get so much more relaxed when Bobby's gone."

"I do?"

"Now that he doesn't take naps anymore."

"Come here, you." Zoe said suggestively.

Joan did, scraping her chair on the red concrete just when Becky called, "Hey Jellyfish! Where are those cards? I thought we had a score to settle. Wishful thinking on your part, of course."

"Yeah, yeah, sure," Joan mumbled, standing behind Zoe's chair, and putting her arms around her neck. Zoe leaned backwards and they kissed, accompanied by Becky's smoky moaning, "Oh dahling, dahling, I love thee so but now I must run and go gamble with the household money...."

When the twosome came up for air, they realized that Roxanna had come back out and was sitting at the table, shuffling through some papers. Zoe took the hint.

"I'll get the cards," said a sultry Joan, breaking away. "Back to work...."

Zoe grunted, and leaned over the table, trying to focus her thoughts. "Now, about the art department. Who's covering the ceramic exhibit?"

"We took care of that already, Zoe. You don't seem to be with me is what I think."

Zoe blinked, rattled her glass of ice-cubes. "I'm sorry, Rox, I was thinking."

"That's the idea," Roxanna said wryly. "Dare I ask about what?"

"Sex—I mean, sex education. And Bobby."

"Oh?" Roxanna restrained herself from further comment.

"Rox, it's about time I enlightened him. He's at that age. He's giving me funny looks so I feel I have to keep my clothes on all the time. And Joan, she's right, I'm not as relaxed about it as I should be."

"Ah...."

"And he is in a house full of girls who don't go to bed with boys. I can't just leave it in the hands of our trusty educators...school you know? Or handle it the way my parents did,

50

unable to handle weird questions. The teacher doesn't know how to begin—so you find out in the school yard, or the back seat, get pregnant...."

"Zoe, you're babbling. Bobby? Pregnant?"

"Well, I'd hold him accountable! Sorry. It's just I've been thinking about the whole thing off and on, and I'm not sure how to handle it. Thing is, how do I tell him about Joan and me?"

"You tell him about sexual preference. It's not like it's news to him," said Roxanna patiently.

"You mean, put it into words? He's only seven."

"No, Zoe. You wait until he's thirty." Sarcasm dripped in the cool summer afternoon.

"Very funny. Sometimes I wonder if it's any of his business, or that he'll hold it against me when he is thirty....Hey, you've got a curious daughter to deal with yourself, you know."

"I know. But right now I'm more concerned with keeping her alive and well than telling her who I roll around with." Roxanna's hand cleaved the air as she quoted authorities, "'In the family where a child has cancer, life has to go on as normal as ever. This is important for the child, and the parents, blah blah blah.

"But I'd tell her, or Bobby for that matter, about the birds and the bees, if she should ask. And she will. And he will, soon. Haven't you discussed this with Joan? Enlighten him together."

"Joan...." Zoe sighed dramatically. "She'd draw him pictures. Why she isn't on the Board of Sex and Health Education I'll never know."

"So? Why are you breaking out in hives over this? The three of you are inseparable, family, you know."

Zoe smiled tenderly at recollections. "Yeah. Bobby was two months old when Joan saw him again. He was only a little older when we started living together. Hell, she has been there from the start." She looked fondly over to where Joan and Becky, aided by a six-pack, were slapping down cards noisily in the scant shade.

For a while Roxanna helped her look over, then snapped out of it, especially when she realized it wasn't Joan she was looking at.

"Look Zoe, I think we have the golden opportunity here for an

51

editorial, perhaps a forum, a letter write-in. It's an important issue. Let's find out what other families do. The successes, the failures—learn from the experts."

"I knew I wanted you on board. Will you write the lead article?"

* * *

Late that night before she went to bed, Roxanna checked in on Melissa. She rearranged the sheet around the small shoulders, and for a while, listened intently to the child's breathing. Satisfied, she rose, began to leave the room, then went back to the bed. Ever so gently she brushed her fingers along the top of Melissa's head. She didn't need to see in the dark to know that silk hair came away with her hand.

She left the room with a heavy feeling in her chest. Sitting in her den, she stared out into the quiet night at the lonely pinpoints of light from neighboring houses, lights blinking through the stately swaying elms.

Her fingers toyed with a pencil; it rolled against an ashtray filled with paper-clips and thumbtacks; it rolled back again. You've got a curious daughter to deal with yourself, you know. The pencil tapped against the wood of the desk, was dropped, picked up, and then strong fingers broke it in two with a sharp crack.

In the dead stillness of the den the sound was as lonely as she felt.

Chapter 7

A few days later Roxanna came home to an unusually empty house. She knew Joan was on the late shift and that Zoe was attending a cocktail party for public relations. She had declined the invitation, choosing to spend the evening with Melissa.

It had not been an easy evening; Melissa's mood had been sour, rebellious. Roxanna believed her daughter's present state of mind had to do with the loss of her Gypsy-black hair. They discussed the why and how of it--that her hair would grow back, perhaps thicker, blacker, and that her hair would not fall out again. As if she hadn't told Melissa this ten times before. She was certain Melissa understood, but her rebellion had not diminished. And soon she would be feeling too sick to bother decorating the nearest nurse or herself with food. Roxanna could not suppress a tingle of a smile as she rifled through the mail on the hall table. There was a letter from her mother, but also an official looking envelope, undoubtedly a bill. "And a fat one you'll be," she muttered to herself. She ascended the staircase in darkness, expecting to find the second floor dark too, but Becky's door stood ajar, and a streak of light poured out of her room.

Roxanna went into to her own room, placed her briefcase beside the desk and took a can of light-beer out of the cooler there. She kicked off her shoes, sat down and opened her mother's letter:

I have enclosed bills we've been expecting, and a reminder from the bank that the first payment of the Monte Cristo loan is due next month. Roxy, do you think I ought to sell the house? It's getting to be too big for me and after my last boarder turned out to be wanted for armed robbery—he was such a nice young man—shows you can never tell—I've become reluctant to let strangers into the house. What do you think? I'm waiting for your go-ahead. How is my baby? Is she adapting to the new clinic?

Has she made new friends?

Roxanna folded the letter slowly, methodically, making a mental note to call her mother when Mel was home so the two could chat. A bittersweet smile played across her lips. The house for the life of my child. It would break her mother's heart to part with the colonial monstrocity and its ghosts. Mom, could you part with all the blood, sweat and tears that kept those walls together? That keep you together? Where will you go then?

We were happy in that house, Roxanna thought. Pa, Jonathan, you and me. We were poor, we struggled, we were eager to survive. Then one day Pa went and fell off the roof, broke his neck, and died right then and there in the backyard. It was harder after that, but we managed. You dragged both Jonathan and me through college. My thank-you was the child you kept while I came and went in search of my own tools— hoping they would bring me wisdom. Although you must have disapproved, you never stopped me. How you wanted Jonathan and me to have a future--while you stayed at home with Pa's ghost, and the memories.

Roxanna rubbed the bridge of her nose, her eyes squeezed shut, a thick frown cleaving her forehead. One thing at a time, she thought, please. First the bills. The house? No. Not the house. Not my mother. At least, not yet.

Impulsively she shoved everything aside, the letter, the bills, the unopened envelope. She stood, hunched over like an old and weary woman, and willed herself to tune her mind into what she needed to do next. Yes, a shower, a long, cold shower to wash away the grime of another day of hurried existence.

She undressed, shrugged into her robe. After an impatient search for her slippers, she sashayed through the hallway to the bathroom. Reaching for the door, her hand wavered. She heard her name, a weak call, but she didn't know where it came from. Roxanna cocked an ear, listening. Silence.

"I'm hearing things," she said to herself and pushed open the door.

"No, you're not," came a distinct reply. "It's me, Becky. Please come here for a minute?"

Whatever she expected when she entered Becky's bedroom, it was not the wreck lying prostrate between disheveled, sweaty sheets. Sudden, inexplicable icy fingers clutched at her stomach, at her heart, and she felt her knees grow weak. She squeaked, "Becky?"

"It all looks worse than it is," said Becky simply.

The skin-colored bandage above Becky's right eye seeped with a brownish stain. Below the rim of the bandage, the perfectly shaped eyebrow was parted by a small vicious cut which did not bleed. The right side of her face was a bit swollen, and inundated with the angry orange of iodine. And that wasn't all. Except for a flimsy top, Becky wore only gaily flowered underpants. The protruding right leg was bandaged from half way up her thigh to below her knee; the unbandaged flesh of her thigh was also yellow from iodine.

Sitting down carefully on the edge of the bed, probably afraid it would break, Roxanna's horrified eyes swept Becky's half-nude, battered body. "Not a fight, was it?"

"No, no! Can you get me a glass of water, please?"

"Sure. Sure."

Roxanna was gone and back so fast that Becky was still in the act of unfolding the little envelope with its comforting white powder. She shook the contents into the glass greedily. "A painkiller. Joan gave me tons of this," She gasped afterwards, then allowed a small painful grin. "I'm a mess, huh?"

"What happened?"

"My windshield exploded on me," Becky said in a tone of voice which could make anyone believe it was the most natural thing to happen.

"Your windshield exploded? Just like that?"

"You know Atlas Crossing, right? There's this bend in the road—everybody wants a two-way mirror there...you know, so you can see what's happening on the other side? Or a traffic light. Something. Well, I was turning the corner and there was this dog sitting right in the middle of the road. I swerved and hit a parked car. And then there was glass flying all over the place. I think the heat had something to do with it." After this barrage, Becky looked as smug as Melissa would with one of her innocent 'see-I-had-nothing-to-do-with-it' smirks.

"How fast were you going?" Roxanna asking, thawing.

Becky shrugged airily. "It's a bit downhill there...."

55

"Which answers my question. And the dog?"

"I don't know. I was kind of dazed. They patched me up at the clinic. They wanted to keep me there, but because I didn't have a concussion, I persuaded them to let me go. Joan gave me a ride home. She went back to work."

"Do you want something to eat?"

"Joan fixed me something, thank you."

Roxanna returned Becky's rather shy smile, relaxing the muscles in her shoulders, and glanced around the room.

Except for the bed, it was an exact replica of Becky's dressing room back at the club. A wicker chair stood overloaded with discarded clothes underneath the window; an old vanity was burdened with paper; a night-stand contained more scribble paper.

"It's the car I'm worried about though," Becky sighed, breaking the companionable silence between them. "It's a '69 Ford Mustang, you see."

Sensing this had to have some sort of effect on her Roxanna sighed and nodded in understanding, thinking, Mustangs and Sun people were a breed to behold. Her eyes fell on a row of photographs pinned to the headboard of the bed; they were of a dark-haired woman, a strikingly beautiful woman.

Roxanna lifted an appreciative eyebrow. "Who's she?" She asked before she could stop herself.

"Oh, Audrey?" Becky tried to turn her head, instead brought her hand to her neck, wincing. "Friend of mine. She was like a dream...."

"How was she in reality?" Roxanna asked, looking straight at a blinking Becky.

After a pause, Becky said, "Reality cures many a dream."

"Why do you keep her pictures?" Will you shut up. Why do you care? Roxanne thought.

"I'm sentimental," Becky grinned suddenly, all teeth. "I loved her once.... Do you have any dreams?"

Roxanna saw Becky's grey eyes study her the way they had before. As if she can see straight through me, she thought uneasily. Suddenly, she was tongue-tied, awkward, not the Woman-of-the-World. She wanted to stand up and walk away from this invalid who so wordlessly disturbed her, and she knew she would tell one dream only. "I want Melissa to live a decent life, but you know that already." Then Roxanna heard herself rattle. "You were lucky not to have glass in your eyes. You have beautiful eyes." Oh my God, why did I say that. She must have heard this three thousand times before.

"Thank you," Becky said as though it was real news. "I was wearing shades. Thank god, my reactions are flawless. I used to race cars you know. Drag-racing."

"I'm glad you don't anymore. You don't, do you? Can I get you something? Something more to drink?"

"No thanks. I think I'll try to sleep. I hurt all over."

"I bet you do." Roxanna was about to give Becky's leg a reassuring pat, but remembered just in time that one did not pat a bandaged leg. "I'll get you a fresh sheet. Where is your linen?"

"In the other room. Watch the wires; it's dangerous in there."

*　*　*

The tending of Becky proved to be a problem. Joan was on the late shift, and Zoe, up to her ears in work, could not possibly volunteer. So Roxanna did. She volunteered to cut short her midday visit to Melissa and change guards with Joan who left at three-thirty.

The day after Becky's accident, Roxanna came home early, as was agreed upon. She consulted the message board attached to the refrigerator where Joan had thumbtacked a note with instructions. Reading the note with half an eye, Roxanna fixed herself a late lunch of left-over salad, sardines and buttered crackers. She used her brief-case as a tray to carry the loaded plate upstairs.

Becky heard her. "'Are you who I think you are."

"I'll be right with you," Roxanna answered, opening the door to the den while balancing her case on one hand.

"Does all this service include holding my hand for about fifteen minutes?"

Roxanna didn't answer, but a small, furtive smile played around the corner of her mouth. It disappeared altogether and was replaced by an alarmed look when she finally laid eyes upon the prostrate victim who asked, "Can you help me out of bed?"

"Joan said you were to stay in bed for another two days,"

Roxanna said sternly, the way she did when she tried to squelch rising discontent in Melissa. "And so you will. I follow orders to the letter."

"Oh? And if I wet my pants? Joan tell you where she laid out the Pampers?"

"Oh, I'm sorry. Can you stand up?"

"Maybe, but it'll take awhile. I don't think I can wait."

"All right, let's get that leg out of bed first."

Very carefully, Becky slid her injured leg out of bed, aided by Roxanna's helpful touch. "Good. Now put you arms around my neck and I'll lift you to your feet."

"B-but I'm heavy," Becky protested.

"I'm as strong as I look. Come on, I'm not going to bite you."

"I'd bite you back," Becky muttered, her eyes downcast. "All right, all right, I'm coming." She placed her hands on Roxanna's shoulders, and remained there.

"Around my neck," said Roxanna patiently. "That's better." Roxanna put her arms around Becky's waist and straightened, bringing Becky to her feet.

There was an easier way. They both knew this. Even so, each displayed an ignorance which surprised Roxanna certainly. I'm not going to live through this, she thought, pretending that the hobbling embrace in no way interfered with her heart-beat, that her straying eyes were blind to Becky's tanned, scarcely dressed body, that she was not hoping its suntan-lotion scent could stay with her forever. She was also fervently wishing her hormones would stop forcing her fingers to fully feel, or grip, the hip they had to support.

"Can you manage from here?" She hoped she asked casually as she opened the bathroom door.

"Sure." Becky leaned against the wash basin, and started to strip.

"Don't hurry," Roxanna said, turning away. "I'll straighten out your bed. Holler when you want me to pick you up."

"It's a deal."

Back in bed between well-tucked sheets, Becky's ordeal was only beginning. At the sight of the green and white tube of rubbing ointment, Becky moaned, "No, please. That stuff stinks. Besides, Joan rubbed some on my neck this morning."

"Sorry, but it's like I said: I follow orders to the letter."

"You're being mean to me, is all," Becky pouted.

Roxanna kept a straight face, but laughter rang in her voice when she spoke, "Turn your back to me...bend your head...that's it...."

Roxanna's able fingers massaged the greasy cream into Becky's neck with strong, even strokes. Soon she felt Becky relax underneath her kneading hand. "Now lie down on your stomach. You'll make it easier for me if you take off your shirt."

Becky obeyed grudgingly, reminding Roxanna of Melissa when she had to do something against her will. Once again Roxanna's hand worked Becky's flesh, along Becky's spine she rubbed, down the small of her back. Curvy hips, strong thighs, she thought to herself, and terrific legs, at least, the unbandaged one.

"That shit burns," Becky said with an edge to her voice. "We're finished, right?" She didn't wait for an affirmative, but turned her back carefully, winced when she moved her injured leg. As she reached for her shirt, Roxanna's eyes, like her mind, strayed again. Becky's breasts didn't spill like water-filled balloons, as her own did.... They'd fit in the cup of her hands.... Becky's stomach was flat, not an inch of fat, and she was a true blonde all right.

"Feel any better?" Roxanna asked, dropping the top of the tube for the second time.

"I feel fine, thank you." They were avoiding each other while they shared this politeness. "Joan said I was going to be black and blue all over the place," Becky was mumbling.

"I'm sorry to hear that," Roxanna answered perfunctorily. "I'm going to have some lunch, do some work. I'll come look in on you before I leave for Mel tonight."

On an impulse, Roxanna bent forward and brushed her lips along Becky's cheek. She only barely brushed at the last minute, because a Melissa-smooch would have been too much, too fresh even. But her lips kissed the softness of peach. A butterfly nudged deep down in her stomach. She raised her eyes, surprised at this reaction—surprised at the impulse—and for the first time she was close enough to see the depth in those playful, seemingly shallow grey eyes. She knew she gasped like a mouse caught stealing the cheese, and she tried to blink her eyes away, away from the trap—quick before it snapped shut to wound her forever. But the butterfly stirred again, and then she was too late, too slow, too weak to withstand the magnetic pull of Becky's darkening, tell-tale eyes. Their lips met, and for seconds unending, there was no world, no sickness, no threat; they were alone, silent. The sweetness of the kiss caught them both unaware--a little breathless, each moved away to let the world back in, still clinging to the magic of those brief seconds of unanticipated pleasure.

* * *

"No one told me there was going to be a party up there. Did you?" Roxanna blurted as she marched into the living room late in the evening after visiting Melissa. The unmistakable sound of raucous laughter and music filtered down stairs through open doors.

Zoe, lazing on the couch, enjoying Stephen King's latest horror story, thought, My, my the lady is in a terrific mood. Not being used to an agitated Roxanna, Zoe didn't know how to handle the situation, and so decided to use the Joan treatment. She kept her mouth shut.

It was a mistake.

"I asked you a question," Roxanna said tersely, towering above her.

"Oh, excuse me. No party, Rox. It's visiting hours." Zoe waved a thumb over her shoulder, promising herself never again to mistake Roxanna for Joan. "You missed the five hundred phone calls."

Roxanna nearly stamped her foot. "For your information, there are three cars heaped on the driveway, one car blocking the sidewalk, and I had to park a mile away. No way could I get into the garage."

"I'm sure you can't blame the shortage of parking space on four women looking up a sick friend," Zoe said soothingly. "I didn't even know we had one around here. Have a cold drink, Roxanna. Relax, okay?"

"It's about time you had a good idea."

Roxanna headed for the bar. Behind her back Zoe let out a silent sigh. She listened to the ice clinking into a glass. Liquid gurgled. She remembered that Roxanna's warm temperament—as Roxanna chose to call her outbursts of extreme impoliteness—did not flare up without plenty of provocation, but when it did, cats tiptoed.

Roxanna fell down in a corner of the sofa, barely missing Zoe's feet, and only grumbled when Zoe asked about Melissa. "Are you sure she can take all that?" Roxanna asked after a refreshing slug of cold ginger ale.

For a moment Zoe was at a loss. "Who? Oh Becky? Sure. She's limping around on that crutch like there's no tomorrow. Hey, you want dinner? I'll warm it up for you."

"Thanks but no thanks." Roxanna tapped Zoe's foot and sighed wearily. Her eyes were downcast.

In fact, Zoe noticed, her whole appearance had a morose look about it. "How's Mel?" she inquired once more. "Has she been giving you trouble?"

Roxanna rolled her eyes and said, "Trouble is not the right word. She isn't feeling well and she wants to come home and feel sick where I am.... I can't say that I blame her, that's what she's used to.... I always took care of her. Later, when she was feeling a little better, she wanted to know why she couldn't go to a farm like Bobby." Her voice faded away. She leaned her head backwards, and didn't speak again.

"Roxanna, dear heart...." Zoe sat straight and said, earnestly, "One of these days, you're going to go under. Do you want to know why? Too much business and no pleasure."

Roxanna drew her legs under her and curled up into the corner of the couch where she seemed to shrink within herself.

"You're worried about Mel's operation, aren't you?"

But Roxanna shook her head. "Actually, I'll be glad when it's over. It's the thought of the pain and the physical rehabilitation she's going to have to go through that's killing me."

"Are you sure they'll...amputate?"

"I hope the fuck so," She whispered, as if to herself.

For a tick of time Zoe looked down at unseen words printed on the page in front of her. She knew what Roxanna's fervent wish meant. "When are they going to operate? Do you know yet?"

"Next week, Thursday or Friday."

Zoe opened her mouth to speak again when the sound resembling a pack of panicked zebras startled them both. Four women trooped loudly down the stairs, still bantering with the one left up top, and through the living room. Roxanna stared, felt her stomach sink way down low.

The first one was a tall brunette who carried herself like a practicing model. The second looked like her younger sister, and Roxanna forgot to look at the third, because she recognized the fourth. It was Stace, Becky's ex. Or were they all? Stace smiled, waved, said, "You're still it, huh? Bye, soap-opera...."

Roxanna strained to keep herself on the couch and not go punch the woman in the face. She turned to Zoe, "How can someone be so habitually rude?"

When the front door slammed, Zoe obliged: "Stace, Marilyn, Pat, Kenny."

"Did I ask to know?" Roxanna snapped. "Am I missing something here? I thought she was through with this Stace?"

"Don't ask me, I only live here," Zoe muttered, her mind elsewhere. Something nipped at her brain. Oh what was it? Didn't it concern Roxanna? So the woman was depressed and ill-tempered, Melissa must have been a difficult tonight. In a better, more flippant mood Roxanna would have nailed Stace with a sharp, witty come-back, instead of rage.

Even so, Zoe came away with the distinct impression that she was missing something, and that something was right under her nose.

Chapter 8

Roxanna closed her eyes and lifted her face to the sun, letting in the sounds of her surroundings. Footsteps hurried by; behind her in the distance, children laughed. A wheel chair crunched by slowly, a creak in one of its wheels; high above an airplane droned. A safe sound way up there, so far removed from the planet earth with its trials and tribulations.

She opened her eyes and saw a grey speck in the cloudless, immense blue sky. The sound brought back memories. She needed them, so they assaulted her—memories of how she had scrambled into an old, barely functioning Dakota on an airstrip, God-knows-where in the Nicaraguan jungle. She hadn't done so alone. She had scrambled not onto a seat but onto the laps of three other terrified reporters. She hadn't known them, but once the airplane was airborne, they had whooped, laughed. Some had shed tears of relief.

That antique had flown them to other battlegrounds where Latin American dictators drew blood trying to squelch spontaneous or planned revolutions. Nicaragua, Argentina, El Salvador— hell, she'd been there. But not alone, never alone.

She had slept between safe, isolated walls of Hilton Hotels, but also crowded with others in decrepit hovels where the next whoosh might be an anonymous Molotov cocktail sailing through debris-scattered streets. She had run through these badly lit streets in the dead of night, had stumbled over corpses—men, women, children. Day and night righteous cameras clicked, registering anything that moved—or didn't.

Others without those impudent instruments, had gone around mumbling into their pocket-sized cassette recorders— like herself—always witnessing the aftermath. Even though other reporters wanted a scoop, it didn't matter, you were all in it together. Wasn't it someone from a competitor's weekly who

63

had told them of the Dakota's presence in the first place? And they would have done the same for him, because somewhere, somehow, you were together, you were doing your job; informing the western world about the atrocities being committed in its back garden. And you did it. Together.

But she had never been in hell alone before. Nothing, but nothing could compare to what she was going through right this minute. Here she sat, in that so-called civilized world, so very, very alone. God, she wanted to pace this beautifully kept lawn. She wanted to stomp her feet, wring her cold, clammy hands, hyperventilate, weep. She, who had seen the anguish of people at war, seen the depth of human loss, felt as desolate as the detached nouns and pronouns she had so often spoken into her tape-recorder.

Her friends tried to be supportive. Zoe had come by this morning, but she was forgotten the minute she left. Joan had been next, told her she'd be the live-in spy and keep Roxanna posted.

How long ago was all this? A half hour ago? Ten years ago?

Crawling, sneaky tentacles of anxiety slammed Roxanna's eyes shut. She reminded herself again—she had been in worse situations. And then she wanted to laugh. Did she do so out loud? Nothing had prepared her for this. This grieving solitude. Maybe she should have joined the support group. Maybe someone would have helped her to handle all this with less pain....

A telephone rang somewhere, penetrating Roxanna's private hell. She realized she needed that sound—any sound—to take her mind off the present—off Melissa, a small child in a great sterile room, a small child covered with antiseptic green, surrounded by antiseptic chrome, rubber gloves poking, knives cutting. She wished she had a less vivid imagination, one which was not functioning full speed, laying out the scene in Operating Room 2A.

In spite of the heat Roxanna shivered. She opened her eyes a mere inch, turned her face away from the sun. A too warm, dry breeze made the hundred tiny shadows thrown by the overhead leaves dance on her skirt. She thought about her mother, wishing she was with her. Then again, she had kept her away, called her much too late to tell her the date of Melissa's operation. Her mother would have taken the first plane out to be by her grand-daughter's side, and Roxanna hadn't wanted this, at least, not yet, not so soon after their separation. The parting had been raw enough then, painful. And her mother couldn't afford the air fare. The last thought made Roxanna feel less guilty. She looked at her watch; she had promised to call. She would do so soon.

Two nurses sauntered by, deep in conversation. One of them had sandy-colored hair, reminiscent of Becky.

She remembered the past weekend: Melissa was at the clinic, Roxanna staying with her as long as she had been allowed to. Only after Melissa was already half-asleep did she leave. Upon her arrival at the slumbering house on Van Buren Street, Roxanna found she couldn't work, couldn't sleep, and then of all things, she had taken Zoe's advice and gone in search of pleasure—wasn't that how Zoe put it? She had picked someone up at one of the women's bars, or let someone pick her up, it didn't matter. Performed with perfunctory perfection. She had left the stranger's apartment at three in the morning, careful not to wake her up.

Roxanna shifted uncomfortably on the bench. Guilt was trying to make her squirm, and succeeded. Never before in her life had she done such a thing. Why hadn't she gone to one of those places where gratification was for hire? She shouldn't have used that sweet body simply for an act—there had been lust but certainly no love—and sneak away like a thief in the night. But the most disturbing thing was yet to come—it hadn't been the stranger's softness she had been kissing, it wasn't the stranger's young and restless body she had been making love to—oh please!

Roxanna jumped and crossed her legs. It had long since dawned upon her that she was physically attracted to Rebecca Morgan, then again, so was half of Straker's female population. For Chrissake, Roxanna thought, annoyed with herself, I'm not a school girl. I refuse to succumb to some dumb crush, especially if the crush consists of seeing a pair of beautiful grey eyes all over the place....Just because I kissed her once or twice, yes, I remember one kiss, one memorable kiss....I don't want to be another plaything for Doña Juanita Morgan, thank you very much. I'll get over this thing. I hardly see her anyway.

* * *

"What? Where'd you get all that information?"

"Well...." Becky cleared her throat which did not need clearing. "She said I could get beer out of her cooler any time I wanted one. So I did....Each time I wanted a beer...."

"Yeah, yeah, but instead of groping in her cooler, you groped around her desk."

"They were on the desk, Zoe. There were pictures of her family and I went over to look at them."

Zoe squinted at the buzzing madness around them which was Maywood at lunch-time, then turned the squint on Becky. "Okay, I'm the only person outside of her family who knows. What I didn't know was that they are considering selling their house." Zoe picked up her sandwich and took a juicy bite. After the urgent hunger sensation had dispersed, she asked, "Why do you want to do this? Roxanna is anything but friendless. She has been offered loans—I offered her a loan. I don't think she wants strangers poking around in her affairs. Doesn't that sound familiar?" And as an afterthought, Zoe said, "If I were you, I'd listen to what I just said."

They were silent among the babbling tongues. Zoe was recalling her visit with Roxanna at the clinic that morning, how she had found Roxanna in the waiting room, staring at nothing. Even though she must have been tight with anxiety, she had not shown any of it. She had seemed pretty cool even to Zoe who knew her well.

Then Roxanna had asked her for a cigarette. Zoe had realized then that appearances were not always what they seemed; Roxanna had not touched a cigarette in ten years.

Becky picked up an aging slice of tomato from her plate with the nail of her index finger, and took a deep breath. "Zoe, haven't you noticed that she's working herself to death? I mean, the woman hardly ever smiles!"

"Oh, I get it. You want to see her smile? Becky, here's a news flash: we're not put upon this earth...."

"Oh cut the crap, Zoe. Look...when I saw the bills.... It will

66

cost her an arm and a leg. Now, if I can put a stop to this, I will. It's donation time anyway."

"Okay. Great. Do what you have to do." Zoe wiped her mouth with the sandpaper napkin and asked, "Can you go over to the clinic and bring her some lunch? I'm sure she forgot all about food. Will you do that?"

Becky remarked testily, "Don't change the subject, Zoe...."

"I said—do what you have to do! I'm not your mother, sweetheart." Zoe suddenly lowered her voice, "Listen, you can't buy Roxanna Vaughan to make her like you any more than she already does—yes, I mean no, don't shake your head, it's true." Zoe was ready to climb on her soap-box and do what she so loved to do—give long speeches—when something made her hesitate. Becky didn't seem to be the Becky who had joined her for lunch twenty minutes ago. No, now she hung her head and slumped her shoulders.

"Oh sweet Jesus! Are you in love with her? Is this another one of your one-night stand crushes? Becky...."

"Zoe, she's being taken for a ride! I don't want that, okay?" The hardness in the voice made Zoe shut up, and the latter raised her hands as if to ward off oncoming missiles. "The donation is going to the National Children's Cancer Fund. I'm making it out in Melissa's name."

"Fine. But be careful, Becky. You can't buy a kid's life. Hey, are you going to discuss this with...."

Becky moved uncomfortably, said, "Of course I am. You like her a lot, huh?"

"Yes, I do. I can't begin to tell you what Roxanna and I have been through together...." And Zoe began to tell. "She was the editor of a leftist newspaper we used to run on campus, and I organized demonstrations. I don't know how many times we licked each other's wounds, bailed each other's asses out—I don't know how many times, over one issue or another.... We cried us a river when I got married, and then Roxanna went home, already pregnant with...." Suddenly Zoe looked at her watch. "Honey, I've got to run. I'll get some Take-out for Roxanna, then I'll go get you a taxi. Don't go away."

* * *

"Hi."

Roxanna's eyes fluttered open, but narrowed instantly to the cruel glare of the afternoon sun. She smiled a little as she watched Becky sit down beside her and stretch her injured leg out like a flagpole.

"Here's some lunch."

"Thanks, but I'm not hungry. Your face looks better."

"Yeah, it does, doesn't it? At least the swelling is gone and I look less like Darth Vader's twin sister. How about some milk? Zoe told me you didn't have any breakfast either."

And so they conversed, like careful friends, Roxanna offering her face to the sun again, Becky trying to fill in the silences with chit chat.

"How long has the operation being going on?"

"Close to two hours," Roxanna answered, glancing at her watch.

"What did you tell her?"

"The truth. I started preparing her last week. She accepted it like that!" Roxanna snapped her fingers sharply. "When I told her she looked at me as if I were...crazy—stupid is a better word for it, like she has always known about an operation. She knows from the other children what goes on. And she has seen amputees by now—she knows about that possibility. And she knows that sometimes when children have left, it wasn't to go home....But do you think Melissa knows about the death of these children and what it means? All through the week she tried to comfort me."

Becky smiled, "She's a remarkable kid. You know, I found her ploinking away on the clinic's piano in the sunroom—the sound turned my ears inside out, but you know, there was a method to her playing, a phrase here or there. That's why I want to teach her. If I play something, she plays it—she definitely has an ear."

Roxanna looked at Becky through slit eyes. "Think there's something there?"

Becky nodded. "Oh yes. There is something there. It might just be her age—curiosity. But there's always a method to her playing. She tries out tunes she knows, hums to get the notes."

68

Becky laughed, but sudden thoughts about the matter at hand, sobered her. "I don't understand. Don't the x-rays show whether the malignancy is spreading? Do they have to go in to have a look?"

"I'm sorry, Becky, but they're not going in just to have a look." Roxanna glanced at Becky again, found the woman studying her sunglasses entwined in her fingers.

"Yeah," Becky sighed, looking up at the sky. "She knows you're having a hard time, you know. Sometimes she talks about you."

Their eyes met across the bench, Becky's darting away furtively. "Don't think she's too young to feel how you suffer for her. She feels it, you know. It has...made her...unhappy...and I hope..." Becky raised her eyes and gazed once again into the expanse of peaceful sky above. "...I hope that in the future you'll be less worried about her and everything else."

"Why, thank you," Roxanna replied, amused by the stammering, amused also because Becky was once again telling her how to live her life.

"I mean it," the woman beside her said defiantly.

"Okay, I'll accept that. Melissa likes you, doesn't she?" Or she likes your guitar.... "In spite of...." your obnoxious behavior on Day One, she was going to say, but she felt the uncomfortable silence beside her, saw the glance in the direction of the white, squat building. "You've been a hell of a support for her, and for me. Why?"

"Wh...why?" Becky blinked and looked at Roxanna with (Roxanna thought) incredible, piercing grey eyes.

"Yes. Why? I never had the feeling Melissa and I were particularly welcome at your house."

"Well, you thought wrong. My mother died of cancer. Of the intestines." Becky let out a short snort. "It's not a nice way to go. Especially if you have a strong heart."

"I'm sorry."

"So am I," Becky answered in a mere whisper.

"Hey, come on, let's go inside. The heat is getting to be something fierce." Roxanna rose to her feet and held out her hand to Becky. She pulled her to her feet; their hands lingered, their eyes never met. Roxanna handed Becky the crutch, and they

69

started up the gravel path, making their way to the West Wing to await Dr. Henninger or Norma Lewis, someone to tell them how Melissa was holding out in O.R. 2A.

They stood just outside the room glimpsing, when someone went through the door, the narrow railed bed where Melissa lay sleeping a deep sedated sleep. Green clad shadows glided around the bed, left to right they floated, mumbling, reading charts, nodded to one another.

"Are you all right? Do you want to sit down?"

Roxanna didn't hear her. Tears shimmered in her eyes, she placed both her hands flat against the wall for support, suddenly remembering a line which had been haunting her all week, all day: 'I am your sister and I need to pray for you; tell me, where do I find a prayer?'

"Hey...." The voice beside her was soft. "Norma will be here any minute and you can go in."

Vonstaff was suddenly telling her things she probably already ought to know—the crack in his face was moving, smiling, and then it walked away as unannounced as it had appeared.

The sound of the wind grew louder as someone put her in a green smock, strapped something on her face, and then she was at Melissa's bedside. Roxanna's eyes travelled along the length of the bed until they fell on the square mound at the foot. Her hand crept to her throat and she must have made a sound, because Becky, standing beside her, gently touched her arm. For a long moment she stood looking down on the totally composed face. Then slowly, as if waking from a trance, her mind and her eyes began to pick up the details: efficient looking and sounding machines lined the wall beside the bed; two infusions hanging above the bed, one containing a transparent liquid, the other dripping the thick red color of blood; a handful of colored antiseptic rubber tubes going in or coming out from under bedcovers, or Melissa, Roxanna couldn't tell and she didn't want to know.

"Roxanna, do you have a minute?" Someone said somewhere. The sound of wind picked up volume as it took her by the elbow, led her out of the room into a familiar matchbox of an office. It bade her to sit, asked her if she wanted a cup of coffee, something she didn't quite hear. And while it waited for Mister Coffee to brew its concoction, it spoke again, louder, "How do you feel?"

"How do I feel? Do you want to hear the honest truth?" Had she she spoken out loud?

The head nodded, positioned itself and the steaming cup of coffee against the window sill of the open window. The head smiled suddenly, and she could not help staring; the smile remained on the scrubbed face as if waiting for something— something to come through—a message? The smile remained— until she wanted to slam if off his face.

"You look just about ready for business," Dr. Henninger said crisply, pushing himself off the windowsill. "I have seen the diseased tissue, Roxanna. The surgeon believes...."

"Excuse me, why didn't Vonstaff amputate?"

"It wasn't necessary."

"It wasn't necessary?"

Her mind began to turn pages of a book she had read; her mind conjured up words The Team had spoken.

"Look...." The scrubbed face sat down. "The tumor was discovered in time. We operated in time. Ms. Vaughan, please sit down. Sharon...."

Was there someone else in the room? She turned her head sharply and saw the pediatrician hovering in the back, near the filing cabinet. Up near the ceiling. Something was not right here. So she sat down. But she had found the page, the paragraph.

She stood up again. "You told me that if Vonstaff did not amputate I could wave good-bye to my daughter...." which was not how the book put it, but they got the message.

"Roxanna, will you shut up and listen," Dr. Henninger said brutally. He must have done it before because it worked. She did as she was told; she listened, weeping, frightened, exhausted.

"The therapies are working. We're going on with the treatment. Just as if nothing happened. Do you understand me?"

"Did Vonstaff take out the tumor?"

"Yes."

"The book says, 'The affected cells have spread all over.'"

"Yes, and that is why it's important that we continue the therapies, and her medication has to be changed, and if there is a remission, she can go home, and come back for regular check-ups. I do mean regular, Roxanna." Dr. Henninger leaned forward over his sterile desk, his voice had a razor-sharp edge to it. She knew he was the best. She knew he wouldn't lie to her.

"We are going to beat it. She has a chance, Roxanna, and she will get it...."

"What are the odds—fifty-fifty?"

"You got it." Henninger smiled again. "Let's stay optimistic, shall we?"

She had said nothing. She thought, I'm still exhausted, Doctor, as if I just finished digging a grave.

Chapter 9

Two days later, on an early Wednesday morning, Roxanna took the elevator to the fourth floor of the Old Stockholm Building and walked into a deserted office. Someone had already been there; the air-conditioners were turned up high and the screen was alive in one of the computer carrels at the back. She groaned at the stack of folders on her desk.

Somewhere a lonely telephone rang; she paid it no heed. She sat down and stared for a silent moment at the pile, wondering how on earth two days of absence could create such a pile. The first folder, begging to be handled, stared right back.

The staff began to arrive; 'Good mornings' rang out, jangling telephones were answered, punctuated with the ping of computers going on. All this harmonized with the teletype writer outside Zoe's cubicle.

Roxanna found herself answering endless questions about Melissa, and soon everybody knew why she was at the office and not with her daughter. Melissa needed all the rest she could get and Roxanna was getting in the way of the nurses.

Zoe was the last to drop by—she was late for work as usual. She asked all the same questions since Roxanna had been staying overnights at the clinic. She left with, "I want to discuss that *Save the River* piece that Marjory wrote...."

A few feet away from her own desk, Michelle Demsey turned from the lay-out she was working on to start a discussion with Dianne Marshall on the other side of the room. Being used to Michelle's and Dianne's eternal discussions in which one tried to outsmart the other, Roxanna hardly listened. Calls came in for her. Memos piled up. Everybody passing by needed something right away.

She caught flashes of their conversation. Michelle said, "How can you be a lesbian by choice?"

73

Dianne replied, "You're right. If you're gay, you're gay. You can't escape the feeling. It's the call of nature, like salmon tracking back up river to die. Like sex is a call of nature."

Roxanna suddenly thought of the conversation she had had with Joan the evening before. "They didn't lie to you," Joan had told her. "They didn't—I read her chart; they're even thinking of lengthening the times between chemotherapy treatments. Your live-in spy, is what I am." And Joan had chuckled.

Across the room Dianne continued "...you have a monopoly on sex."

"Sex, sex, sex, that's all you ever think of...," exclaimed Michelle.

"...using their infinite researcher's wisdom," Dianne said, "the medical scientists and the psychiatrists are making one lamentable mistake...."

Only when the conversation had let up, did it strike Roxanna that Joan's polite reserve towards her was...envy? She and Zoe had a bond that years of separation could not break, certainly Joan must know they had never been lovers? Never would be, not with Zoe's life so centered on Joan, Bobby and work.

Melissa and I, Roxanna thought ironically, trouble in paradise. Wordlessly, Joan had come around. And Becky?

Who knew but Becky herself?

The argument was still going on. "...They compare the lesbian woman with the homosexual man. They wouldn't dare do that when they're researching heterosexual men and women, now would they?" Dianne continued.

"Rox...." Michelle, who had noticed her listening openly, turned to her, and at that precise moment her line buzzed. Phew, Roxanna thought, and picked up the receiver.

"Do you know the one about Mister Silverstein's last will and testament?" Said a familiar male voice.

"I beg your pardon?"

"Being of sound mind while I was alive, I have, before I died, spent all my money."

"Very funny, Jonathan. Hey, big bro, what are you doing up so early?"

"Early? It's nearly quitting time over here. It's you people living backwards. Ma told me about Melissa. How is she?"

Roxanna told him; yes, she has come through just great. Now if only her white blood cells would cooperate; yes, she could sleep again, perform in her work; how were Sally and the kids....

Roxanna pictured her big, hairy brother behind his executive's desk, and as always, found it difficult to do so. She remembered his boyish, flamboyant style; she wondered often how a clown like Jonathan got into the clutches of office work, and managed to get himself the title 'Consulting Manager to the President' of Northern Atlantic Bank. It certainly wasn't by playing practical jokes on the boss, she was sure, but maybe it *was* his dinner jokes....

On Jonathan's advice she had opened an account with this bank, a thriving family business. Again it had been Jonathan who had suggested its Loan Program. He had played a dominant role in advising her, and getting her accepted.

"They were both arrested for vagrancy...."

"Jonathan, I'm busy...."

"...and brought before the judge. 'Name and address,' thundered the judge.

" 'I live everywhere' said the first hobo; 'I live in the streets, in the fields, in the woods and on the beach.'

" 'And where do you live?' the judge asked the second hobo. With a straight face, the second guy answered, 'I'm his neighbor.' "

"Great. Is this why you're keeping me from my work?"

"I know your sense of humor died with Lenny Bruce, but laughter is healthy, Roxy. Anyway, Ma is glad she doesn't have to sell the house. You were on the phone with her yesterday—why didn't you tell her?"

Tell her what, Roxanna wondered, nodding her thanks to the mail carrier who dropped a fat package wrapped in brown paper on the in-coming tray.

"I'm her ear." Jonathan continued, "Was it Megabucks? You had me up the creek with the brass for a while. I mean, did you read the contracts before you signed them last year? The amount of money due on a specific date?"

Roxanna remained silent. She had lost her brother way back, and sat hoping he'd say something to bring her on track. She figured she had to be patient because Jonathan always took an hour, even if he could get somewhere in fifteen minutes.

"Hullo? Roxanna? Are you still there?"

"Jon, pray tell, what are you babbling about?"

"Oops, it's a secret?" Jonathan asked loudly. "The IRS? Seriously, now that we've received the redeemed loans in one great bunch at the same time, we've lost money on you—the money we call 'interest.' But I've done some fast talking, and the reputation of the Fund also helped."

Roxanna laughed a little, the sound of someone who had not liked the joke but was too polite not to make an appropriate noise. "Jon, can I get a word in edgewise? For the love of God, what are you talking about?"

"Oh, hey, your loans. As in l-o-a-n-s, you know?"

"No, I don't know!" Roxanna lowered her voice. Michelle and Dianne were trying hard not to look at her, and others were also pretending not to hear.

"Give me a break...." Jonathan requested, but she heard the change in his voice. Approximately three thousand miles away, Jonathan Vaughan perceived something was askew. The Consulting Manager to the President rose on his tiptoes instantly, and switched to a flat business tone. "There was a computer print-out on my desk this morning, telling me contracts 55561 and 555672 are no more. These are your contract numbers, yes? Do you understand me? Your loans have been redeemed!"

Roxanna: "You're joking. Both the Monte Cristo loan and the Specter loan?"

Jonathan: "Both."

"Jon, there's been some mistake. I don't have that kind of money. Who authorized the payment?"

"Our main branch in Straker."

"Someone had to put money in the bank, right?"

Jonathan's voice conveyed impatience, "Well yeah...."

"Who?"

Jonathan made a noise like a snort, or a giggle.

"Who?"

"Let me see here—*The National Children's Cancer Fund of the County of Riverside*...."

"What? Jonathan, there's been a mistake...."

"It's no mistake. Believe me. I could check of course...."

"Check. How come they knew about these loans. Why have they acted without asking me, without *telling* me...?"

* * *

"Zoe?"

When Roxanna rounded Zoe's partition—even though Zoe had hung out her 'Do Not Disturb' sign—something she did when it was serious dead-line time—Zoe hardly looked up from her legal pad. She waved Roxanna in the general direction of the only other chair. "I'll be right with you. Do you think we should endorse these two women on their publicity rafting trip down the—sit down, you're making me nervous. Please...." Zoe looked up. Roxanna was staring at things that she alone could see, her eyes big and round, her mouth on the verge of falling wide open. *Melissa?* Zoe corrected herself. *If it is what I think it is, we're going to have fire-works.*

When Roxanna's voice started to drone over Zoe's head, Zoe listened for a while. The further Roxanna got, the more Zoe's brain churned. Tiny waves of approaching panic rippled along Zoe's spine as she thought—something was wrong. How on earth did Roxanna find out so fast? Becky fixed the whole thing just a day ago. Granted, maybe the Northern Atlantic was aiming for a notation in the *Guinness Book of World Records* as the fastest bank turn around, but this was ridiculous. Surely there were hundreds of bank statements to come out of computers, to be folded into envelopes, the envelopes to be stamped....

Zoe became aware of silence and her friend's glazed eyes as she placed both hands, palms down, on Zoe's desk. With her head between her shoulders, Roxanna was trying to ape a vulture. "Did you do all that?" she asked primly.

"Aw, it was nothing. I mortgaged the house, sold my car. By the way, I threw in Joan's Toyota, so when she wakes up will you tell her she's minus a car? Oh yes, and tell Becky about the house."

"So it wasn't you."

"How could it be? Even my insurance settlement wouldn't cover that. Besides it's all tied up in this."

Roxanna spread her arms in a gesture of despair. "Things

like this happen to other people, not to me...." She leaned over the desk again. "Do you know that with this...this *whatever it is,* Melissa's treatment has been paid for? Anyway, Jonathan promised to check out who authorized the payment."

"Jonathan?" Zoe hoped her voice didn't squeak.

"Yeah, Jon. I just told you. Weren't you listening to me. You remember him, my big brother. That's why I have my account with N.A. Bank to begin with—because he works for it. And it put him in an awkward position, I might add."

Zoe repeated the name to herself: Jonathan. Holy shit! But of course. She nearly groaned out loud. Oh, Rebecca, for once couldn't you have consulted your brain instead of your wayward heart? All right, you are no medium and you couldn't have known that Roxanna's one and only brother is Consulting Manager at one of the twenty-one branches of the Northern Atlantic. What a load of bad luck! And now Roxanna is looking at me, and I'm trying to act as if I'm not dying to pick up the phone and call you quick. But I act so together, and yes, Roxanna has the mind of a sober detective—she is a journalist after all and knows how to get a story. So count your blessings.

Then Roxanna was on her way out, saying, "I can't make lunch today, Zoe. I'm going to visit Melissa. Can I count on you to help?"

"Help? What for?"

"You've got plenty of tentacles walking around Straker. I might need some. Okay?"

"Yes, sure." Zoe said weakly. She waited for Roxanna to leave the office, then reached out for the telephone, and dialed rapidly.

* * *

"Her brother? Why didn't you tell me she had a brother working in the bank?"

Zoe waited patiently for the screech to fade away. Then she said patiently, "How could I know, Becky? My correspondence with Roxanna did not include her brother. Listen, marble-brain, I've been thinking. If I were you, I'd call Patrick...."

"Patrick and I are not on speaking terms."

"Whatever. She'll be knocking on his door any minute now."

"How do you know that?"

"Do you forget she's a sleuth by vocation? She'll find out. There's one thing that can keep you away from her and you know what that is, don't you?"

"Yes, I know."

"Let's hope she won't get that far."

"For all the banks her brother could be working for he had to pick N. A. Zoe, don't you breathe a word, you hear?"

"I have been and am as tight as a clam."

* * *

It did Roxanna's heart a world of good—more than did the knowledge of redeemed loans—when Norma Lewis informed her that Melissa had perked up considerably during the night, and to the nurses' surprise and satisfaction, was recovering rapidly. Norma credited this speedy recovery to the change in medication. There was some color on the much-too-white face, her moodiness had vanished, but the nausea brought on by the change of medication was beginning. If she believed the head nurse, it would hit her with a vengeance.

She was still in pain, Norma warned; sometimes not even the world's supply of painkillers seemed to be effective.

Melissa was leaning on two fluffy pillows decorated with tiny Donald Ducks rushing around in various stages of panic and triumph. Carefully, tenderly, Roxanna hugged and kissed her. "I'm proud of you, sweetpea," she whispered with another kiss for the small ear. "Norma tells me you're feeling a lot better. Are you?"

Melissa nodded her head, yes; when she spoke her voice was weak, "Will my leg stop hurting too? They didn't...they didn't take it off, huh?"

"No, they didn't." Roxanna had told her this the day before, but Melissa had probably been too doped up to remember even her own name.

"It's not only the stupid leg that hurts." Mel sighed deeply, almost philosophically.

"No?"

"Nope." Melissa suddenly raised something she had been holding in her hand to show her mother. It was a remote control. "They let me play video games and I'm good they say. When can

79

I go home, Mommy?"

"In a couple of days. I thought you'd rather stay here forever and play all those games. Honey, what else hurts?"

"Everythin'," Melissa mumbled. She moved her body languidly, as if she did not really want to, and said no more. Roxanna sensed Melissa shouldn't be overly reminded so she dropped the subject. Right then, Melissa became more interested in finding the correct button to switch on her small TV set. Roxanna suspected she loved punching all those buttons and didn't really care if the screen came alive.

"Zoe and Joan promised to come visit you," Roxanna said. "They'll probably bring you a present. So don't forget to say thank you."

"What kind of a present?"

"How do I know? And even if I did, I wouldn't tell you. Wouldn't be a surprise anymore, would it? Did Becky come to see you?"

"She was here. I want to play the piano with her." Melissa suddenly lost all interest in the remote control. "She singed into the intercom. Wanna know how she sounded?"

"It's sang, Mel, and yes, I want to know what she sounded like."

"Like Daffy Duck."

They both giggled. But not even this brave attempt to cheer themselves up could bring a light to the child's eyes which were dulled by painkillers. Roxanna tried to keep the inevitable tears away, but she could not reason with a surging, choking emotion. She laid her hand on Mel's bald head, kissed her forehead, her cheek. Brave, hurting child, she thought, what I wouldn't give to be in your place.

"Mommy, don't cry," Melissa pleaded, eyes huge, suddenly shy.

"Mommy is a great big baby," Roxanna sniffled through a smile. "You know, cookie, I'll be glad when this is over and you can come home, get better and go to school."

"Mommy?" Melissa, knowing a good bargain when she saw one, squirmed, laying the charm on thickly. "Mommy, when I get outta here, can I have those strawberry shakes and stuff Becky always buys me? You know what she promised? She said she was going to buy a new car, and when I got outta here, she's going to give me a ride with the top down and everythin'. She says she's going to buy a black Cher'kee Chief, you know, a jeep? With lots of gold on it...."

Roxanna left Melissa after seeing that she ate her lunch of yogurt, a squashed banana, a cracker or two. She talked Melissa into keeping the light food down by distracting her with a story-book description of the day-care center where she would go for a while after the clinic.

Her child dozing off, she left the ward quickly, badly in need of fresh air. She wanted the open, blue sky above her, wanted space to rid herself of yet another soul-searing picture of Mel's I'm-sorry-Mommy look, because she had to throw up anyway.

She parked a few blocks away from the office and stared through the windshield. The glare of the sun reflected on the hood of her car went unnoticed. Her weeping was silent but bitter, her eyes wide open. Ridiculous thoughts pranced through her mind. Becky buys her strawberry shakes? (As if you didn't know.) Didn't Becky care that Mel was on a special diet—were there vitamins in strawberry shakes?

* * *

While Roxanna's colleagues rushed around the office with an energy that spelled 'closing-time,' Roxanna sat at her desk thinking, and she thought hard. Jonathan had volunteered very little, if putting his job on the line could be called just that, but he had given her a name—O'Sheary.

Oh who? The name ran in circles around her head until she nearly swatted it. Jonathan, in parting, had said something else respectfully, not that it helped much. "I didn't know you had such powerful friends." So before she consulted the ordinary phone book, she called a Mrs. Gladzek from the *National Children's Cancer Fund*, only to be told that an anonymous donation had been given, the bulk in the name of Melissa Antonia Vaughan, presently being treated as the Children's West Wing of the George Straker Clinic.

Driving home that evening, her mind still working over-time, she wondered where she had heard the name before. O'Sheary. She knew it. And if they were so powerful, so rich, okay, they probably gave to charities, but to redeem loans? It was, Roxanna decided as she killed the engine in the garage, ridiculous. Or a mistake. But Jonathan had been so adamant....

Later she tried to discuss it with whoever was around, but found little help.

Zoe asked, "Rox, didn't you tell them there might have been a mistake?"

"Oh they checked; no mistake. Thing is, it's in their favor. They won't run too hard to find it...."

"If you say so," Zoe muttered, glancing at Becky who sprawled in her favorite armchair in the living room. If Roxanna had been less preoccupied with the day's miracle, Zoe was thinking, she'd have found Becky's presence at home and at dinner highly irregular.

Suddenly Becky said, "You know what I think? Sounds like someone had an interest in the case, friend of the clinic—doctor or something—someone interested in funding research on whatever kind of tumor she had. I think that if something like this ever happened to me, I'd sit back and enjoy it."

Zoe, a *shut up* look on her face and a disturbed Roxanna stared at Becky who stumbled on. "W-wouldn't you, Zoe?"

"Maybe," shrugged Zoe, offering no help. "Why not let it rest, Roxanna? At least until Monday. You're driving us crazy. I mean we should be celebrating!"

"Yeah, you're right. I'm sorry." Roxanna stepped through the wide open glass doors into the coolness of the evening. Behind her back Zoe managed to catch a pair of grey eyes which were just waiting to be caught. She smiled without showing her teeth, opened her paperback-thriller, relaxed into the armrest of the chair emphatically. Becky answered with a snort, dangled a leg over the armrest of her own chair moodily.

"I heard a car in the driveway," Roxanna said as she returned, "it's probably Joan."

"Are you sure it isn't Cagney and Lacey?" Mumbled Zoe. "Oh, Rox, by the way, we're getting together one o'clock next Saturday for a house meeting. Also we need to clear out the basement, see if we can get rid of the mice in this house. We're going to need all of us. Think of a time you can be available, all right?"

"Sure." Roxanna looked at her watch. "I've got some work to do, so if you'll excuse me...."

When she was gone upstairs, Becky stirred. "She doesn't really have to help, does she? Mel needs her more than we do, and the basement can wait."

"I don't agree," Zoe retorted. "She needs more than just Melissa, her job, Melissa, paying the rent, Melissa, her job...."

"Okay, okay, I didn't think of that. I'll be out of town for a couple of days, but I'll see you Saturday at one," she said, retreating.

"Goodnight, Becky." And when Joan entered, Zoe smiled. "Hi honey, how was your day?"

"Yuk." Joan plunked down on the couch and kicked off her shoes. "So yuk I don't want to talk about it. It's too quiet in this place. Like a mausoleum." Then picking up her shoes, she stood.

Zoe eyed Joan as she walked away, grinned at the sour echo left behind, then suddenly shut her paperback. Joan was right; it was quiet. Roxanna and Becky were upstairs; Bobby was way out in the mountains with his Dad, and here were Zoe and Joan, all alone. Together.

What Joan needed, Zoe thought as she followed in her lover's tracks, was a night of fun, fun, fun.

Chapter 10

A pile of junk squatted in the backyard. Two rotting tennis-nets covered half a dozen over-flowing cardboard boxes, a disabled Ping-Pong table balanced on top. Three rusty garden chairs with their zig-zagging match-stick legs sticking out into the air formed the beginning of a separate heap of trash. Becky swung a squeaking water-hose over the chairs. Humming she went back inside the basement, her still sore knee causing a slight limp.

Joan and Roxanna were bent over cartons in the corner, talking. "They used to be readable, last year's and this year's editions, I think," Joan said. "I don't know what they're still doing here, but then, Zoe can never throw magazines out...."

"What are they?" Becky looked over Joan's shoulder. "Never mind, I know. You're right, what are these still doing here?" Just as instantly, she lost interest; Zoe was calling her from the other end of the basement.

Joan followed, and left alone, Roxanna inspected a moldy *Evening News Magazine* out of the box. The cover was done in eye-catching yellow on a black background:

Three Die in Blaze. The High Price of Joe's Revenge. Read Why He Did It!—Page 3. Excl. Story by....

She shook her head; to think her agent had sent an article on lesbian motherhood to this sensationalist magazine! How would the title have read: *Woman Couple Raises Kids*. See details! She replaced the magazine, but in her amusement, couldn't resist a glance at some of the other catchy covers:

Triple Murder: Baby Found in Blanket in Empty Well. Race Car Driver Burns Beside Wreck; Actor's Son Caught on Yacht Full of Cocaine and All Male Cast; Magnate's Daughter Starts Riot at Folk Festival.

"...shouldn't carry things with that knee, Becky," Zoe said.

"I don't carry things with my knee," Becky gasped, falling all over the box she tried to pick up.

"You know what I mean. Let me help you carry it up the stairs."

"I can manage, thanks."

And she did. She came back inside the basement, walked in just in time to hear Roxanna say, "Here's the one with the fight at the Folk Festival. Isn't that the one Becky got involved in?"

"Joan, wasn't that the year we went to the Virgin Islands, missed the whole affair? I remember the court case was in August when we got back, wasn't it, Becky?"

"I forgot," Becky said loudly, and then emphatically, "Where's the can of kerosene? We'll burn baby burn...."

"Oh well," Zoe was saying, "the poor thing didn't get compensation...." And for Roxanna's benefit: "For her broken arm. Broke it in the fight."

And Joan rattled, "Poor Rebecca Morgan, no wonder she...."

"*Joan, don't!*"

Both Joan and Roxanna jumped and stared at Becky; Zoe who read Becky immediately, sent Joan a warning look, but Joan was gawking at Becky, and didn't notice.

"All I was going to say, was...."

"Well, don't, okay?"

This time Zoe's *shut up* look helped; Joan clapped her jaws together, shrugged her 'Oh well' shrug and continued with what she had been doing, rummaging through a box full of Bobby's old, forgotten toys.

As if nothing had happened, Zoe piped, "Oh Becky? There's an old amplifier back there. It is yours and what do we do with it?"

"It belongs to my brother, Michael. I'll ask him about it. Joan, can you help me carry this box?"

Suddenly Roxanna said, "I'm not finished yet."

"Yes, you are," Becky answered without a second thought. "Joan, are you going to help me or what?"

A minute ago you managed just fine with a box twice its size, Roxanna thought. "I said, I'm not finished yet."

"And I said...."

"I know what you said." The sound of sizzling sparks in

Roxanna's voice startled Zoe. She sent Roxanna an alarmed look, then glanced at Becky, hoping Becky had not heard what she had heard. But Becky was straightening slowly, looking at Roxanna in a wondering way.

"Why on earth do you want to read those magazines?" she asked. "Don't you know what's in them?"

"I don't need you to tell me about it."

"Oh, excuse *me*."

"Girls," Zoe tried. "Let's not...."

"You just want to be nosy, right? I should have known...." Becky placed her hands on her hips and Roxanna knew what this meant. She also knew that no upstart was going to lay down the law for her, even if she was the landlady.

"Nosy?" Roxanna chirped, throwing all caution to the wind. "I'll show you nosy." She flipped through the magazine to find the article. "Page 25, 32, 46, here we go, page...."

And then Becky moved. With one flowing movement, Roxanna hid the magazine behind her back. She pointed a long finger into Becky's face, and said, "You touch it, you eat it."

Roxanna resumed her search for the article, and when she opened her mouth to announce the anticipated title, Becky snaked out an arm and snatched the magazine out of Roxanna's hand, upsetting the box.

"Thank you." Becky turned on her heels, but Roxanna's fingers curled around Becky's upper arm, and stopped Becky right in her tracks.

"Give it back to me."

"No, I won't and what if I don't?"

Roxanna opened her mouth to speak when something shone through her anger, and she saw it. Why was Becky so frightened? She saw it in her eyes. She was looking into those eyes much too long.... They were going to make her give in...yes, she could feel her insides melt already, taking away the sharpness of her anger.

"You're hurting my arm," Becky snapped, and Roxanna jumped to attention. She let go of Becky's arm and picked up the July edition from the floor. "The trial was in August, right? Well, here's July. There must be some mention of the massacre."

But Becky didn't move. Roxanna wondered why Becky was

not interested in the July edition, when in the next instant, Becky dropped to her one good knee and began to search for the June edition. Becky began tearing off the front pages of *The Evening News* with comical dedication.

"You're going to have to read through a lot of them, because I'm tearing up the index. Read them all! You'll be on top of the *Evening* scheme, now won't you?"

"What, if I may ask, is going on?" Zoe asked. No one except Joan heard and she wasn't even sure of that. Joan, a head taller than Zoe, had moved behind her as if for protection. Joan was not a fan of disputes and sought to steer clear if one was threatening. More than once, she measured the distance between herself and the exit, but like Zoe, seemed too fascinated by the whole thing to leave now.

Roxanna dove for another magazine; Becky jerked her arm away, and Roxanna was left standing with the cover in her hand. This seemed to nettle Roxanna to the extreme. By now they were both sweating profusely. The sweat trickled along their temples, down their necks and dampened their already smudged T-shirts.

"What are you trying to hide from me?" Roxanna demanded, raising her voice. "What's in there?"

"And why the hell should you want to know? —when you know already. Why don't you go smell someone else's dirty laundry? That's what you do anyway, isn't it?"

"The two of you are being pretty childish," Zoe tried once more.

"Yeah." This was Joan throwing in some weight.

The reporter in Roxanna was growing more curious by the minute. She grabbed for a butchered magazine; the poor item was ripped apart in front of her very eyes.

Now, as Becky jerked her arm away, Roxanna yelped as she slipped on one of the magazines on the floor. But before they both hit the ground, Roxanna made for the magazine once more. Speechless by the behavior of her grown-up friends, Zoe began to see that the importance of the magazine had long flown out the basement window.

"It's because one of them has hot Spanish blood running through her veins," said Zoe knowingly, like a wise grandmother.

"What's that supposed to mean?" Joan ask, her voice brittle.

"Well, the other is an Irish thoroughbred. That doesn't mix, no way."

"Irish?" Roxanna succeeded in standing while Becky was still trying to get her knees off the floor. Holding the remains of the front page of the June edition like it was a parchment scroll, Roxanna read aloud: *"Singer, Rebecca Morgan involved in riot at Rocky Gardens. Ends lover's quarrel with iron hand. Victim to sue Ba....* Here Roxanna stopped reading simply because the rest was ripped away. Muttering, "Is this why she's kicking up such a fuss?" she tried to find the number of the page they were looking for. She thought she discerned the number twenty-four in the index, and said, "We shall find...."

Once again Becky reached out her hand swiftly, but Roxanna, expecting something from that direction, reacted flawlessly. The magazine disappeared behind her back, out of Becky's reach.

In a deliberately clear voice, Roxanna said, "I am going to take this with me. Short of breaking my legs you can't stop me."

"What makes you so sure I won't?"

"Because I'm a whole lot stronger than you are."

"Roxanna..." Becky blocked her way, swallowed hard, reached out her hand, pleaded, "Please? Give it to me."

"Oh? Switching on the old Morgan charm?"

"I don't think you should...."

"I'll have you know that the old charm don't work with me."

"I bet it don't," Becky bristled. "You are so enchanted with yourself you make me sick. You're as arrogant as...."

"*You* are!"

"*I am not!*"

"Let me help you. You are an insolent little snot-nose! Grow up! And let me tell you something else...."

"Can't we stop this?" Zoe was aghast now.

"It's getting way out of hand." Joan agreed, but she was less alarmed than Zoe who already sensed that Roxanna's anger had faltered, perhaps died. Roxanna was no fool; the fear in Becky's face was palpable, showing she had something to hide. And Roxanna was certain it wasn't only the contents of that article.

"I'll tell you this," Roxanna raised the disputed magazine,

and slapped it into Becky's arms. "What's in there? Who cares?" With that she brushed passed Becky, clattered up the basement steps and was gone.

* * *

"That was to teach you not to mess with her."

"Oh, go away. Leave me alone."

"There, there, don't cry." Zoe rocked Becky in the circle of her arm, comforting her as if she was a sad child. Becky, teary and frumpy, sagged against Zoe.

"I don't know how it started. I honestly don't know."

"Will someone tell me what the hell that was about?" Joan asked.

"I'm beginning to believe," Zoe said, "that your chemistry just doesn't mix. Maybe someday the two of you will be able to live together in peace, and I sure hope it happens before Bobby comes home. I don't want all this shit when he's around."

"G...go tell h...her," Becky sniffled. "Why do you always pick on me?"

"Becky, don't you think you ought to tell her about the donation?"

"Tell who about what donation?" Joan wanted to know.

"Tell her?" Becky whispered, horrified at the thought. She stared at Zoe. "What do you think she'll do? What do you think she'll say?"

"Who?" Joan wondered.

"I can think of any number of things, Becky," Zoe said. "Will you look at this place?"

"Yeah, I don't believe it." Joan talked to herself as she kicked out at the scattered magazines. "I thought we were supposed to be *cleaning it up.*"

"Oh, shut up," Becky said with a tremor in her voice. Zoe was about to nod in agreement when Becky made a choking sound. She spread her filthy knees wide apart, bent her head deeply, and giggled.

"Sweet Diana," Joan said to the spider webs above her head. "A loonie."

Becky looked at Zoe from under her eyelashes; Zoe's lip trembled as she said, "Did you see how she went for the magazine in mid-air? Girl, that was home-run material, for sure."

Becky tried to suppress another surging giggle when Zoe covered her mouth. They looked at each other and exploded into laughter.

Joan, feeling completely left out, was not amused. "Oh God, it's catching."

Chapter 11

Roxanna toweled her hair vigorously as she walked barefoot from the bathroom to her bedroom. She peered from under her towel at the digital clock on the night-stand and was dismayed to see it was already four-thirty. Mel must have wakened from her afternoon nap by now and wondered why her mother wasn't there, the way her mother always was. Roxanna decided to give herself a half hour to get ready. The children would be playing, and she didn't want to interfere with that.

Her robe fell open when she sat down on the bed and continued to rub her hair. The luxurious scent of apples coated her body; her hair so clean it squeaked. The stale smell emanating from the moldy magazines had been everywhere, and sitting there she could still smell it. Must be my imagination, she figured, trying hard to keep her mind closed to everything else, knowing her mind would not cooperate. She shook the moist strands of hair out of her eyes and curled the towel around her neck. She lay down backwards on the bed, closed her eyes. '...You're just like your father,' her mother used to say, 'temper, temper. So what if Jonathan takes the first ride on the bicycle? He's a lot older than you are. Help your brother to his feet. Pick up the bicycle. Roxanna, you can't even ride the damned thing!'

Uncomfortable with her thoughts, she was all too aware of her temper. It wasn't easy to bring out though, but Becky seemed able to do it. Roxanna could only hope that Melissa hadn't inherited any of it.

She knew she had to apologize to Becky. She hadn't meant to be rude; she just couldn't figure out what had happened down there in the basement. Did 'Freedom of the Press' and 'I can read anything I damn well please' really have anything to do with it?

Getting up from the bed, she walked slowly into the den, still towelling her hair and thinking absent-mindedly how that wretched moldy smell was everywhere. Then she frowned; it wasn't her imagination—the smell was heavier in the den. Disturbed, she jerked the towel off her head, sniffing loudly. Then she saw it lying on her desk.

An "Oh no" broke from her lips as she walked to the desk and almost reluctantly stared down at the maimed magazine. She didn't want to know what had taken place between *The Evening News* and Becky—a broken arm, a court case—never really wanted to. What had happened in the basement just...happened. I must be more tense over Mel than I thought, she admitted. Obviously the article remained Becky's very own personal trauma, and would explain why she was so hysterical. The magazine was open to page twenty-four or what was left of it, but did she give a damn what it said?

Trying to read the caption done in small black letters through the wrinkles of the page, she found: *Prodigal daughter food for scandal. Will Daddy cut off funds? Read all about how we found out that popular singer Rebecca Morgan is not Rebecca Morgan. Well, she is and she ain't!*

Half the page was ripped away, leaving but one photograph. As crumpled as it was, Roxanna could make out a yearbook picture of Becky. Jeez, these guys did go all out, Roxanna thought as she stared at the beautiful young face, stared too long of course, She blinked her eyes away, shook her head, thinking she had better things to do than try to read a torn up account of an incident and trial she wasn't really interested in. It wasn't as if Becky had started the fight at the festival....

Roxanna glanced at the waste-paper basket, dropped the idea of throwing the filthy magazine in there. And then suddenly she found herself wondering why Becky kicked up such a fuss, and what she had prevented Joan from saying. This last thought stayed with her as she blow-dried her hair.

By the time she was dressed, the thought had become a frown. And there were other things: If Rebecca Morgan wasn't Rebecca Morgan, then who was she? Perhaps it was a stage name, but did artists keep it up in their immediate surroundings? If so, why hadn't she been told Rebecca's real name? The article's caption '*Well, she is and she ain't!*' was beginning to make sense....

The knock on the door was so soft; it was almost inaudible.

"Come in," Roxanna said, turning away from the mirror, clasping shut her earring.

Becky closed the door behind her and stood awkwardly, still filthy from the scuffle in the basement. With a sparkling, clean Roxanna in the room she shrugged, seeming to scrutinize her condition, reminding Roxanna of a line from Jon's hobo joke. 'I'm his neighbor.'

"I'm glad you're here." Roxanna smoothed her skirt which didn't need smoothing. "I'm sorry I blew my top down there. I don't know what came over me...."

"It's all right, Roxanna. It wasn't your fault. I shouldn't tell people what they ought to do. You'd have found out anyway."

"Yes. There's always microfilm at the library. And really, I'm not interested—it isn't any of my...." She was suddenly aware that Becky was gawking at her incredulously. "What's the matter?"

"You didn't read it. You mean you don't know?"

"Know what?"

An apparent relief washed over Becky's face as she leaned against the door and crossed her arms. "Which means I still have to tell you. Oh boy. You know, sometimes I think I've committed a crime...."

Roxanna thought about this one fast; she felt she had to say something, "It wasn't your fault about the incident...."

"...ever since, I can't eat or shit or sleep, and I desperately wish I never did it. OK, it was a foolish thing to do, I know, but Mel needed—you needed...." Becky stopped short. "I wasn't referring to...."

"Becky, you don't have to explain...."

"My name is Rebecca Morgan O'Sheary."

Roxanna's jaw unhinged, her eyes popped. "You?" The something slammed into place. She had dropped her last name. Magnate's daughter! So that's what she had prevented Joan from saying!

Watching Roxanna approach her, Becky croaked, "I have a trust fund and every year I'm supposed to give to charities, and I do. Save the Whales, stuff like that. This year I gave to Mel. She was unhappy because she knew how unhappy you were. She

93

isn't unaware of your moods, you know. And you need a break. No one appointed me, I know, but I guess you realized it's hard for me to mind my own business at times. But who made it a law no one could help you out?" If Becky hadn't run out of breath, she still may have been talking at nightfall. Abruptly, she shut her mouth.

Rebecca Morgan O'Sheary. O'Sheary! Of course, the letterhead on her bills.

"Jesus, Becky...." Roxanna's lips moved like a fish urgently in need of fresh air. And when the air filled her lungs, her brain, there was an exclamation, "But you have hardly made peace with us as your tenants. Yes, you've made friends with a musical and very sick girl, but throwing all this money around. I mean *money* —why?"

"Roxanna, I know it was probably uncalled for, but I'd do it again. Please accept it as a gift for Melissa's future."

"Becky, I...oh, damn it, I don't know what to say...." Roxanna sat down on her bed, glancing at the digital clock on the nightstand. "I've got to go...I've got to go...." She muttered, not moving.

"Me too." Becky, ready to open the door and get out, was held back by a look in Roxanna's eyes.

"Where did you get all the information? I mean, how did you know about my loans and everything?"

Becky looked uncomfortable. "I don't think we should get into that now.... Excuse me, I really need a shower." But before she left the room, she added, "Straker has always had an anti-gay chapter, and they infiltrated the festival which was billing a lot of gay singers with the straights, and started trouble. It had been a really great feeling until then. Fantastic. It was partly my rage that people would come in and spoil a good time that got me involved. The *Evening* never mentioned that, even though I made a statement. They just wanted sensation—a way to get at my family, smear the name around. I had always been careful to have my own identity, separate, for a lot of reasons. It was my parents they hurt—that's what hurts me still."

* * *

Zoe closed the front door behind her, gathered the day's mail

94

from the hall table, and walked into the living room. Wondering why no one had sorted out their mail, she walked towards the couch where a table lamp was on, shining like a beacon in the darkness. Bruce Springsteen's *The River* infiltrated the otherwise dead quiet. Zoe glanced over the back of the couch knowing she'd find Joan. Which she did.

Joan opened her eyes, smiled a little, but said nothing.

"Hi." Zoe bent over and they kissed in greeting. Zoe stared at her lover a long silent second. "What's the matter?"

"Nothing. What time is it?"

"Eight-thirty. Thereabouts." Zoe straightened, still staring down at Joan. Your nothings are sometimes everythings, she thought. "Have you seen Becky?"

"No."

"When I do see her, I'll kill her. It isn't nice to disappear for days and not let us know where she is."

"This isn't the first time, Zoe." Joan sounded weary. "She's probably at her brother's place, cooling off, although for the life of me, I don't know why she seeks him out to solve her problems. He's no big help...."

"I wish she'd call." Zoe took off her blazer and threw it on the armchair. She tapped Joan's knee and Joan pulled up her legs so that Zoe could sit. "Had a hard day?"

Joan shrugged. "So, so."

They were silent then, Joan listening to the end of the song, Zoe wondering what was wrong.

"Mel is home," Joan said after a while, breaking the silence.

"Have you been up? How is she?"

"They're fine, thank you."

"I'm glad for Roxanna." Zoe put an arm around Joan's knees, said, "God, I'm tired. I'll probably go to bed after my shower. Did you change your shift for next Sunday?" When Joan looked blank, Zoe repeated, "Next Sunday? Your birthday? The barbecue?"

"I forgot. And right now I don't feel like—I don't want to...."

To Zoe's consternation Joan's eyes filled with crystal tears. She covered her eyes with her hand but Zoe had already seen. Zoe moved closer, passed her hands along Joan's upper arms once or twice, squeezing gently. "What's the matter?"

"It's nothing," Joan sniffled, passing her hand under her nose. "I...I feel stupid. If I cried for everyone who died in that place...*mierda!*"

"You mean the clinic? You don't cry for everyone who dies in that place. The way you handle your emotions have always amazed me." Zoe took Joan's face into her hands, and whispered, "Do you need a little help now?"

Joan's eyes filled abruptly; she cried, "He's dead."

"Who?" Zoe felt her heart give a painful thud.

"Reginald. He died in agony. What on earth was that good for?" Tears suddenly streamed down Joan's cheeks, and words spewed out of her mouth. "I told you about him, don't you remember? He used to be in my ward. When he turned seventeen, he was transferred to the ward for bigger kids...."

"Oh yes, didn't the ward throw him a birthday party?"

"He was doing real fine, the cancer was in remission. He was making plans to go to Art school. He was talented, you know. The wall behind his desk was full of water-colors he painted. Horses and cats. He loved cats and horses."

"What happened?" Zoe pressed as Joan fell silent, eyes turned inward, remembering perhaps, a particular painting.

Joan suddenly looked weary and spent. "Did you know that if Melissa's cancer had not been discovered and taken care of so fast, it would have shown up some place else in a couple of years or so?

"In Reggie's case it showed up in his left jaw. The pain never went away."

Zoe felt goose bumps underneath her fingers as she stroked Joan's arms. "He died today?"

Joan nodded while a fresh flow of tears wet her smudged face. "Why does one person get hit by a car and die instantly? Why does another have to suffer seven days and seven nights before he can die? You know...I wonder...you can laugh as much as you want to...but I wonder...Does the soul that suffers the most go to heaven as a deformity, and the other as an anger? Or is it the other way around?"

Zoe was moved beyond words. She would have connected this strange observation with Bobby, when Bobby in a moment of small-world philosophy, would ask her the impossible questions she could not answer. Except that Bobby's philosophical questions did not include sickness and death.

"Joan? What was so special about Reginald?"

Joan shrugged impatiently. "I don't know. But his dying was such a waste...a waste of talent, a waste of a sweet, loving human being.... We called him the Guru. The name followed him into the other ward, everywhere he went for check-ups...."

Zoe listened to Joan confess the tenderness she had felt for Reginald during the year he had been in her ward. The other nurses were equally charmed by the soft-spoken boy. She felt less guilty of betraying herself, because those other nurses were also betraying themselves—letting down their professional defense against attachment to particular patients, the defense being there to stand guard against burn-out, or insanity.

Even after Reginald left the ward, the nurses hung onto his memory. They would visit him. They threw him a birthday party, did him little favors, watched over his well-being like mother hens.

"I shouldn't have let him into my heart. This is too painful, too tiresome...." Joan ended with a sad, tired voice.

"You let me into your heart," Zoe said quietly.

"And look where it got me," Joan hiccupped. The attempt to joke did Zoe a world of good. "And now...," Joan sounded as dramatic as she had meant to, "...I have this shit at home. Not only that, Becky and Roxanna aren't a match made in heaven. You know what I want?"

"The good old days?" Zoe tried to grin. It turned lop-sided.

"Well, it's not *that* bad." Joan buried her long fingers in Zoe's hair, caressing her neck absent-mindedly. Her voice was low, sincere when she spoke again. "I want to come home and know everything is all right. I don't want to feel like I'm sitting on a powder keg all the time. Roxanna is your friend, right? I'm sure she can be my friend too, because she's nice, you know? But are we going to have to take this for a whole year?"

"They just got off to a bad start," Zoe suggested hopefully.

"What the fuck happened in the basement the other day, anyway? You never told me."

"Becky didn't want Roxanna to know she was an O'Sheary."

"And that's supposed to explain everything?"

"No, it is not." Zoe sighed, and told Joan what Becky had done behind Roxanna's back. In spite of her forebodings, her depression, Joan chuckled.

"What ever happened to 'let's mind our own business?' "

"Actually, I thought it was rather sweet," Zoe mused, realizing she was sagging deeper and deeper into the couch. Vaguely she thought she ought to stand up and go take a shower. But this time alone with Joan—this peace and quiet—yes peace, no matter what subject Joan was broaching or was sure to touch on in the next minute—well, this time was precious. She tended to forget that Joan needed this, that it wasn't a coincidence that Reginald's death had upset her so.

And Joan could mind-read. "You know, this about Reggie has set me thinking. How are we going to deal with...well, suppose Melissa doesn't make it?"

"We've talked about that...." Suddenly that shower was very important to Zoe and she began to sit straight.

"Yeah, and maybe we didn't know what we were talking about. You certainly didn't. Melissa was just a name then. Now there's a child up there...the flesh and blood kind, you know?"

"Do we have to get into this now? I'm tired. I want to take a shower...."

"There's something else," Joan began carefully.

Zoe groaned out loud as Joan knew she would. "I didn't know we were having a meeting at nine o'clock this evening. What is it?"

Joan, used to Zoe's melodramatics, wasn't ruffled in the least. "We've agreed, oh, a long time ago, not to get all passionate in front of Bobby—I wasn't even allowed to look your way...."

"Don't exaggerate," Zoe mumbled.

"Okay, not to show signs of too much affection, like kiss you if he was watching—something I've always thought ridiculous because I believe children need to be taught affection...."

"I don't care what you do in front of him after we tell him about the facts of life. I thought we agreed on this."

"We do. Now for the *moment supreme*: what about in front of Melissa? Do we know Roxanna's stand on this?"

Zoe, ready to roll her eyes, didn't. "Oh Christ!"

"Yeah. Think he'll help?"

Zoe stood up, saying, "Are you finished wondering about the universe for now? Yes? Well, take my hand—good—stand up, like I'm standing now, and follow me to the bedroom. When we get there, we shall take off our clothes, take a shower and then, we'll go to bed. I'll kiss you good-night, tell you how much I love you, and then blissfully fall asleep. Understood?"

"Yes Mom," Joan said obediently, and just as obediently, began to follow Zoe. "But promise me we'll talk about all this someday soon, okay?"

They fell asleep in a warm cocoon, safe in the knowledge that their love—this complete rapport—would not only carry the nights, but also the days, because their days and nights had not always been so safe.

Chapter 12

Unknown to Zoe, after Bobby's birth, Joan had seen her at the Merry-Go-Round a number of times. Zoe came there with a group of women; they sat in the back of the establishment quietly chatting among themselves.

Sometimes Zoe came alone. Joan didn't approach her, not until much later. It wasn't that she had been overcome before, rather she had been mystified if not cautious. You didn't visit the Merry-Go-Round on such a regular basis if you were straight. And Zoe was married, had had a baby not two months before. Whatever her motives were, she wasn't cruising. Was Zoe coming out of curiosity, to experiment? Joan was intrigued, remembering what they had been through in the delivery room, remembered Zoe particularly. And it wasn't as though there hadn't been many difficult births since then.

Joan became familiar with how Zoe spent the evening at the bar when she came alone. She'd sit at a table where there was enough light and where the speakers weren't bellowing directly into her ears. She'd read leaflets, scribble notes, have a couple of drinks. She relaxed. And didn't accept any offers to dance.

At last Joan could stand it no longer, and dared the approach. "I know you don't dance so I'm not asking." Joan thought the line unique, if not clever. Zoe took her time to look up from her notes. When she finally did, she recognized Joan immediately. Her smile was wide; she seemed pleasantly surprised.

"Hey, you're my breathing therapist! Sit down, have a drink."

Joan did all this without a second thought. And the talking came easily.

"I was in the clinic the other day with Bobby for a check-up. I thought maybe I'd see you...."

"Bobby? Oh, your son. How is he?"

"He is a very healthy baby." Zoe smiled at Joan.

Joan fidgeted. "After what you went through he had better be, right?"

"You remember us? You must have delivered a thousand babies since then." Zoe didn't fidget, she stared. Maybe that was why Joan fidgeted. The face Zoe saw was young, had a high, smooth forehead, a perky little nose, a self-assured line to her mouth, full lips which smiled easily, smiled often. And there were innumerable questions in those eyes.

Zoe remembered. Yes, green and brown speckled eyes, dark in the bad light of the bar. And the shoulder-length hair which Joan kept curling behind one ear. Zoe thought her beautiful.

Joan learned that the women who joined Zoe those other evenings, had asked her to become the editor of a feminist magazine which was failing due to bad management. They met at night because most of the women had day jobs. Sometimes Zoe brought her baby along.

"Then you've seen me in here before? Why didn't you come and say hello?"

Joan shrugged it off. "You're always so busy...I didn't want to bother you."

"You wouldn't have bothered me. It's nice to see you again."

Susan Laroche, one of Joan's bar-hop friends, didn't think so. "She has a baby for chrissake. See how we're all steering clear? Stop ogling her. The two of you sure hold co-ozy conversation. Joanie...." Susan, all of nineteen, placed her hand theatrically upon Joan's, "Don't mess with straight women. I'm telling you I know what I'm talking about. I've been there. If it's kicks she's looking for, she'll be looking for you. When the kick gets out of hand or too much of a hassle, well, it's Heart-break City for the kickee." Seeing Joan's drop-dead look, Susan became exasperated, even frantic. "Joan, there's plenty of trouble there. A husband. A baby...."

"She's divorcing her husband."

"Oh, great! That leaves the baby. Think of the competition. It'll always come first in her book...."

"It is a *he*."

Susan had apoplexy, as had Joan's other friends. So it wasn't as if Joan hadn't been warned.

There were the pleasant memories. The three hour trip down for their first memorable long week-end in Little Town at the beach house (the salt-encrusted monstrosity Zoe had gotten in the divorce settlement) was uneventful but companionable, as if they were going fishing and someone brought a two month old baby along....

"Ever go to Little Town before?" Zoe turned the radio down.

"A couple of times. Moonlight parties. My family lives on the other side of the county."

"Think you're going to leave home soon?"

"Yes. I had to stay until I was twenty-one." Joan grinned as her eyes met Zoe's, shook her head. "I promised my mother. My father made me. I mean, the fuss they made when I had to be in a dorm during my training at Riverside Memorial...."

"Are you going to stay in Riverside or will it be Straker?"

"I'll probably move to Straker. The clinic is recruiting."

And so they talked their way to Little Town, and into the beach house, through checking all the rooms for bugs—especially Bobby's. Talked while they unloaded groceries. Then while Zoe fed and put Bobby to bed, Joan went down to the beach and discovered the silence. She stood in the shallow water, her pant-legs rolled half way up her calves, gazing at the ocean. Where she stood, the water was as dead as a blanket, but restless up ahead. She had stopped walking, glanced at the rock formations on each side, looked up at the cloudless, blue sky above, then over her shoulder to check how far from shore she was. Just then she spotted Zoe sneaking up behind her.

"Oh damn!" Zoe exclaimed in disappointment. "Why'd you have to look?"

"What were you going to do, push me under?"

"Yell 'shark' and bite your butt." Zoe reached over, and putting her arm around Joan's waist oh-so-naturally, she observed, "Beautiful, don't you think? You should see the sunset. Fabulous! Oh, I know—" She suggested they watch it from a miniature beach just behind a rock on their right. Joan followed reluctantly, frequently glancing at the house.

"What about Bobby? Suppose he...."

"Bobby is fed. Bobby sleeps. Believe me, we'll hear him if—I iid if—he wakes up. Want to know why?"

"Because Bobby has a big mouth," Joan said concentrating on the path Zoe was following. First they went up, then, after a couple of downward slides, they unexpectedly came upon a horse-shoe patch of sand.

"I think we'll fit," said Zoe, gasping slightly. "Jeez, I should stop smoking."

The sunset was as beautiful as promised. As a cacophony of colors washed over the horizon; beauty forced them into silence. Joan almost forgot to breathe. At that moment, she felt closer to any human being than she ever had before in her young life. So she accepted Zoe's expected pass, didn't object to the steamy kisses, the roaming hands. The virgin in her welcomed Zoe, agreed wholeheartedly to the pleasant sound of an unzipping zipper. There was one tug, then another, and another; the zipper remained stuck. By then, they were both looking down. There sat Joan's belly button and the top of her underwear. Then their eyes found each other, and they snickered, embarrassed suddenly.

"Oh well, I had planned a romantic dinner first anyway," Zoe sighed in Joan's hair. "Remind me to set an extra place—for a set of pliers."

Joan still screamed with laughter when she remembered that scene, and much to Zoe's embarrassment, found greater satisfaction in telling every willing ear that the, "buttering up and taking advantage of Joan Rodriguez sure came to a screeching halt right there."

But not all the memories were pleasant.

When Bobby was four months old, he started teething. They crooned over the first two teeth which had come through easily enough in his lower jaw. Then all hell broke loose. Bobby's next teeth hurt and the poor baby didn't know whether to shit or run, so he bawled. He whined all through the day and all through the night. He chewed on anything he could reach, clean or dirty. Fever and diarrhea plagued him. Visits to the doctor were frequent. Bobby was susceptible to diaper rash, no matter what material the diapers were made of.

And of course, Joan, a rock in the turbulent sea ('The most together person I've ever met,' Zoe often announced proudly.) spent most of her days and nights at the Conaught Apartments where Zoe was living at the time. The Rock began to wear away, the Rock was growing tired, especially because this together person gave more than she received.

Joan was always tired—had started sleepwalking to classes and back. Exhaustion became second nature. She had to study, and had a hard time doing so. Bobby simply didn't stop screeching. By the time his teeth had come through, she wished she had never heard of him. She was taking her second year exams.

In the beginning of her happy union with Zoe, she had dutifully and lovingly taken care of Bobby—fed him, cleaned him, baby-sat him or hurried him to the doctor so Zoe could start her newspaper job. Now Joan couldn't find enough excuses to stay away from the apartment.

Zoe found herself toting Bobby around Straker, or trying not to break her neck over him in her cubicle of an office. She didn't mind; Bobby was her miracle and she loved him more than anything or anyone else in the world. But Zoe had forgotten to tell her Rock, Joan, that she was deeply loved and appreciated for all the trouble the Breckners had put her through. Zoe failed to understand why talking to Joan became more difficult. Why she seemed superficial, cold, even distant, and she did not understand Joan's frequent absences from the apartment.

Oh, but deep in her heart, didn't Zoe know? And wasn't she too busy, too tired, too occupied with Bobby to take on another cause called 'co-parent' too?

One day Zoe came home from a long day at the office, and she found Joan bouncing a delighted Bobby on her knee. She could have danced for joy at the sight because Joan looked as if she felt at home again. But the urge to dance became a scream in her brain when she saw the suitcase next to the chair. The echo of *No* vibrated intensely, and for a moment she thought she must have screamed out loud. With something close to terror in her eyes, she watched the tall woman carry Bobby across the living room and lower him gently into his play-pen.

Straightening, Joan said, "Zoe, I'm going to stay at Susan's for a while. I've got to get ready for my exams and I can't do that here."

"I know." Zoe threw an armful of paper in the easy chair, and fell on the couch with a heart-felt sigh. "I know."

"I know this is a bit sudden, and I'm sorry. I want you to call me when you need a baby-sitter or something. I'll come."

"That's nice." Zoe closed her eyes, feeling defeated and old.

"Thank you." Joan refused to give an inch; then she did. "Zoe, I can't study here. It's too noisy, too *small*."

"And Susan is a big help, I'm sure."

"Susan?" Joan didn't understand for a moment. "Oh, Susan offered me a place to stay. I mean, I could go home, but it's too far away...."

"Susan wouldn't care if you had rabies!" Zoe snapped. "So run to her. Something you can't handle around here?"

Joan rolled her eyes. "I need to study, okay? I can't do that with him around fussing. You know that."

"By all means, go!" Zoe glared at Joan, knowing damned well she was being unreasonable. And very insecure. She had seen Joan's need, knew it has been festering deep down inside someone who took on so much without really being prepared.

And now she knew exactly how to get out? Time out, buddy, she needs time out. Great. But would she be back? "When do you think you'll be back?" someone asked.

"When I think I'm done studying." Joan kissed Bobby who was standing, wobbling to and fro. She kissed him again and crooned, "I'm going to miss you." Pretending the storm wasn't going to reach the shore.

Politely Zoe asked, "Can I, at least, have your share of the rent?"

"Oh yeah, I forgot. I'll drop by tomorrow. When do you think you'll get home?"

"I'm not sure. I'm going to have to find a day care center for Bobby."

The storm had nearly reached the beach.

"Oh? You're going to find a day care center for him? Now that I'm leaving." Joan was livid.

"Now that he's old enough," Zoe corrected patiently. And just as patiently and self-righteously, "You are leaving, aren't you? What do you want me to do with him? Leave him here to play with the roaches?"

"We could have worked something out."

The storm hit with all its might—months old, pent-up frustration exploded, and what could have come out in a normal day-to-day conversation, came out in lung-searing shouts.

"*When?* You just dropped the bomb!"

Joan gave it back. "You think this is a bomb? Sweetheart, wait for the fall-out. Let me tell you something you already know, Zoe. I have moved from this side to that side—even considered moving under the bed. I have asked you to take him out of here—to the park or something, so I could *study*—but did you allow me space? *Nooo....*"

"I didn't hear you ask me anything! When did you ask? When?"

"You could have known, couldn't you?"

"What?"

And then two things happen simultaneously: someone banged on the wall, and Bobby started howling. He had been sitting in his play-pen, hugging his teddy bear, staring wide-eyed. He had never heard voices raised in anger before, especially not coming out of the faces of his parents.

"See what you have done?" Zoe hissed, picking him up. "You scared him."

"I scared him? *You* started to shout."

"Oh, give it up. Go to that Susan woman. What the hell should I care? There, there, it's all right." Zoe rocked the frightened child, shushed him. Bobby tightened his arms protectively around his mother's neck, hiccupping. His big brown eyes sent Joan a begging, if not forlorn look.

It broke the storm.

Joan slid along the wall to the floor, sat down with a splat, and started bawling. Immediately, Bobby bellowed and reached his stubby arms for her, nearly falling out of Zoe's unprepared arms. But Zoe was so moved, she brought him over, let him go and joined the chorus. And so they sat, sobbing like three sad and weary, but, most of all, lost, children.

This unusual marriage ceremony didn't bring an instant solution to their problems, but it did teach them what they meant to each other; it taught them that they could not forfeit their own needs and at the same time, that the child they both loved, needed their love.

Zoe snapped out of her career-oriented haze, her taking for

106

granted attitude towards Joan and set out to find a bigger place.

She placed Bobby in a day care center for a couple of hours a day, but if she thought that did it, she was mistaken.

They were asked to leave their new apartment within two months, the landlady getting wise to them pretty quickly. Sporadically, this continued to happen and not wanting any more trouble than they already had—like the courts taking a good look at Bobby and who was actually raising him—they moved around Straker and lived like thieves in the night. Even though Bobby didn't seem to mind this nomadic existence, they knew they had to settle down; they needed a secure place, a home, not only for Bobby, but also for themselves.

After Joan came through with flying colors and was a Registered Nurse, Bobby a year old, and Zoe's newspaper beginning to break even—the circulation growing—the need became more urgent. It was Joan who put her back into the search. They decided to be upfront with prospective landlords, which didn't help much, until Joan found out about Rebecca Morgan's offer.

Life wasn't easy yet. As Bobby was growing up, the question of a male role model became an issue. Joan kept insisting his teachers, his friends—Freddie next door—were plenty male models for him, but Zoe didn't agree. Zoe contacted Bobby Senior and he came to the house to discuss what was on her mind. And while Joan sat fuming upstairs, downstairs it was agreed upon that Senior would not only take Junior for the summers, but also spend pre-arranged weekends with him. Joan fumed because Zoe refused to come out to Bob Senior, only told him she had women housemates...the boy needed....

And on and on it went. The boy needed—the boy was growing up—the boy fell and broke his arm—the boy had been fighting (which one of us is going to the teacher who wants to speak to his mother). Even though Joan picked Bobby up from day care many times while Zoe was oh so very busy, what the hell did his teachers know, really?

Joan wanted to answer questions. Zoe didn't. 'It's none of their business,' was her motto. As long as no one asked outright, 'Does Bobby have two moms?' she didn't think it necessary to broadcast the fact that he did, indeed, have two moms. To placate Joan, she finally did tell Bobby Senior who, after this, didn't skip another weekend. He started a strange relationship with Joan, one Zoe began to recognize as being out of curiosity. He was the drill sergeant, she the soldier. Would all hell break loose if she didn't come through?

Zoe had sleepless nights, fearing the man would start doubting the validity of the arrangement his son was part of. Joan didn't lose sleep: 'because he likes me.' But that wasn't good enough for Zoe, a daily ache of worry lodging deep in the recesses of her mind.

Neither Zoe nor Joan kidded themselves that because their days flowed like water to a peaceful shore—even though sometimes those waters were choppy—their troubles were slowly coming to an end, or that they would have great solutions for those to come. The hard times still came and went, no less turbulent than those before, but all the while, the bond strengthened between them, and in their unity, a boy flourished—a child they were ready to give their lives for.

Chapter 13

"Oh, my God! She remembered!"

Roxanna nearly dropped the earthen plate heaped with peanut-butter cookies at Joan's exclamation, and looked up to see Becky stride around the corner of the house towards the small gathering.

"Hi." She placed a giant bouquet of flowers on the garden table right in front of an open-mouthed Joan—the spare-rib she was about to bite into hung in mid-air in theatrical paralysis. Becky bent from the waist to kiss Joan shyly. "Happy birthday. Hey, would I forget your birthday? Say hello to Cindy, half the bouquet is hers."

Only now did Roxanna realize Becky wasn't alone; so did Joan who called a greeting as Cindy appeared from around the corner to deposit a kiss on her cheek.

"You did last year, Becky," Joan said wryly. "The flowers are beautiful, especially the tiger-lilies. Thanks."

"I did not forget your birthday last year," Becky scolded. She led Cindy towards the grill where meat sizzled: steaks, hamburgers, plenty of spare-ribs, the latter being Joan's favorite. "I was only a week late. Bobby get here?" She asked this of Zoe who was forking meat onto a paper plate decorated with pale red roses.

"Yes—eat and run as usual. He's already over at Freddie's. Why he doesn't just move in I'll never know. Here Cindy, grab a plate. Beer's over there. Why didn't you let us know where you were, Becky? You were gone the whole damn week. Suppose something'd happened to you."

"Nothing happened. I was rehearsing with my brother."

"What did I tell you?" Joan mumbled, licking her fingers. "So, how about the hamburgers?"

Becky held out a garden chair for Cindy to sit on, then sitting down herself, she said, "Relax, they're not burnt yet." As she poised a spare-rib close to her lips she said, "I thought there'd at least be a party going on at this place."

"We're saving it all up for our anniversary celebration, remember?" Zoe called over from her hot, smoky corner. "And it'll be Bobby's birthday too. Who do you think we are, hot-shot?"

"Who do you think we are, hot-shot?" Becky mimicked towards Cindy who was already giggling. "Don't let her fool you, sister. This is actually her house. And those cars out front—you know the brand new one I'm driving...?"

"And we just had a hot-tub installed too," Joan picked up on the bantering. "We start work on the green-house next week...."

Roxanna left the hilarious foursome to check on Melissa who had gone upstairs for her nap. Hilarious, of course, is a big word, she was thinking as she closed Mel's bedroom door behind her. Cindy thinks everything Becky says is hilarious, hanging over Becky in a fawning way. And if she isn't thinking everything Becky says is hilarious, she's sitting there smiling dopelly into the distance. High as a kite, Roxanna was sure.

Not that I care, she thought as she sat down in the den, planning to do this for a few minutes and make sure Melissa was falling asleep. To keep busy she pulled a folder from a small stack on her desk—short stories she had to edit for the coming Wednesday deadline. Might as well start reading something now that she had some time.

But her mind kept straying, her eyes glancing once or twice at Melissa's closed door. The treatments Mel was receiving were going well. The operation had been a great success, partly because even though Melissa looked frail, there was an iron will in there, probably installed by her grandmother with whom she had spent a great deal of early life. Roxanna took some of the credit too for bestowing her with love and truth, a healthy attitude and confidence in life. Yes, Mel's iron will would get her through.

Melissa was to remain at home for at least two weeks, but Roxanna had the feeling her daughter was waiting for something. She was awfully quiet, disappointed even. Roxanna credited this to Becky's broken promise to take Mel for a ride in her new Cher'kee Chief. Becky had never shown up, hadn't the entire week. How to tell a six year old that adults broke promises? Would Melissa understand if Roxanna said Becky had probably just forgotten?

But Roxanna had been in for a surprise. The night before she had asked Mel why she was so quiet—wasn't she happy to be home?

"...Course I'm happy to be home," Melissa answered, and then, even though she didn't look unduly unhappy, Roxanna could see something was bothering the child.

She tucked her in, pecked her forehead, and asked, "Has Becky been to see you?"

Melissa shook her head and Roxanna got the feeling Mel didn't care when Becky was going to show up. So that wasn't what was on Melissa's mind ever since she came home.

She fussed around Mel's bed for a while, waiting, showing she was willing to stay and listen. Then at last....

"Mommy?"

"Yes, sweetheart?"

"Mommy, is Bobby still at the farm with his Daddy?"

"Bobby? Yes, he is. Do you miss him?"

Melissa shook her head, no, said shyly—eyes blinking at her mother, "Joshua has a Daddy. And Petey too...."

Roxanna's hands stopped fussing. Melissa had seen Daddies at the clinic; she knew Bobby had one, so where was hers? *Oh Mel, why so soon?* Roxanna looked into the eyes of a child who expected an explanation. Even though Roxanna knew she was going to answer the question truthfully, she was also going to lie.

"Why doesn't Bobby's daddy live with Bobby. Doesn't he love Bobby?"

"Of course he does. But Bobby's mom and dad are divorced—" *Great, this is the best you can do?* "They stopped loving each other. Sometimes that happens between grown-ups. Bobby's father still loves Bobby, and they see each other on weekends, or they spend the summer together."

Melissa's much too wise eyes searched Roxanna's face seriously, thoughts jumping into line to be turned into questions. "And Aunt Zoe loves Joanie?" She tried. "And then you live together, right?"

"That's right."

"Did my Daddy stop loving you too? Cause he isn't living with us, huh?"

Roxanna was dismayed. The kid was only six. Her sense of logic wasn't supposed to be working yet. She made herself comfortable on the bed, leaned sideways on her elbow, and so had Melissa imprisoned in her arm. She looked at Melissa who knew both the posture and the look: Mommy was going to tell her a story.

"Mel, honey, I love you very much. You know that, don't you? Good. Do you love me?"

Melissa nodded, and shrieked when Roxanna tickled her, squeaking, "Are you sure sure *sure*? Do you love Becky? Yes? Aunt Zoe? Joanie? Bobby?" Here Melissa had to think about it.

"I guess so," She conceded.

"They all love you too. The only difference is that I love you a whole lot more than all of them put together. That's because I'm your mother. My love for you is a special kind of love. Not that Becky's love or Joanie's love doesn't make a great big difference, but mine is...is so...it's so big I can't even begin to explain it!"

"Your daddy loved you like that..." God forgive me, she thought. "...Oh yes, he did. You were so small you can't remember him. He loved me as much as I loved him."

She didn't say, he took me by force when he couldn't have me for free anymore.

"He was tall and he had green eyes and brown hair, and he had a mustache and spoke Spanish very well..."

He hadn't shaved for days, he had been drinking, his breath stunk to high heaven, the stubble on his face was like pin-pricks on my skin, but I'm not going to tell you that you were conceived that way...you don't deserve it.

"He worked for a newspaper, was very dedicated, and had to travel a lot to get his stories like I used to. Right? Sometimes dangerous places. Well, one day in another country when he was on a story about a war going on, the car he was in had an accident...."

* * *

Later, sitting at her desk and staring at a short story she was supposed to edit, she remembered how the serious listening look

112

on Melissa's face had waned, and then Melissa yawned.

She had actually yawned, Roxanna thought wonderingly. She knew children did unexpected things—they weren't as polite as grown-ups. But her heart was bleeding when she was telling that lie....

Roxanna dropped the pen she was holding poised above the paper. Until next time, Mel, she thought. You'll probably fall asleep when I tell you about the birds and the bees, and that this bird was doing it with other birds, not with the bees.....

"Hi...." It was Zoe.

Roxanna jumped; she hadn't heard the knock—what was wrong with her concentration? These days she caught herself staring at flies on the wall. She was being honked at too often at traffic lights. Once she had forgotten to turn off the shower, and now she had drifted off again, hardly hearing Zoe's voice: "Can I come in?"

"Sure."

"Hi. What are you doing up here? Don't tell me you're working. Weren't you enjoying yourself down there?" Zoe hoisted one hip on the edge of the desk, drank out of her bottle of beer.

"I was coming down in a minute. I've been sitting...thinking."

"Uh-huh. About the return of the Prodigal Daughter?"

"You mean Becky? No. Why should I?"

"Vaughan, I saw your body language when you left. And I know why you left. Woman, you are a bad actress."

"What are you babbling about? I came to—are you drunk?"

"I sure hope so. How's Mel? Sleeping?"

"Yes." Roxanna couldn't help sighing. "I must tell you, I'm a bit worried about the medication I have to give her when she's in pain and can't sleep." Roxanna's voice lowered still more. "I mean, she's only six and all that chemical stuff they're pumping into her.... God knows what it'll do to her further development—physically, emotionally."

"Rox, isn't there a risk with *anything* they give her? Do you think sitting up here, depriving yourself of some fun...a diversion...is going to give you access to what the future holds for her?"

"Oh Zoe, you don't understand."

"Yes, I do understand," Zoe said more vehemently than she

meant to. "You're sitting here eating yourself up. I don't want to be in your shoes, but I've learned something—I've learned it from my lover downstairs, and that is never to *bottle* things up, and there is a time for everything—Joan would kick my ass if I didn't let go at least once a day. There's a sort of party going on downstairs." Zoe punched Roxanna's shoulder playfully, affectionately, "*Come on down!* A friend of Joan's came by and she's sitting with me. She's telling me everything I never wanted to know about calluses. Trust Joan to have a podiatrist as a friend."

"It's better than having a serial murderer for one." Roxanna smiled.

"Okay, let's quit beating about the bush here." Zoe took a healthy slug from her bottle of beer. "Do you want to know why she stayed away for the whole week?"

"Pardon?"

"You heard me."

"Zoe, I don't give a fart in outer hell...."

"Hey..." Zoe clucked like a mother hen. "You've been bad tempered all week, and it sure wasn't Mel's fault."

Roxanna looked genuinely upset. "I was? I'm sorry...I...."

"I don't know what's the matter with the two of you. You're both peeling off in different directions as fast as you can. What are you scared of? Hasn't it occurred to you that Becky is trying to get through to you through Melissa? Why do you pick a fight or withdraw a mile a minute the closer she gets? Roxy, why don't you ease up a little, make a little more space in your life...."

"Zoe, you don't understand," Roxanna said with sudden urgency. "Because she throws her money around I'm supposed to get all chummy here? How would it look—dammit, Zoe, it's made it hard for me...to...uh...to...."

"To start singing serenades under her window? Oh, I get the picture. You being anything but a Casanova...or a Valentino—tina? You stiff piece of brick."

Roxanna, unaware of Zoe's flattering outlook on her feeling for romance, said righteously, "I'm not going to compete with half of Straker's lesbian population...."

"Now it's competition she's afraid of." Zoe took another swig

114

of beer, tried hard to disguise a burp, but didn't succeed. "You break my heart, Vaughan. She should live in celibacy like you do?" As an after-thought Zoe wondered aloud, "You do, don't you?"

"Look, I'm taking your meddling because you're drunk...."

"And because you love me." Zoe tapped Roxanna's hand affectionately. "I'm sorry, but I'm taken. Listen, let me tell you about Becky and her money...." Zoe ignored Roxanna's rolling eyes, "What she did wasn't very calculated, now was it? She did it with heart. If she used her marble brains, you would never have found out she was the one who did it." Zoe leaned towards Roxanna and rapped her knuckles on the desk. "You could do a lot worse, you know. Rich lover, a house, great car, a yacht...."

"Becky owns a yacht?"

"Yup, but she doesn't use it any more. One of those countless brothers of hers does. Or it isn't hers. I don't know."

"You're way off, Zoe. She likes Mel a lot because Mel is musical and doesn't whine, but that doesn't mean...you heard what she thinks of me...don't I make her sick?"

"Oh God, Roxy, you weren't being very angelic yourself. Why don't you go and make up. Remember how to kiss? It goes like this." Zoe puckered her lips, squeezed her eyes shut and blew a kiss into the air.

"Thanks for the instruction," Roxanna remarked dryly. "Look, I'm not ready for Rebecca Morgan O'Sheary, and I doubt she's ready for Melissa and me." Suddenly Roxanna lowered her voice. "You could have told me the landlady just climbed out of the cradle, you know."

Zoe chuckled. "And spoil the surprise? I didn't tell you she was blond either, now did I. Think I forgot your preference for...."

"Zoe...." Roxanna changed the subject. "How did Becky survive these five years with Bobby, Joan and you?"

"By leaving the room when Joan did." Zoe thought hard for a minute. "Okay. You have a point there somewhere. About Becky not being able to handle you. You were always so damn *heavy*. About Mel...."

"Joan walked out on Bobby and you at least twice, right?"

Zoe bent her head in shame. "She had reason to," she

muttered. The next instant, she brightened. "She always came back, and that's how—or when—we learned to talk to each other. The point I wanted to make was that yes, Joan came to me and my little family when Bobby was still a baby, but Melissa is six, and you wonder how Becky is going to handle a lover with a kid that old—Rox, don't under-estimate Becky."

"Zoe, put a cork in it, okay? Go back to the party. Have fun. I promise—no more quarreling with the landlady. I'll behave from now on."

"Oh, please *don't!*"

On her way out the door, Zoe heard Roxanna's amused, if not surprised little laugh. I hope me and my big mouth have set things rolling, Zoe thought as she clattered down the stairs.

Chapter 14

The last week of July announced itself with an unexpected surge of heat which turned into a heat wave lasting well into the first weeks of August. The dogged heat slowed down what was left of Straker's working population, one person being Zoe, this, much to Joan's delight as she watched vacation coming nearer and nearer. The first Saturday of August found Zoe and Joan in deck chairs on the porch where they pored lazily over a calendar, trying to set a date on which to leave for the beach house in Little Town. Joan insisted she wouldn't mind if they left the minute her shift ended on Monday the twenty-first so that her vacation would begin immediately. They'd pick up Bobby at his father's farm, as agreed upon before he had left. Maybe Becky would also want to come along. It was during the lull in their conversation that Roxanna appeared around the corner of the house pushing a small wheelchair with Melissa in it. Roxanna was wearing a knee-length T-shirt, and there were three wet patches in three significant places. Her hair was still wet, but fluffy where it had already dried.

"Hi," Joan called, asking the obvious, "been swimming?"

"Yup." Roxanna braked the wheelchair next to the garden table under the shade of the beach umbrella, and went inside to fetch a glass of apple juice for Melissa, iced-tea for herself.

"When are you allowed out of that thing?" Zoe asked, reaching out to pat Melissa's hunched shoulder.

"When I'm in the water."

"Oh. Good."

Joan laughed, sitting up. "Does your leg still hurt? Can I see it?"

The scar was the size of a full-grown centipede, bright pink mostly because of her stay in the swimming pool at the clinic.

"It doesn't hurt any more. Only when we exercise. Thank

117

you, Mommy." Melissa held out eager hands for the full glass.

"Hell of a tan you've got there, Rox," Zoe said with a look of envy. "I wish I could get that copper tan. You know what I get for all my trouble? The look of a boiled lobster. Then if I'm lucky, I don't start peeling right away...."

"Don't exaggerate," Joan mumbled as she picked up the calendar from the ground where she had dropped it. "You manage."

"Do you remember what I have to do for it? Sometimes I ask myself if it's worth it. Roxy, we set a date. The twenty-first. Little Town. Wanna come along? Can Melissa?"

"August?" Roxanna looked at Melissa, her brain ticking. "The fresh sea air would be great! And it'll be just after your August treatment, Mel. What do you think?"

Melissa finished her juice with a gasp, nodding at the same time. Roxanna drained her own glass and rose from her chair. "Time for your rest and then we'll start dinner. See you folks later."

When they were alone again, Joan held out the calendar so Zoe could see where she was pointing to. "What does this 'R' mean? It's in your handwriting."

"Let me see. The sixteenth? Oh, Roxanna's birthday." Realizing what she had just said, Zoe's eyes widened as she whispered, "Roxanna's birthday." She glanced up at the open balcony doors on the second floor. "Why the sneak. She didn't say anything at the last house meeting. Or maybe she forgot?" Then Zoe wondered. "Can someone forget their birthday?" She looked at Joan. "Wednesday. What's your shift on the sixteenth?"

"Seven to three. I have a friend who doesn't even care, and I don't think she knows how old she is. Can you understand something like that?"

"Listen...." Zoe leaned sideways and Joan met her halfway. "If she hasn't said anything by Tuesday, it means she has forgotten. Either that or she's keeping it quiet. She probably doesn't feel like celebrating."

"But she must," Joan said earnestly. "What could be better for Melissa? Children want to know these things...they love parties. Birthdays are important...."

"Okay, so what about grown-ups and surprises?"

It wasn't until late in the morning of the sixteenth when her mother called long distance that Roxanna remembered. At lunch time she tried to find Zoe, and invite her for lunch and a drink, but Zoe had left for some unknown destination shortly before lunch. She decided to forget the whole thing. Why bother?

Later in the day Joan called to tell her that she would pick up Melissa at the clinic's day care center since she was on the early shift and so could spare Roxanna the ride. Joan often did this, especially when she took her turn to go shopping. Melissa enjoyed going along, riding the aisles—Joan pushing Mel's wheel-chair which pushed the shopping cart. They made up complete meals. And more often than not, they let it get completely out of hand, much to their own chagrin when, at the end of the month, the house-hold kitty looked bleak.

So Roxanna didn't think it unusual for Joan to give Melissa a ride home, except that on the sixteenth, Mel had left the center long before Joan made the phone call. She lunched with Joan and Becky, and they bought the biggest coffee flavored cake Melissa had ever laid eyes on, together with an expensive music-making machine. Melissa and Becky spent the rest of the afternoon executing the plan.

* * *

"Mel? I'm home."

Roxanna examined the mail on the hall table, bent down, took off her shoes, and walked into the living room. The room was silent, abandoned. She knew there had to be somebody at home—both Becky and Joan's cars were in the garage. At the foot of the staircase, she called out, "Melissa? Joan? Are you up there?"

No answer.

Roxanna tried a meek, "Anybody?" then thought they were probably outside on the patio, and was halfway across the living room before she saw them. She jumped and nearly screamed.

The three adults were standing behind Melissa who was squirming impatiently in her wheelchair and who, delighted with her mother's complete surprise, if not shock, joined in singing with all her might, Happy Birthday to you!

"Hip, hip hooray!" Joan yelled with abandon, and after

another series of 'hip hips,' Becky pushed Melissa towards Roxanna. Only then did the mother notice the enormous cake sitting on her daughter's lap—a cake as big as a tray and supporting thirty-five flickering candles.

"Your wish, Mommy."

"All of them," Becky grinned.

Roxanna beamed, took a deep breath, but she had to break off to smile again; she smiled for Becky. Oh God, those eyes...painful eyes, inviting eyes....

"Blow," Melissa protested.

"I'm blowing, I'm blowing." Hell, this isn't a school-girl crush. Accept it. Roxanna blew out all the candles—I wish the naked look in your eyes to be what I wish it to be. I've seen that look before; has it been there ever since? Forgive me then, I've been blind. I've been a fool, yes, I wish, I wish— There was still one wish left for Melissa.

Then there were hugs all around; Melissa's was smug, Zoe's soft and well-meant, Joan's shy but strong. When this ceremony was over, Becky took her turn. What Roxanna thought would be the quickest of hugs got completely out of hand. Becky kissed both Roxanna's cheeks—so far so good—then brushed Roxanna's lips with her own, something she should not have done, because Roxanna found their lips lingering, her own especially, then Becky's. A sudden flare of fire turned their touch into a full-bodied, take-me-in-your-arms kiss. They stood there, oblivious of everything around them.

Joan's mouth sagged open, and Melissa's followed suit. Only Zoe seemed not to notice anything out of the ordinary. She cleared her throat to catch Joan's attention, who, alerted, wheeled Melissa swiftly into the dining room. "Mel, you're going to break your neck. Sit still," Joan advised as the child craned her neck curiously.

"Why is Mommy kissing Becky like that?"

"Because it's her birthday. Anything goes." Joan decided not to say that it wasn't only Mommy carrying on. She sat Melissa in front of the cake that Zoe had set on the table. As long as the cake remained in sight, Melissa behaved like an angel.

Zoe and Joan took their respective places at the table and waited in silence.

120

"I hope they cut it out soon," Zoe mumbled after a while. "Dinner is getting cold."

"Did you know anything about this?" Joan asked in a low, urgent manner. "Are they having an affair or something?"

"Yes. They just don't know it yet."

"Things that go on in this house.... Hands off, Melissa. You can have all the cake you want after dinner." And to Zoe, Joan complained, "I hope they don't decide on a follow-up...."

"I hope they do. Lots of them. Not right away of course...." Zoe started to snicker but suddenly the leering expression on her face changed to that of Sister Holy Innocencia. "Oh, here comes one of them. Hey, where's Rox?"

"She went upstairs to freshen up," Becky muttered as she sat down.

She's in a stupor, Zoe noted. I wonder if she can remember what time of day it is, where she is at the moment, and what she's supposed to be doing here.

Presently, Roxanna came to dinner. She seemed cool as you please, the way she always was, but Zoe knew better. Too cool after all that heat in the living room. There is a shine in your eyes dear heart, Zoe thought, where there was none only minutes ago. You grope for your knife twice. You spill your wine and laugh it off. You hardly notice Melissa looking at you, wordlessly trying to remind you to help cut her steak. She knows it's not like you to be anything but attentive to her. Are you tasting the tuna in your tuna-fish salad—your favorite, by the way? Only when you sink your healthy teeth into that delicious corn-on-the-cob do you realize you are actually eating.

You spoil your desert, accept a second glass of your favorite Riojas red wine. Your eyes try not to stray to Becky's who's trying to so the same. Then your eyes do meet, and you don't hear Mel telling you we have gifts for you. Luckily, there is still the table between the two of you, but I know your feet aren't tucked under the chair. Oh yes, Becky has snared you. All of you. I believe nothing has been left intact, not even a blood vessel.

After dinner they grouped in the living room where Roxanna found herself unwrapping the gifts she had not expected. Her admiration for the two handsome quilts, gifts from Zoe and

Joan, was genuine. Zoe had remembered how Roxanna adored the mighty sight of eagles in flight, and these birds of prey—sap green feathers on a white background—adorned the quilts which Zoe had picked out, even though Joan wasn't enthusiastic about the purchase— "I wouldn't be caught with my eyes closed under one of them." Zoe could tell that Roxanna's obvious pleasure didn't change Joan's mind.

Without ceremony Becky plunked a cardboard box on the bar. "And this," she said, placing a flat, square package on top of the box, "is a joint effort from Melissa and me."

"Hey, the cake." Zoe, a bit off-base because of the heady wine, remembered desert. "Let's cut the cake, already."

"Can Mommy play it first?" Melissa begged.

"No, Mommy can't play the cake first. Anything but the...."

"Zoe," Joan began. "Mel means...."

"I know what she means. I'm only joking. Do you think I'm drunk or something?"

"Well, either that or you have engine problems."

Lifting the stereo cassette recorder out of its box, Becky said, "Any time you want to listen to that..." Roxanna was tearing the paper off the flat package which revealed a tape, "...you should do the following...."

Roxanna looked over Becky's shoulder, and said, "I know how to operate a tape-deck. What's on the cassette?"

"Sit down and I'll play it," Becky urged emphatically, putting a hand on Roxanna's upper-arm, and trying to push her in the direction of the couch. Roxanna refused to budge, and pretended to check the buttons on the recorder with lively interest. Becky's confusion, she was thinking, was comical. Only when Becky said, once again, more urgently, "Sit down and I'll play it," did she move away to sit beside Melissa on the couch.

Melissa snuggled closer, saying proudly, "I helped her make up some of the words."

Almost apologetically Becky went on. "I play the guitar. It was too big for her."

"I understand...."

"The chords are easy. Like, listen to the melody."

Joan had heard enough. "Can you get going? La Boracha is falling asleep here."

"No, I'm not," Zoe said thickly, sitting up abruptly to prove her alertness.

Quickly Becky jabbed at one on the buttons on the tape-deck, and after a small pause, a Spanish guitar uttered a hesitant tune, and Melissa's child-voice recited more than it sang:

"I am a hungry cat
prowling in the street
but I know I have a warm place,
somewhere I can be safe;
I've seen signs of love on your face..."

Roxanna, at a loss, put her arms around Melissa, knowing she was going to cry any minute, when her eyes caught Becky's.

"The hungry cat is hers...and a warm place to be safe...."

Suddenly Roxanna loved her, the landlady, Rebecca Morgan O'Sheary, and this sentimental love song.

"Oh my, do I have talent on my hands?" She mumbled against her daughter's nearly hairless head.

"Here's where the piano comes in," Melissa said as she tried to squirm away from her mother's arms, acting as if what she was reciting was a recipe. "Listen, listen, Becky's in the background...."

"You are a short, sweet song
sung in a candle-lit room...."

That night, after Roxanna put a weary but satisfied Melissa to bed, she came out into the darkened hall and knew instantly she was not alone. Nor was she for the rest of her birthday.

* * *

The next morning Roxanna arrived a half hour late for Zoe's last meeting before she left on vacation. In one go Roxanna crossed the office, dumped her briefcase on her desk, snatched a folder out of it and, a little breathless, barged into the conference area where Zoe held her meetings. Zoe never broke off what she was saying, "...performed by a group called The Purple Furrow. It's a short play about the experiences of three gay men and one

123

lesbian. Amber?"

"Just a minute." Amber shoved her chair forward, making room for Roxanna. When Roxanna was seated and greeted by the rest of the staff, Amber continued, "I enjoyed the play, in as much as I can enjoy other people's misery. The players portray middle-aged homosexuals and tell about their experiences—the breaking up of their marriages, the why of it, how they told their children—how the children reacted, the usual stuff. I particularly like The Nightmare—I'm stretching this into an article, all right? It's about a forced admittance into a home for the elderly. The whole thing was original, believable, well-performed. And funny. It was very funny."

"What's the idea? Simply...entertainment?" Zoe pretended not to notice that Roxanna, sitting diagonally from her, wasn't listening to a word they were saying. Her showered, perfumed and dressed body is present at my conference table, Zoe thought, but she has left everything else at home.

"It's not simple entertainment," Amber was saying. "Their aim is to raise issues facing older gays and lesbians. Because of the heavy taboo on homosexuality when they were young, this group, even today, is still isolated, if not forgotten. I recommend it."

"All right, that's it for page nineteen. Marigold? Page twenty-twenty-one...?"

Roxanna tried hard to concentrate on what Marigold was saying. She heard but nothing registered; Marigold may as well have been speaking Cantonese. Somehow the transition from bed to work had been too quick. It seemed to be only a moment ago that she woke up in Becky's arms, Becky's warmth, and now, one way or the other, here she sat, barely able to function in the capacity she had been hired for.

"...The Sleeping Lessons are given by a Doctor Lloyd Wheeler. They're based on the simple principle: you learn to fall asleep by learning not to lie awake!"

"And how much do I pay this Doc for this simple principle?" Dianne asked, skeptical as usual.

"I heard fifty bucks," Lee, one of the reporters, remarked as she slapped some papers around in search of a specific piece of paper.

"Does any one here have sleeping problems, and want to check out the treatment?" Zoe asked the five women sitting around the table. The head-count was actually six but who was counting?

"Uh-uh, not for fifty bucks, I don't," Lee muttered, and the others chuckled.

Marigold continued, "Here's another example. If you are unable to sleep because your partner is snoring like a buzz-saw, you...."

"Throw another piece of wood in," Lee guffawed and they all laughed.

"Lee, please," Zoe clucked. "Stop it or we'll be here all day."

"...you look at this person with the most tender, loving look you can manage...."

"At two in the bleeping morning?" Lee looked at Zoe. "Are you allowing this to be printed? I mean, who is this guy? A saint? Saint Wheely?"

"Lee!" Diana jostled her neighbor. "Please?"

"...and you think, isn't she adorable in her sleep?" Marigold rattled. Lee and Diana fell all over each other laughing. "Hey!" Marigold called out, "You ought to take Roxanna as an example. She's had too much Wheely I'm sure...."

Roxanna sat remembering how she had tried not to wake Becky, but there were too many arms and legs so she had not succeeded. It had taken pains to leave that bed, and only the thought of Melissa wandering about the house in search of her mother had made her tear herself away. And now here she sat, trying to remember what she had done with Melissa.

"I'm sure Doctor Wheeler has another simple principle for people having trouble waking up. The minute Rox does...." Zoe reached out to tap Roxanna's hand with an index finger. "Roxanna, Amber will take over my desk while I'm gone—Lee will take over yours. As of tomorrow I'm officially on vacation. I'm going to pick up Bobby, and get things ready for Little Town. I'd appreciate it if you'd cover for me tomorrow, and take care of last minute details, but...," Zoe eyed the others, "...knowing my staff, I'm sure everything will go very smoothly, and there won't be much to deal with tomorrow. That's all, I guess." The women all got up to troop off to their tasks. "Not you Vaughan. I would like to have a word with you." Zoe opened the folder Roxanna had placed in front of her, and began to turn the pages.

"Oh, Zoe, if you're looking for the review," Roxanna began apologetically, "It's not finished yet...I mean, it is, but not...it needs polishing. I didn't get...."

Zoe ignored her, until everyone was gone. Then she said in a low, no-nonsense voice, "I want to hear it all."

"...uh...it's all in there." Roxanna flustered, pointed to the folder. "I didn't get the chance...."

"I don't give three hoots about the review, Rox. Don't be so stuffy. Come on, tell me. About last night."

Roxanna's lips formed an 'oh' and Zoe was sure she blushed underneath that tan. "What's to tell. You were there."

"I was? Did I enjoy myself?"

"Hell of a birthday party, don't you think?"

They stared at each other for a tick of a second, then grinned, saying nothing—understanding all.

"Are you two babies going to have an affair?" Zoe probed. "Please answer me, yes. Please. You have been driving me crazy."

Roxanna tried to dodge all this nosiness. "Maybe. Well, before you make it a house rule...."

"I guess now I have to keep you on my good side, huh, you fooling around with the landlady? Pfff, you know how to make your bed."

"Hey, you were the one...."

"I know, I know. I have a big mouth. Good. Onward, oh soldier. When you're finished with the review, let lay-out have it. I don't have time to check it. I trust you to bring me no shame."

And before Roxanna left, Zoe said, "I hope it works out, I really do."

Roxanna winked as she turned. "So do I."

So do I. So do I, played like a broken record through Zoe's mind. Oh, my God! Me and my big mouth, indeed.

It wasn't Roxanna she was afraid for; it was Becky. But hadn't she herself once said, "Don't underestimate Becky."

I must have been out of my mind, Zoe sighed.

Chapter 15

Like a great, big beetle, the station wagon inched its way along the dusty, rocky trail, snaking though the thirsty hills. Zoe was glad she had to come this way only once a year, and it wasn't only because of this...rut. She was glad to come this way only once a year because of Claire. The woman always worked on her nerves. Three hills it took for her nerves to settle, but today, today was special. Claire, Robert's second wife, bulging with their second child, was always so damn friendly (like a viper). She was so...tolerant...so patronizing in her acceptance of how Zoe had chosen to raise Bobby, so damn understanding of what Zoe was, and that she chose to live it. Well, Claire with her holier-than-thou attitude had gone and done something absolutely stupid. Claire, whom—Zoe was sure—held nightly conferences with benevolent Robert as to how to get Bobby into the clutches of her nuclear family camp, well, Claire had gone and done something absolutely marvelous!

So marvelously had she gone and done it that Bobby couldn't wait to get into the station wagon, and get the hell out of there. He did pause to wave to his father and yell that he'd see him in September. He did wave vaguely to Claire, and he had had his seat-belt on (for the first time in his life without his mother having to remind him twice) before Zoe had stepped into the car.

"...You know that white stuff, that crunchy stuff—yuk—you know, what Joanie always throws into the soup...you know, it's got all these wrinkles in it."

"Leeks?" Zoe tried.

"Yeah." (What did he care?) "But raw? And then the red stuff—beets? Well, they are hard, not boiled so they were eatable, and tomatoes...."

"I thought you liked tomatoes." Zoe stopped the car at the intersection; she had to turn left to head for Little Town where the others had probably arrived by now. She had wanted to help Joan pack, but Joan knew this routine. Zoe would be too anxious to get Bobby out of Claire's jurisdiction to be of much help, so had told her she'd do the packing. She had said, "Zoe, please go, you're working on my nerves."

After her last shift, Joan would ride up with Roxanna and Becky looking after Melissa during the three hour drive, something she didn't mind doing.

Bobby still rattled on, "And there was this stuff they grow in the garden behind the house? Green stuff...like grass...and she put that in the food and I couldn't eat a hamburger...Daddy told me they were vegetarians now. He said it was good for me to eat all those vegetables. Mom, I hate vegetables."

Zoe kept a straight face. "Vegetables are good for you, Bobby. I always told you that."

But she thought, thank you, Claire.

"Well, I'm not going back there if they make me eat that shit."

Where did he learn to say that word? He never used to.

"Bobby!" Be stern. Joan would. But she couldn't. It was hard enough keeping her face in line.

Then Bobby giggled behind his hand which he placed modestly across his face. "Daddy took me to McDonald's twice and we didn't tell her. Mom, all that ve-ge-ta-rian stuff made me shit funny...."

Zoe turned the car onto the highway and pressed down on the accelerator, speeding things up a bit. It was getting harder and harder to keep a straight face at Bobby's stand-up comedian act, especially since he wasn't trying. She couldn't wait to tell Joan about Claire's blooper, but she knew she had to say something in Claire's defense. Well, she did say 'vegetables were good for you....' "You mean diarrhea? When you change your nourishment so abruptly, it does happen that you...shit...funny."

"Oh brother, I was always hungry. Yeech." Bobby looked out the window at the parched land speeding by. "I told Daddy I didn't want to eat all that stuff...." And on and on the boy went until Zoe was ready to turn the car around, find Claire, and wring her neck. Bobby hadn't had what he was used to at home: good, solid protein. Just looking at him made her hate Claire.

128

Bobby had gone cold turkey; Bobby had lost weight. Bobby fidgeted.

Damn them to hell. If Robert wanted to keep seeing his son on weekends, he had to start taking better care of him—not turn his world upside down like he—they—had done.

"Don't worry, sweetheart. You should see what you're going to eat tonight!"

"What?" He grinned—like a shark ready to attack, showing his strong new teeth.

"It's a surprise!" It would be a surprise even if it killed her. She paused for a moment, wondering whether it was time to change the subject, and whether or not to tell him what she had wanted to talk about on their way. "Remember Melissa?"

"Yeah, she eats funny stuff too." Bobby chuckled; Zoe could have smothered him to death right that very minute. That was how much her heart went out to him, how much she loved him.

"We've talked about her being sick, right?"

"She had to go to the hospital a lot, huh? Is she dead?"

Zoe nearly choked. "Bobby, that's not funny. No, she isn't dead, but she's still sick. Something has happened and I don't want you to be afraid of her, or think she's some sort of freak or something, or that it can happen to you all of a sudden, because it can't. Okay?"

Bobby nodded, looking at her in suspense.

"Well, sweetheart, Melissa lost all her hair." She glanced over at him, sensing he didn't quite take it in. "The medicine she has been taking has made her lose all her hair. That's why she was wearing the baseball hat at Joanie's birthday, remember? She's bald. You know, like Freddie's father? Only she's completely bald. Get it?"

"Like a marble?" He asked seriously.

Zoe took care not to roll her eyes. "I don't want you to start inventing names for her, you hear me? Like marble-head or something...." Great! Put the words in his mouth.

"Oh, we've got one of them in school. Melissa is one of them too?"

"Yes, but as soon as she gets better, she'll have her hair back. Maybe sooner."

Bobby mulled over this information in his head, and Zoe

129

noticed that the further they were getting from High Chaparral, the less he fidgeted. In fact, he stopped.

Gently, Zoe said, "I'm glad you have someone like that in school, so you won't be shocked when you see her. But no calling her names, you hear?"

"They call him UFO," Bobby hee-hawed, saw his mother's displeased look, and stopped abruptly. Then he remembered another one, "Onion-head."

"Bobby, no! Okay? You'll hurt her. And Roxanna. I don't want that. Is that understood?"

"Okay. Did you pack my fishing gear?"

"I'm sure Joan packed your fishing gear. She can't wait to see you. And I'm glad to see you...." She ruffled the silk on his head. "Sorry you didn't have a nice time at the farm."

Bobby shrugged. "Oh, it was all right. Just the food...." And again he yeeched, then to Zoe's relief, started to relate how Robert had taken him along to find a goat that had run away into the mountains, and how they found the poor thing in a cave they hadn't known existed up there. And now that he was a year older, could he go on Donald's yacht with Don's parents, and fish like she had promised?

* * *

Roxanna looked over the edge of the magazine she was reading when she heard an angry, somewhat frustrated howl coming out of Melissa who sat surrounded by half-collapsed sand-castle towers near the water's edge. Bobby was performing a rain dance around this tub of children's handicraft, fast hands darting towards a checkered ball Melissa was desperately clasping to her bosom. When Bobby finally succeeded in slapping the ball away from her, it bounced into the air straight into Bobby's eagerly out-stretched hands. With arms still out, ball imprisoned between those agile fingers, he zipped away, then remembering that Melissa could not follow, he braked slightly, turned around and almost looked sorry.

"Well, it was your idea," Becky commented sleepily as she lay back down on their shared beach blanket again. "You wanted Bobby and Mel to get reacquainted now that he's back."

"I think he's playing with his life. Wait until she can run again."

"Here she comes," Becky said out of the corner of her mouth.

Melissa scrambled out of the sandy tub, and instead of standing up, started to crawl towards the two women sunning themselves.

"She's doing that again," Roxanna muttered, and raising her voice, she called out, "Mel, your leg hurting?" She saw Melissa shake her head and crawl on. "Walk, baby...stand up...." Melissa pretended not to hear, and Roxanna watched her getting closer without saying another word.

Becky said, "Roxy, it won't kill her to obey. You know, sometimes I don't recognize her...."

"Tell me about it." Roxanna sighed, shaking her head. Mel had never given up her one-girl crusade for a puppy, (every other word she said spelled 'doggie') but after she had returned home from her operation, during the time of her recuperation, the doggies next door were being shipped off to their respective owners.

One day the insistent, enthusiastic yapping (Freddie's included) that they were used to, had stopped. After Melissa held a conference with Freddie over the backyard fence, she was disconsolate, fretful and disobedient for days. Roxanna comforted her as best she could, reminding her gently that at this stage of her treatment, she wasn't allowed to have pets, but, maybe later, much much later she could. Gradually, Melissa made her peace with the whole thing.

Until Freddie's sister's cat had kittens. This was around the time Melissa was allowed to walk on the recuperating leg. She had graduated to taking short walks with her mother, or to visit Freddie. Melissa wanted a kitten. Not only did she come to loggerheads with her mother, but also with Joan. Secretly relieved, Roxanna left the explaining to Joan, not wanting to be the bearer of bad news yet again. Joan adored cats. See? She had a whole collection of cat stuffies, all sorts of sizes and colors in her bedroom. Pictures too. She had always wanted a real cat but alas, she was allergic to the cute little things.

"What's that? Allergic?" Melissa had asked suspiciously.

"An allergy is an...uh," Joan faltered, seeing Melissa's attitude, but went on bravely. "Well...not everyone has it. It's a sort of... reaction my body has to certain...stuff, like in the fall when there is all this pollen in the air? I start to sneeze, my eyes start to water, I can hardly breathe, and sometimes I get skin rashes. Cat hair does this to me too. That's why we don't have a cat around here."

Melissa decided there was a conspiracy going on. No puppy? No kitten? She went on strike.

Roxanna remembered her embarrassment—and Becky's badly concealed grin—when she was on the phone with her mother, telling how Melissa was reacting to her bi-weekly chemotherapy, telling how disobedient the child had become, when she realized her mother wasn't particularly stirred by the lament–especially not with the last part.

"Honey," she said in a dry, ironic voice, "when you were eight you went on a hunger strike because your father bought Jonathan a bike without your permission. You didn't eat for a week! Did I tell you about the rollerskates you wanted but we couldn't afford to get you? Remember? Roxanna. This child is really yours."

Roxanna shook her head again, this time to dislodge the insistent memories, and didn't notice Becky's stare as she sighed deeply. It was hard, she was thinking, to stay strict with a once model child who was starting to act her age, who was becoming difficult in a way she had not thought possible. If she could be honest with herself, she had to admit that this situation baffled her. But apparently, not Becky. Then again, Becky had easy living.

Roxanna gave up the memories and looked around. The late afternoon sun hovered above the stretch of private beach and she enjoyed listening to the murmur of tame waves a few feet away. Benign looking rocks hemmed in this part of the beach and the house, built high up against a rocky wall, perched on its weather beaten, salt encrusted foundation of piles like a vigilant pirate. The covered veranda was deep and wide. Because it only caught the late afternoon sun, it was usually cool and dark in there, a place of repose, a refuge from the midday heat.

The walls of rock also formed a natural barrier which kept out wandering tourists and lovers searching for romance or privacy. It protected this part of the beach from buffeting inland winds, allowing only a slight breeze from the sea. The water was calm, its waves sluggish. The lack of impudent ocean wind and unwanted visitors created a serenity Roxanna had forgotten existed. And then there was Becky sharing her towel.

"Mom, tell Bobby to give me back my ball!" Melissa demanded as she sprayed sand all over the place.

"Since when was it your ball, Melissa?" Becky said before Roxanna could open her mouth. "History has it that it is still Bobby's ball."

"No, it isn't." Melissa looked at her mother, thinking she'd get better results here. "Aunt Zoe says the ball belongs to all of us. Aunt Zoe said Bobby can play with his sailboats and I can play with the ball."

Roxanna held up her hand, silent warning for Becky to stay out of it. For suddenly Roxanna could hear her mother again: 'I never tried to break that iron will of yours, Roxanna. I guided it. I believe I've done well. I trust you'll do the same for Melissa because she is her mother's daughter.' And Roxanna found she could believe her mother, always had in fact, but she had never needed to act on that faith—until now.

"Aunt Zoe said that?" (Thanks a lot, Aunt Zoe) "That still doesn't make it your ball. I bet Aunt Zoe forgot to tell Bobby about the deal. You tell him the minute he gets back. And tell him—Melissa, are you listening to me?" Melissa sighed the dramatic sigh of a child misunderstood, and was about to turn to Becky in search of a better ball player. "When he gets back, tell him he's not to climb over those rocks and disappear, okay?"

"Mommy...."

"You have things to play with. Get back near the water where it's cooler. Are you too hot?"

"No," Melissa grumbled, ill-tempered, and in her childish anger, forgot to crawl back from whence she came; she walked.

"It's amazing how she resembles you, tantrums and all," Becky snickered and grinned only wider when she saw Roxanna's wordless look. Their eyes met and what Roxanna wanted to say to Becky fled her mind, perhaps because it was still a fleeting, undefined thought. Like Becky, she reacted to the pull of the magnet and turned to meet Becky who pecked her nose.

"You're beautiful with your peeling nose," Becky whispered

in the intimate space of two inches or less separating their mouths, "and I love you."

"You haven't..." Roxanna murmured, planting a tiny kiss on Becky's lips "...seen my other..." the next kiss, soft, melting, not so tiny "...peeling parts yet."

"Oh, but I will."

Their lips met and they kissed, almost sisterly at first, then their lips parted and their kiss deepened. The kiss was long, and Roxanna felt it could go on forever, but she was the first to break it up. She took Becky's face in her hands and tore her mouth away. "We're supposed to watch the kids," she breathed.

"What kids?" Becky lowered her face to Roxanna's neck. She pressed her breasts against Roxanna's, moved longingly as if she hadn't had enough the night before. Roxanna wouldn't have minded all this wriggling had Becky not been nude from the waist up. She was having trouble keeping her hands to herself, what with Becky's suggestive look. Roxanna thought she could see the sky in those deep eyes. "Let's go to the house," Becky whispered. "We can watch the kids from the window...."

Roxanna gave Becky another dry, wordless look, and Becky giggled, "You're right. The house could be on fire and I wouldn't notice."

"You'd probably think it was me." Roxanna let her eyes run along Becky's golden body when Becky moved a safe distance away, turning on her back. Roxanna reached out and brushed at the sand congregated around Becky's belly button, as an excuse perhaps, to touch her.

"Oh, God," Becky said suddenly. "Zoe and Joan'll be back with the shopping. I promised to have the potatoes peeled by then. Come up to the house with me?"

"So you can ambush me...."

"You wouldn't like it," Becky sing-songed as she rolled off the towel, and rolled and rolled, laughing. "Well, it was a nice try."

"You're a sex-maniac." Roxanna muttered, burying her head back into her magazine.

"And whose fault is that?" She pushed herself to her feet in the abrupt way she had when she made up her mind to do something she was not looking forward to. "See you later, beautiful."

134

"You can't do that Zoe."

"And why not? You didn't see him like I did. He was...he was...jeez, one more week and he would have been a basket case." Zoe slapped her T-shirt into the old rocking chair, started to strip her jeans, then realized she had forgotten about her sandals. With a harassed sigh she plumped down on the big double bed and unlaced the straps. Joan, a seasoned coparent, knew when to keep her mouth shut because it took a whole lot for Zoe to rant and rage. It took her less time to undress because she was wearing a whole lot less than Zoe. She lay down on the bed, pulling a single sheet over her body.

"I'm going to call that man tomorrow and tell him in what state I got my son back. You know what I don't understand? Robert is as big a meat gobbler as Bobby is. You know how many barbecues we had when we were married? Every weekend we had half the population of Straker trampling about the house. So I don't understand how that woman...."

"Her name is Claire, Zoe, Claire. Robert's wife. Don't call her *that woman* in front of Bobby. He'll think it'll be all right to treat her with as little respect as you are treating her."

"Oh, my God, Freudina in my house!"

"I'm sure Claire had as much trouble with Robert as she had with Bobby...."

"Bobby is a kid for Godsake!"

And a spoiled one at that, Joan wanted to say, but nobody messed with Zoe when she was on the warpath. Joan said, "That great big T-bone steak you served him for dinner will constipate him. All that meat all of a sudden—a small civilized steak would have been enough. He hardly touched his potatoes, ignored his vegetables completely." Joan chuckled suddenly. "He was looking at the salad as if it had just landed from Mars. Anyway, I don't think breaking your agreement with Robert to have Bobby for the summer is going to help your cause."

"What cause?" Zoe pulled her sheet over her nude body about to switch off the light. She didn't.

"Cause. Cause. You think I don't know you don't want to send him up there. That you're afraid Claire'll brainwash him? Zoe, some good clean country living isn't going to hurt him.

135

Especially not the vegetables...."

"You didn't see him the way I did. He was...."

"I know, I know, ready for the loony-bin."

"Have you thought of the fact that he might not want to go next summer?"

"What about the weekends? Robert would want him for the weekends."

"There are three MacDonalds between the ranch and Straker."

Joan rolled her eyes, settled her head comfortably into her pillow, showing she was ready to go to sleep.

Zoe, supporting herself on her elbows, looked down on her: "You don't seem overly worried," she said accusingly.

"The day a bunch of vegetables hold a conference on how to launch an attack on humankind and wipe us all out, then I'll worry. Right now I want to go to sleep. I want you to promise me you're not going to call your ex and complain about the vegetables he makes his son eat. Leave it alone, Zoe. Don't start rocking the boat. Claire'll jump at any excuse to let the public know that you're bringing up a male child in an all-woman camp, a lesbian one no less. God, the press will love it! Do you want all the hassle? Get off it. Promise me."

"You didn't see him the way I did," Zoe persisted and this time her voice was dangerously calm.

Joan took heed. She wouldn't win; she knew it. "Okay. We'll undo the damage that was done. I'll fix him a gourmet dinner tomorrow that'll make him forget all about Claire's vegetable garden. I'll camouflage my veggies in the sauce or something. Now stop worrying. Switch off the light, will you? Listen, sweetheart, I understand your frustration, but let's not make a big deal out of it, okay?"

Zoe shrugged.

"Switch off the light. Spoons?"

"No, it's too hot."

But it took Zoe ten seconds, and she did.

Chapter 16

Three days later all hell did break loose, but much closer to home than Joan could ever have imagined. The kids had been romping on the beach all day, especially Bobby, and had the two mothers thought that ravishing hunger would have been the result of this romping, they were mistaken. Dinner progressed in a tiresome, untidy manner. Melissa complained of painful, sunburned shoulders and made sure her Mommy saw just how painful by pointedly cringing each time she brought her spoon to her mouth. Roxanna was sure the overdose of baby powder sitting on Melissa's shoulder had taken away most of the irritation, so she let her daughter perform, until Mel's attention began to stray from eating. This was brought on by Bobby who was sitting opposite Melissa. Bobby, ignoring his mother's frequent requests to eat, had found a way to pass the time by hula-hooping an onion-ring around a greasy index finger, before finding it suitable for consumption. Melissa, always on the go to try out new things, poked her finger through one of her onion-rings, and was ready to start twirling, when suddenly, Zoe's hand shot out and tweaked Bobby's ear.

Bobby howled.

"I told you once, I told you twice, do not play with your food. Eat it! Now do you understand me?"

Both Bobby and Melissa nodded their heads and stuck their onion-rings into their mouths. That both children actually agreed on something was worth applause, and the Laurel and Hardy act was not lost on Roxanna. But one look at Zoe's face told her that, dare she laugh, Zoe would lovingly aim an onion-ring at her. To her own dismay, Roxanna felt her face flush, and then while she tried to suppress her laughter, Joan snorted like a pig.

Roxanna broke up. Joan covered her teary eyes with a hand,

137

ashamed at herself, but unable to stop sputtering. And so they sat, shoulder shaking, laughing almost apologetically.

"What's with them?" Becky asked, mildly astonished.

"Sunstroke." Zoe glared at Joan.

Bobby took advantage of his mother's distraction to make the next onion-ring disappear, and Melissa realized that if she tried really hard, she could hula-hoop three onion-rings on three different fingers.

"Melissa, stop that," cried Roxanna, voice still weak from laughter. "Eat! I don't believe you guys...."

"They're just tired," Joan remarked.

"All that sun and water and swimming is supposed to give you a snappy appetite. Aren't you kids hungry?" chimed Becky.

Zoe said, voice icy, "Bobby, I told you to eat. Right now!"

"Oh, Zoe, leave him alone," said Joan.

"I'm showing him some discipline. Do you mind? You're the one always telling me he needs more discipline."

"Why don't you work on your timing?" The sound of tiny icicles jiggling in Joan's voice was not lost on the other members of the table. "Look," Joan went on, "you're exhausted, yourself. Leave him to me. I'll...."

"I am not exhausted. I only want my son to eat, and if you don't like the way I'm handling it, well, tough luck!"

Bobby and Melissa looked at Zoe from under their eyelashes, very much aware that one of them had gotten Zoe annoyed, and that she was taking it out on Joan. During the silent spell in which Joan seemed to be considering whether to be rude in return or not, Becky prodded Melissa to eat. Roxanna said, "What's in the mashed potatoes, Becky? They're delicious."

"Well, there's real potatoes, salt, pepper, and instead of margarine, I used creamed butter."

"Mm, hidden talent there."

"Yeah, I read a mean cookbook."

Melissa's interest in her food, other than the mystery of twirling onion-rings, didn't last long. Bravely, she tried again, so concentrated that she didn't hear Joan excuse herself, leaving both the table and the house. Bobby, after a covert glance at his mother's face, ate his food steadily, without further ado.

Later, after the exhausted children had been dragged to bed,

Becky went in search of Joan who had not returned to the house by nightfall. She found her near the water's edge, watching the mesmerizing phosphoric display on the foaming surface. Becky sat down beside her and silently handed Joan a can of beer. Joan jerked off the tab with a vengeance, and gulped the liquid.

Becky tried, "She didn't mean it, Joan. Those kids were pests tonight and like you said, she's tired...."

"Oh, you don't know half of it." Joan sulked.

"Want to talk about it?"

"No, I don't. Ever since we got here all she's been talking about is how Robert—no, Claire—has been treating Bobby. So I try to make up a little for his lousy summer. I cook him nice things, I take him fishing—I nearly drowned this morning teaching him to dive under water. But do I get a 'thank you, Joan' or a 'great Joan'—does she appreciate what I do for him? Jesus, do you know the trouble you're in for?" Joan steered away so fast, and unexpectedly, that it took Becky a second or two to realize she was supposed to say something.

"I'm the one in trouble here?" She sounded bewildered, if not sorry she hadn't minded her own business.

"Of all the women you could've picked, you picked one who has a child. How could you be so stupid. Let me tell you something. Every time Zoe blows up, it's because of Bobby. You're allowed to love 'em, clean 'em up, pick up after 'em, but you're not supposed to show 'em a little discipline—not in front of Mama, especially when she's too...tired...to do it herself. It's a no-win situation...." Joan flung a minuscule pebble into the dark sea angrily. "Roxanna's got a six year old, and you're going to be in the middle of it...."

"No, I'm not." Becky shook her head. "I'm going to leave her to the mother. I'm going to mind my own business. I'm going for the mother...."

Becky giggled mischievously, quickly noticing that Joan didn't appreciate the innuendo right then. "Joanie, she's just tired. Okay? I've seen you whip Bobby into shape, you know, and I haven't heard a squeak come out of her—or wasn't she looking?" Becky couldn't help but grin again. Anything she saw as solvable she never took seriously. "Remember when you ran away after the gigantic fight you had with her, and you swore you were never coming back? Wasn't that the second time you ran away?"

"Yeah, yeah." Joan grumbled, and finished her beer.

"You came back within a week. Screaming." Becky elbowed Joan, and hee-hawed again. "Face it, Rodriguez. You can't live without your wife and child. Am I right or am I right?"

"Imagine him falling and breaking his arm and blaming it on me...."

"You were baby-sitting him."

"I was co-parenting." Joan half-screamed. "Not baby-sitting. And it's not as if I pushed him."

Becky tapped Joan's shoulder in an effort to calm her down. "Okay, okay, that was years ago. What are you going to do tonight? Sit out here and catch your death of cold? Shall I bring you another beer? A sleeping-bag?"

"Go away," Joan requested in a quiet voice, and as Becky rose obediently, Joan grabbed her by the belt loop, pulled her back down. "Thanks Becky, I know you prefer not to get involved in our family squabbles, and I think you're right, but let's not forget this lesson, huh? Thanks, I do feel better."

Becky went back inside the house, fetched another beer—for Roxanna, and went upstairs. Roxanna was prostrate on the bed, head stuck in the latest Evening magazine.

"Hi, I brought you refreshment."

"Thanks. Where have you been?"

"Out looking for Joan. She's telling her troubles to the fish. Thing is, she's pretty sensitive to people raising their voices at her. Too sensitive, if you ask me."

"There's probably a reason for that."

"Yep. Joan's parents fight like cats and dogs. She grew up in that sort of pressure-cooker atmosphere."

"Does she have bothers and sisters?"

"One sister, married, two brothers. She's the youngest. I guess by the time Joan was born, her parents were really into these yelling matches. Haven't you noticed it takes a lot—I mean a lot—for Zoe and Joan to fight?"

"So maybe they yell quietly."

"Anyway, she's out there wondering whether she's going to sue for divorce or if leaving the room was enough." Having

140

finished her own beer, Becky placed the empty can on the night-stand. Glancing at her, Roxanna realized Becky had dropped the subject completely, in fact, was impishly looking at her as if suddenly she had had a great idea—which she had. "The kids are asleep, so you've got no excuse...."

"I haven't been making exc...."

Becky made sure she shut up, and Roxanna responded, running her hands slowly along Becky's back, up and down. Then took off the flimsy blouse Becky was wearing. The world ceased to exist there and then.

And then Becky's hands faltered. She lay still, listening, trying to breathe normally.

"Becky?" Roxanna's voice, smothered, came from between Becky's breasts.

"What's that?"

"Mm?"

"Listen, can't you hear it? Someone's yelling." Becky slid off Roxanna and was enroute to the door before Roxanna knew what was happening.

"Becky?" she croaked.

"I think it's Zoe!"

Alarmed, Roxanna followed Becky. As they clattered down the stairs Roxanna, buttoning her shirt, wondered astonished, how on earth could Becky have heard anything while she hadn't? How could she have? Not with her blood on fire. Not with her mind set on only one thing....

They burst out onto the veranda, heard Zoe's frantic yelling coming from the direction of the steps leading down to the beach. They were about to head out, into the darkness toward the beach and the murmuring surf, when Zoe catapulted into the light, panting, "Big...black...thing. Jesus God, heaven! Joanie? Oh my God, where's Joanie?"

"What's going on?" Joan came running out of the house, jumped from the porch to the sand and reached for Zoe just before Zoe stumbled. Together they fell into the sand. Zoe clung to Joan, unable to speak. Her face was green-white in the light of the porch.

"Zoe, are you hurt?" Joan shook her gently, looking her over, worried. "What's the matter?"

Zoe finally managed a squeak, saying, "Big, black …thing…It moved!"

"Big black thing? What big black thing?"

"I dunno. I didn't stop to look!"

"Well, was it a person? A Martian?"

"Don't joke about it, dammit." Zoe grabbed Joan. "What were you doing inside the house? I went out there looking for you. You know I don't like you being out there in the darkness all alone by yourself."

"But what happened? Why were you yelling?" Becky asked in a low, urgent voice.

Zoe swallowed, and rattled, "I was walking along the beach, minding my own business when I tripped and fell." Reliving the whole thing made her shiver and crawl closer to Joan.

"And?" Roxanna urged.

"There's nothing on that beach to trip over!" Zoe nearly screamed saying that. "And then…it moved."

"Honey…." This was Joan, patience herself. After all, she was the nurse and had faced worse situations without losing her cool—beginning with seeing Zoe through delivery. "Relax, okay? Tell me—what moved?"

"Are you deaf or something. I just told you, I don't know. The thing I tripped over—it moved, okay? And then…and then I heard it crunch…." Zoe looked into the darkness and shivered again. Above her the threesome looked at each other.

Zoe went on shakily, "…and I could see it was black and I heard it munching. And you wanna know something else?"

"What?" Came the expected chorus.

"It wasn't alone!"

"What do you mean it wasn't…." Becky, never to be listed in the history books for performing a heroic deed in the dark, moved to stand closer to Roxanna.

"Let's go inside and discuss this over a drink, shall we?" Roxanna suggested. She pushed an eager Becky on her way, then helped Joan lift Zoe to her feet. Once inside, she poured Zoe her favorite drink. Still visibly shaken, Zoe took to it with a vengeance.

"Zoe," Roxanna began thoughtfully, "was it hard?"

"Was what hard?"

"Whatever it was you tripped over?"

"Yeah, it was. Now that you mention it. Yes, hard. Round. When I tripped over it, whatever it was...it kind of...came loose." Becky shivered dramatically. "A giant snail?"

"Man from Atlantis?" Joan wondered. "Too bad he landed on the wrong beach."

"But of course!" Becky snapped her fingers and jumped to her feet. She turned towards Roxanna and they harmonized, "Turtles!"

"Some species lay their eggs in the sand of the beach where they were hatched. Right, Rox? We should feel honored!" said Becky enthusiastically.

"A regular biologist," Zoe muttered.

"Turtles?" Joan marvelled. "Wow!" And Zoe had a field day rolling her eyes.

"Becky's right," Roxanna agreed. "At least, I hope so. I don't know if it's the time of year for turtles to lay their eggs or if this is the right continent."

"Whenever or wherever, couldn't they have waited until I went to bed?"

The threesome congregated around Zoe who had taken to the couch, and laughed.

"Oh? You think it's funny? Why don't you heroines go out and take a look?"

"Okay," said Joan laconically and stood.

Zoe's hand shot out and grabbed her arm. "In the morning might be a better idea. Don't you think so?"

"Oh?" Joan's left eyebrow wrinkled. "Do you want to know what I think? I think Zoe made up the whole thing."

"What?" Zoe sputtered.

"Well, it won't work. I will not forget your rudeness—I will not allow you to ease your way into my bed by trying this act."

"You assume an awful lot, lady!"

"I do, don't I." Joan stuck her nose into the air, and followed it all the way to the back of the house—direction: bedroom. When the door slammed all three women winced.

"What?" Zoe grumbled to herself. She finished her drink and sat there, fuming. Becky signalled Roxanna with her eyes; Roxanna nodded. To Zoe she said, "Don't you worry about those

143

turtles. It'll take them days to get up here. Good-night, sweets. Don't let the bed-bug bite."

"If the bed-bug lets me in. Come here." Zoe beckoned Roxanna who obliged. "Closer." And when Roxanna bent over, Zoe whispered in her ear, "Take it easy up there. Your bed creaks."

Roxanna didn't bat an eyelash. "So does yours. G'night."

* * *

A door slammed downstairs. Becky jumped; Roxanna, relaxed in the aftermath of love-making, couldn't be bothered.

"I think they've been at it for a while," Becky whispered. "We were too busy to hear them."

Joan's voice came clearly through, and they found themselves listening to one of Zoe and Joan's unusual, but blazing rows.

"...Ever since we got here all you've been doing is sniping at me. If I irritate you so much, why don't you go away? Because I'm sure not going to. Go back to Straker for all I care. I need this vacation! I need to be away from all the sickness and misery I see every stinking day. I need my two weeks, three weeks if you let me, goddammit!—If I keep you from your rat-race, feel free to go back to it. I'll spend my hard-earned vacation without anyone being rude to me, thank you very much. Conjo! I take enough mierda at the clinic...oh? Okay, go! I won't bother to call you selfish because you know that already—no, I will not lower my voice. I've had it with you, up to here!"

The house shook when a door slammed again. But the door was opened almost immediately. Zoe called, "Where do you think you're going?"

"None of your business where I'm going. You stay there and play with yourself. I'm going to sleep alone for the duration of my stay here too. Don't bother bringing me breakfast in bed either."

Pulling the covers over her head, Becky braced herself against Roxanna for the inevitable door bang.

"There are bugs in there," Zoe sang out loudly.

A door opened and closed once more.

"...I'll sleep on the couch—No, I'm not being childish, only fed up—No, I don't want to talk about it. Leave me alone."

144

"For Godsake," Becky prayed. "Leave her alone."

"They'll wake up the kids," said Roxanna tightening her arms around Becky. "No, wait, I think Zoe's giving up."

They heard a door click shut with unhappy finality, and silence descended on the beach house.

The turtle says, "If you dig deep enough, you'll find them."
Zoe tossed in her sleep as she dreamed.
The sea gull scratches dubiously with its outer toe at the soggy surface of the beach.
The turtle eggs it on. "Will you hurry up? We were interrupted once before, remember?"
"Are you sure they're yours? I don't steal, you know." The gull squawks.
"Sure I'm sure," says the turtle. "How else would I know where to dig?"
"You're doing the digging?" the gull asks sardonically. She cries, fussing, "Hey there's someone coming. Oh, I know her. How are ya? Where are you going? No, you don't wanna go in there."
Joan reaches out and pats the gull's snow white crest, says, "For your information, I need a vacation. I'll rent a condo or crawl underneath a stone; I need to be alone. Who knows, maybe I'll surface in Hawaii, so for now, bye bye."
Joan burrows into the hole
The turtle says, "Oh, let her go. No one will miss her. Uh-oh, there's someone else coming. Jeeheesus. Lookit that!" The turtle spins and with incredible speed, gallops across the beach and plunges into the wild surf. For a while its dark head bobs in the silver reflection of the moon on the water's surface. It calls for the gull but once, then dives under. The gull although fully at ease in its territory, and not conscious of having done anything wrong, hesitates and tries to see in the dark. Then she hears an awful snort and the earth shakes. Thump. Snort. And then another thump. Snort. Whatever it was, it was coming nearer. The gull hears a pitiful wheezing voice moaning, "I musta laid them over here, no, over there? Oh my little babies, oh, maybe over here."
When the sea gull sees the gigantic green turtle, she wants to take off, to get the hell outta there, but once again she hesitates. She only twitches her wings uncomfortably as if someone just

walked over her grave; she's curious at the sound the giant turtle is making. Instinct tells her it is not a happy sound. She backs off when the green monster lays its beady eyes on her.

"Hey, you bunch of feathers," sobs the green turtle deeply, "have you seen my babies? I musta laid them over here some place. Won't you help me look?"

"Not another one," the gull grumbles, and louder, "Sure. Oh, here's our night visitor. I guess she's coming back from her vacation. That's a pretty basket you have there. What's in it?"

Joan says, "Little turtles. I found them on Kahana Bay Beach. I love little turtles. I love little everythings. Don't you?"

The giant turtle demands, "Let me have a look in your basket."

Joan pulls back the flowered cloth and the turtle exclaims. She marvels, she claps her fore-flippers together, flap flap flap, "Oh, goody, goody, my babies. Give give give. I want to take them home. Oh they must be so dry."

But Joan is skeptical. "How do you know they're yours?"

"I'd know my babies anywhere. Give give give."

The sea gull squawks in exasperation, "Oh, give them to her. We've been here all night and I want to get home before daybreak."

"No way. Finders keepers. Let go of my basket, you bully."

The giant turtle is frantic. "Gotta take my babies to Hawaii. If you don't give me back my babies, I'll, I'll..." and the giant turtle raises some blunt flipper and swats Joan with one single thwump.

Hawaii? Zoe stirred, and in her sleep, her hand searched the space beside her; there was no one there. "Joan?" Zoe moaned. Foggy with sleep, Zoe muttered an oath, and turned over into the cool, empty space beside her on the bed.

Chapter 17

The next morning Roxanna was the first to awaken and go downstairs. Or so she thought. Bleary-eyed with sleep, she yawned her way into the kitchen, when she stopped short, blinked, thinking her eyes needed focusing, but the mirage didn't go away. Melissa and Bobby, both wearing their swim suits, sat as sweet as angels at the table having breakfast. Cornflakes adorned the floor but nonetheless....

"Good-morning, guys." She gave them both a random kiss on their heads. "You babies sleep all right?"

"I'm not a baby, Mom," Melissa protested.

"Oh, excuse me."

Bobby put an index finger to his lips and pointed beyond the kitchen counter towards the living-room. "Don't wake up Joanie," he said hush-hush. "Mom told her to sleep on the couch last night. She always does that when she's mad at her."

Amused by his view of the matter, Roxanna leaned over the counter. Joan cocooned in a sheet, was sound asleep on the couch.

"Why?" Melissa asked loudly.

"Why what?" Her mother asked while pouring orange juice for herself and the kids.

"Because dummy." Bobby was exasperated. "I just said so: Mom's mad at her, that's why."

"Mommy, are you going to make me sleep on the couch when you're mad at me?"

"Of course not," Roxanna answered absent-mindedly. "Eat your breakfast."

Upstairs, heavy footsteps came out of the bathroom, went in again—not Becky's. Becky was not a heavy-walker; she moved more like a cat on the prowl.

"Mom, can Bobby and me go out and play?"

Roxanna nodded, thinking about the footsteps which weren't Becky's. "Don't stay in the sun too long, Mel, and don't the two of you go into the water before one of us grown-ups comes down to keep an eye on you, understand?"

Bobby yelled, "Okay" as he thundered out of the house, oblivious to both the slow moving Melissa and Joan on the couch.

Joan jerked bolt upright, and clawing both sheet and hair out of her face, she yelled, "How can one sleep in this house?"

"You could move into the bedroom, Sweetheart. Morning. Want some orange juice?" Roxanna said.

"Yeah, sure. I'll go have a shower first. Scrambled eggs?"

"Okay—and get whoever's up there down here. I'll make a batch á la Salvation Army."

Halfway up the stairs, Joan met Zoe coming down carrying the cordless phone. Her eyes were downcast, her face puffy with sleep. "Hi," she said quietly, but Joan was far too busy watching her own feet move to formulate a decent answer. She pushed passed Zoe, hurrying on and nearly bumped into Becky who popped out of the bathroom like a jack-in-the-box. With toothbrush on hold, she said to Joan accusingly, "Was that the best you could do?"

"Don't start with me. Are you going to be in here much longer? I want to use the shower," Joan snapped, and Becky let her be. "If there's any water left...." Then Joan stopped as if in mid-thought, looking over her shoulder at long-gone Zoe. "She didn't take a shower—did she?"

Becky shook her head. Joan grabbed her urgently. "What was she doing with the phone in the bathroom?"

"Wanted privacy?" Becky offered to a firmly closed door.

* * *

Becky strummed her guitar in the shade of the front porch, and sang, "I seen her late last night under the street-light, I seen her late last night waiting for her lover. Buttons her coat to keep out the cold...."

"Very uplifting," Joan murmured as she clapped lethargically. The midday heat was severe, and she had brought a deck chair onto the porch to lounge in.

Nearby, Melissa leaned with her back against the chair

148

where her mother lay reading; she looked up expectantly at Becky, then at Joan who might ask for an encore. Melissa wasn't allowed out in the heat. Why, the sun had even driven hardened sun-lover Becky into retreat. Only Zoe remained in the water playing ball with Bobby. It hadn't gone unnoticed that Joan and Zoe were still keeping clear of each other, and the rest of the household were wise enough to go about their business.

"How about...?" Joan started, "how about the one about the knock. I like that one."

"Only if you promise not to howl along, okay? I hear a knock on my door, yeah, someone knocking, 'Can I, can I come in?' But I say, I say 'I am not alone'...Joan, you promised...."

"I can't help it. That's how I sing. All right, I'll shut up. Sing the chorus."

Becky took a deep breath to start up again when Joan raised her hand in a stop-sign. "Hey, is that a car I hear?" One loud honk answered her inquiry. "Who the...." She stood up and looked around the corner of the veranda. A green van was backed up half in and half out of the steep gravel driveway. The driver, his head stuck out of the window, saw Joan and called, "Can I find a Joan Rodriguez here?"

"Who wants to know?"

"Ron Daley, Little Town Express Delivery. You got an ID on you?"

Joan looked down at herself—at the black swim-suit she was wearing. "Do I look as if I—oh, never mind. Just a minute."

After Joan found and then showed Ron Daley her driver's license, he handed her a pad where she signed for a large yellow-green envelope. She thanked him and returned to the porch, awaited by two curious friends, Melissa having disappeared into the house after some forgotten toy.

"All the way out here and I still get junk mail," Joan said, flopping back on her chair.

"You don't sign for junk mail," said Becky. "What is it?"

Joan opened the envelope, turned it upside down and let the contents drop out. There was a letter, a smaller, narrow envelope and a brochure showing a bungalow, palm trees, tourists loafing about a long white beach on some obscure island. "Just what I thought. Tourist propaganda. I think this is cruel,

149

cruel, cruel, especially since I can't afford it. Let's see what the letter says." She unfolded a sheet of letterhead paper, frowned delicately, and read out loud, "Dear Ms. Rodriguez and Ms. Breckner, Thank you for your last minute reservation on August twenty-fourth. We are pleased and ready to serve you...."

"Wait a minute," Roxanna interrupted. "That's today. You didn't tell us...."

Joan read on, her voice peculiar, "...your flight leaves August twenty-nine, eleven a.m.... My flight leaves?" She dropped the letter and grabbed a smaller envelope. With adept fingers, she took out the contents—two airline tickets with boarding passes. "Look!" Joan shrieked under her breath.

"I don't believe it—you win something?" Becky picked up the letter and scanned the type-written lines, mouthing, "Where are we going? —blah, blah, blah.... Oh, here it is: *will take you to Kahana Bay Resort*.... Holy shit! You're going to...."

"Hawaii?" Joan squeaked in surprise. Becky stared at her. Bewildered, Joan stared back. Then as if someone invisible pulled their strings, they both turned to look down the beach where Zoe was being harassed by Bobby. "Nooo," Joan wailed suddenly. "She can't do this. She's trying to buy me off. I don't want to go to Hawaii."

"She's taking Joan to Hawaii—Zoe is," Becky said to Roxanna as if Roxanna wasn't sitting two feet away. And quicker, "Hey, don't expect this each time you refuse to make up."

"Damn, you mean I have the wrong lover?"

"I'm telling you, she can't do this. She...she...I don't...says who...?" Joan was speechless.

Roxanna offered, "Joan, if it's a hardship, why don't you give the tickets to Becky and me?"

Becky sighed, "I think this is the sweetest thing anybody has ever done for anybody, Joan. Go on down and make up...."

"No, I can't do that...."

Then Becky lost patience; she shovelled everything back into the envelope and slapped it into Joan's arms. "Will you go down there and make up? This is the sweetest thing...."

"I heard you the first time, Becky," said Joan wryly. Then she grinned. "I know what to do. I know how to handle her. You know

150

what?—I'm not going to tell her that I know what she has done."
Becky scolded, "That's cruel."
Joan's grin widened. "I'm going to let her taste some sweat.
Zoe Breckner needs to be taught a lesson."
"And you're going to teach her?" Roxanna asked.
"I'm going to teach her." Joan agreed.
Becky moaned, "I give up."

* * *

Roxanna heaved a half-heartedly protesting Melissa onto her back and carried her off for a nap. Had she had the strength, Melissa would have strongly objected, especially because Zoe made no attempt to cart Bobby off for his afternoon nap. But Joan's announcement that she was going to her bedroom helped.

Once Melissa was settled, Roxanna made her way to the porch where Becky drifted off on a deck chair, and Zoe lay wide awake. Twice she disturbed Becky by drumming *The Lone Ranger Overture* with nervous fingers, too absorbed in whatever was bothering her to notice Becky's pointed looks. Roxanna had already seen how restless Zoe had become, and when she began to chew on her lower lip, Roxanna knew Zoe was ready to tell her troubles.

"Hey, guys? Didn't...? Hasn't...? Wasn't...?"

"Yes?" Offered Roxanna helpfully. Both turned their heads at the sound of a car crawling on the gravel road, passing high behind the house, accompanied by laughter and loud voices giving directions over a blaring radio.

Zoe rattled, "Was there anything delivered to the house this morning?"

Roxanna and Becky looked at each other, and earned a nomination for performing the best non-committal look ever shared between two guilty people that year.

"Are you expecting something?" Roxanna queried evasively, wishing she had gone for a walk.

"Oh no. Well, yes. Something. It should have been here by now. Hell, I'm going to call and find out what 'Express' means in their motto."

After the screen-door slammed shut behind Zoe, Becky whispered loudly, "I don't like this one bit. Do you know how it makes me feel?"

"Like little Ms. Fink, right? She's going to yell at these perfectly innocent hard-working people...."

"No, she's not because I'm going to stop her." Becky was about to stand up when the screen-door burst open and Zoe reappeared.

"Where's the stupid phone? Listen, I'm going into Little Town. Keep an eye out on Bobby for me?"

"Why are you going to...." Becky began, but Zoe had already disappeared around the house. "Roxanna, I think I had better get Joan."

"I'll go stall Zoe."

"How?"

"I could try lying down in front of her car."

* * *

Drummed out of bed by Becky, and still dopey with sleep, Joan poured herself a soda in the kitchen. She ignored Zoe who, as if on cue, appeared and began to arrange pots and pans in loud fashion. The screen door banged behind kids bound for the beach.

It wasn't until she was nearly out of the house following them, that she stopped, caught by what Zoe was mumbling about to Roxanna. "They were surprised. Hah! If you say you'll deliver, deliver! Right? 'Phone in your last minute reservations. Where do you want to go? The Virgin Islands? Bermuda? Hawaii?' A valid credit card, and presto, you'll have your ticket within the hour. Roxanna, this guy tells me, he says, 'Miss, you don't have any cancellation insurance,' and I say, 'Sure I have. You advertise in my magazine and I'll lower the rate just for you, if you give me at least some of my money back, after all, it's your error.' And so I cancelled."

Roxanna saw Joan turn grey under her tan. With eyes as big as saucers she was seeking out Becky who was standing by the living room window. Becky returned the look, saying nothing, meaning nothing.

"Wh...what did you cancel?" Joan gasped, rooted to the spot.

Surprise at being spoken to by her own partner, Zoe bent over the kitchen counter. "Are you talking to me? Or Roxanna?"

"Zoe, please. What did you cancel?"

"Our wedding. No, seriously, nothing you should worry your pretty little head about. I had this small scheme going, see? But it back-fired. I'll tell you about it sometime, if you deem it profitable to talk to me, of course."

Roxanna dove into a cabinet, muffling a guffaw, but Joan was too far gone to notice. She rushed to the counter, reaching for Zoe. "I think you should uncancel everything. You made a mistake."

"I made a mistake?" Zoe's voice was Arctic.

"Yeah. I mean, no. I made the mistake. I have the tickets. I know all about it. I mean, what your scheme is. I know about it."

"I know you know." Zoe said quietly.

Joan turned and glared at Becky. "You told her!"

"No I didn't."

But Joan wasn't listening. She risked whiplash when she jerked her head round again. "You knew I had the tickets and you cancelled anyway?"

"I'll see if there are any onions left in storage," Zoe said to Roxanna.

"Zoe...." Joan followed her lover like a confused kitten. "Zoe, I didn't know you'd get mad. It was a joke...."

"Mad. Who's mad? I'm not mad." Zoe opened the door to the pantry, switched on the light before entering. "Let's see. Onions...onions, oh, there they are." She gathered up three and made leaving signs. Joan blocked her exit. " 'Scuse me. I have some spaghetti sauce to make."

"I was going to tell you tonight. I meant it as a joke. Honest. I'm sorry."

"You were going to tell me as soon as tonight? Well, like I said, I'm not mad. It was just a little joke."

"That's what I said. But if you aren't mad, why did you cancel?"

"I didn't. Like I said: it was just a little joke." Zoe closed the pantry door behind her and half tip-toed back to the kitchen where she remained standing, waiting.

Suddenly there was a muffled scream. "Zoe, you're going to eat those onions—raw!"

Zoe's reaction was flawless; she threw the onions into

153

Roxanna's general direction.... Roxanna actually caught all three, but Zoe didn't wait to check it out—she turned on her heels and banged out of the house. Joan barged out after her. From the window Roxanna and Becky watched as Joan's strong legs ploughed the sand, racing down the steps like a perfectly oiled machine behind Zoe, also making her way down those steps— but more like a bouncing ball. Zoe miraculously kept her balance until she reached the bottom where she fell flat onto the sand. Hearing Joan behind her, getting closer, Zoe shrieked in cold panic. She jumped to her feet but she was no match for Joan. She yelped when Joan threw an arm around her waist and dragged her down.

Straddling Zoe and feeling her up shamelessly, Joan demanded, "Okay, where are they?"

Zoe pointed an unwavering finger at the house. "Roxanna has them. She loves onions. You're tickling me!"

"How about sand? I bet you'll love the taste."

Zoe thrashed around like a fish on dry land. "You made me do it!" She yelled. "You thought you were so damn smart, huh? Well, you gotta be a lot smarter than that, Rodriguez. Hey, hey, if you feed me that, I'll cancel for sure."

Joan lowered her hand, but not the threat. "You will what?"

"Okay, okay, we'll go First Class, if you want. You're going to turn me on sitting on me like that."

Joan wriggled her hips, looked thoughtful. "Yeah. Hey, I like this."

"Stop it. I bet the kids are watching. Get off me." With one strong thrust of her hips, Zoe pushed Joan off balance. They rolled through the sand; one time Zoe was up, then Joan, until they lay panting in each other's arms, half-heartedly trying to roll over just one more time.

"Woah," Joan gasped. "That was great. Hell of a big bed."

They lay on their backs for a while, trying to catch their breaths. The mighty blue sky with but a few scattered clouds, ballooned above them. It was strangely quiet now that the beach grasses which usually played a constant background music in the wind, had grown still in the evening air. A lone sea gull skimmed the water, screeching, the sound perhaps warning its mate of its approach. The sea-birds had all called it a day, had all retreated to the rocks, to the nooks and crannies they had so noisily squabbled around all day. A handful of loons still scouted the water's edge, wary of any children giving chase, and soon these birds were also gone.

Both women felt this vast silence. Neither wanted to speak, neither wanted to begin, for fear of spoiling the effect.

But at last Joan spoke. "Those kids are supposed to go up for supper," which wasn't what she wanted to say.

"Roxy wants to give Melissa her time on the beach now that it's cooler," Zoe mumbled. She turned her head to look at Joan but Joan didn't respond. "Joan?"

"What?"

"I've been a nuisance, huh? I guess you put up with it longer than you should...."

"Yes, I have."

"You shouldn't have."

"That's right. And now we're going to Hawaii, without you even asking me if I want to. Do you see?"

Zoe's sigh was a defeated one. "All right," she half-snapped, "You tell me how to make amends."

"Take me to Hawaii," Joan giggled, turning her head to gaze at her lover. "What are you going to do with Bobby? Something tells me he's not going to the farm. And if he is, I don't want to go through your rantings and ravings all over again, in Hawaii I mean. To hear you carrying on, you'd think they had him in shackles up there."

"I'll ask Roxanna and Becky to look after him."

"Roxanna has plenty to deal with with Mel. Becky is supposed to get ready for another season at The Blue Notes...."

But Zoe let out a triumphant cackle. "Melissa has to go to the clinic for treatment when they get back to Straker. She'll be away from two to six weeks and Becky—well, we don't really have to ask her, do we?" Zoe started to sound as if she had been too quick on the draw. "What do you think?"

"There's no harm in asking," Joan said with a sort of finality in her voice.

Zoe brushed sand off Joan's arms, her shoulder, slapped gently at the sand in her hair. "You know, it's kind of nice...you know, Roxanna and Becky...."

"Let's hope it stays nice."

"Brother, you're supposed to be the optimist in the neighborhood."

"I don't feel so optimistic right now." Joan sighed towards the sky. She didn't elaborate, and Zoe felt very, very sorry because she knew what had brought this on.

"Oh Joannie, I'm trying to make up. Won't you let me? I love you an awful lot. Please know that. I'll fix everything, okay? I'm a great fixer."

Joan grinned. "I know that."

"We'll go away—you and me—together, alone. You'll relax, I'll relax...."

"Yeah, you'll be in the casino...."

"You too. Did you really think I had cancelled?" Zoe laughed saucily and pushed Joan backwards in the sand unexpectedly. "You should have seen your face."

Joan did her best to remain injured, refused to respond to Zoe's conciliatory kiss. "I don't think you were very funny."

"I think I was." Unperturbed, feeling Joan's momentary dark mood waning, she planted another kiss on Joan's lips. Joan didn't move away, so Zoe was encouraged. But then Joan pushed her away with a hand on her shoulder.

"If you had cancelled, I'd have filed for divorce. See how you'd like the look on your face!"

Chapter 18

Zoe fixed it, but before informing Bobby, she consulted with Roxanna who readily agreed to take care of the boy during the week and a half that she and Joan would be gone. Bobby tried not to be overjoyed when he heard that he didn't have to go to the farm as he had had to a few years back when his mother and Joan had gone to the Virgin Islands. That happiness lasted for about two seconds until he realized he wouldn't be with his mother or Joan. But Zoe talked to him, and his fallen face regained its former cheerful demeanor. On D-day he waved after the car, and the minute it turned the corner, he raced to the beach and into the water to rescue one of his sailboats which was heading out of the bay and into the Pacific Ocean.

For the rest of the household the trip back to Straker proved uneventful enabling Roxanna to slam together a schedule for the coming week and half while she drove. She'd fix breakfast for both herself and Bobby, take care of his lunch box, and cart him off to Christopher's Oval where the school bus met the East Straker children. Becky would make sure she picked him up in the afternoon—Roxanna shouldn't worry, she'd make the time—and have something to eat on the table when Roxanna got home from work. After dinner, since Becky didn't have to start at the Blue Notes for another few weeks, she could stay with him, tucking him in while Roxanna was at the clinic until nine with Melissa.

Dusk was falling when Roxanna turned into the driveway of 68 Van Buren Street. She killed the engine and stretched out thoroughly, looking at Becky dozing beside her with her head against the window. In the back the kids sprawled also conked out.

Roxanna gently tapped Becky's cheek. "Hey, psst, wake up so you can get inside and sleep."

157

"I thought we'd never get there." Becky yawned, stretched, looked over her shoulder. "We ought to unload this stuff."

"Why, yes. I was planning on you doing it. Seriously, the garage is occupied, so...what shall I do?"

"Back up onto the lawn. Like thieves, you know."

"Okay, you got your keys?"

Becky grabbed a ring of them from the dashboard. "If you need me, I'll be upstairs in the tub. Come on, Bobs, you too."

Roxanna didn't see Becky again until later, after tucking Melissa in which proved to be an adventure of its own. "Okay, young lady, stop diddling. Want me to powder your back some more? We've been a teeny careless in the sun, haven't we?"

"Yeah, but it don't hurt so much anymore." Melissa turned her back to her mother, ready to agree to anything because she loved being pampered with the white stuff.

While she applied the baby powder, Roxanna said nonchalantly, "You like Becky, don't you?"

"Yeah, she's my friend. You like her too, huh?"

"Yes, I do. You know, I'm glad you like her...Turn on your stomach...or your side—you prefer that?" Roxanna put the baby powder away, pulled the sheet over Melissa, folded it just below her armpit. "Mel, Becky has become very special to me...."

"Yeah, I know." Melissa brimmed over with sudden childlike smugness. "Becky likes you a lot and you like her a lot."

"That's right. I was going to tell you when she became my friend, but you were having all this trouble with your leg. You were having a bad time, and because you were in so much pain, so was I. I thought we'd talk when you were feeling better. And then we went to Little Town...." Melissa's eyes suddenly drooped and Roxanna wondered if she should postpone this. With the nirvana she had lived in the past weeks, she had placed Melissa on hold—done so too long perhaps. Right now Melissa's child eyes showed her understanding of the mistake and were wide open again, looking up at her mother, waiting. Roxanna knew her daughter; she believed her daughter knew her, and because they had always been honest with each other, trusted her.

"Is that why...you sleep in one bedroom now? To be together?"

"Yup. And now the three of us are going to be all together.

But with you and me it'll be just like before. Whaddayasay?"

"The three of us?" Melissa frowned a little, thinking her private thoughts. Roxanna let her. Then Melissa wondered, seriously. "Becky doesn't mind?"

"Not if you don't."

"Okay. I guess she can live with us," Melissa sighed contentedly, settled her fuzzy head on her fluffy pillow. "She didn't mind before, huh?"

"Honey?" Roxanna tried to keep the bewilderment off her face.

"Mommy...." Melissa, tired of beating around the bush, was exasperated. "She always used your bedroom when we were in Little Town, remember? I didn't mind 'cause I think...I think she thought I didn't know...and that's why she didn't ask...and now you just told me, right? And now you're going to tell her that I don't mind, and she can sleep in your bedroom, right?"

"Right."

Roxanna found Becky waiting outside Melissa's bedroom. She shut the door softly and was about to walk away, thinking Becky would follow her. She heard Becky hiccup and turned for a better look. In the dimness she had not noticed the state Becky was in. She did now. Becky's face trembled and she had tears in her eyes. Seeing Roxanna's miffed look, Becky wrapped her arms around herself, trying not to collapse against the wall with silent laughter.

Roxanna could not appreciate Becky's glee. A snort escaped her as she walked away.

"Hey...." Becky circled her arm around Roxanna's waist, held her back. "Where do you think she's been? She sure surprised you in there."

"I wasn't...er...prepared, that's all. But for the love of the Goddess, I'm never going to underestimate that child again."

"A six year old gotcha!" Becky pushed Roxanna against the wall and kissed her briefly. "We should stop meeting like this," she purred. "My place or yours?"

"Whatever. Right now all I want is a bed—small, large, made of concrete—only a mattress—I don't care."

"Great. You've got a bigger bed. Let's go back."

Roxanna backtracked obediently. The long ride from Little

Town had drained her, and then there had been Melissa's wise-guy act. But the day's hardship became yesterday's memory when the big bed came into view. She let herself fall backwards onto it, vaguely aware of Becky throwing a sheet over her prostrate body—of Becky pecking her cheek, saying that she loved her. Then she slid mercifully into sleep.

* * *

At noon the next day, Roxanna turned her Chevy into the driveway, honked once to announce their arrival, and started to speak to Bobby. But the boy had already opened the car door and was on his way to the patio, direct to the kitchen and refrigerator. Shopping, Roxanna thought to herself as she left the car, hadn't been invented for this boy. First Bobby had dragged his way out of bed and into the shower, taken forever to get dressed—all the while mumbling about why Roxanna couldn't go shopping for his back-to-school supplies all by herself. She had the list from Zoe, didn't she? And then, at the mall, Bobby had behaved as if he had invented the act of reluctant purchase. He had needed shirts, but none of the colors pleased him. Melissa had hung around in her wheelchair, resignedly waiting her turn for some attention. That never came, because while Bobby had been figuring out which lunch box he wanted, her mother had plenty of time to get her what she needed.

Then there had been the watch incident. He was supposed to buy a watch, an ordinary, inexpensive watch. But no, he had wanted a huge digital watch with the date on it, which as he had tried it on, ate his wrist, and his arm had suddenly become one big weighted calculator. "Awesome!" He had crowed, the loose monstrosity dangling while Roxanna had handed him a much more ordinary watch to match his size.

When they had finished and Zoe's list finally all checked off, it had been time to take Melissa to the clinic to leave her there.

Now Roxanna followed Bobby's tracks calmly, opened the screen door calmly, and zeroed in on the boy hanging over the kitchen table, drooling all over a plate of cooling pancakes. (She should never have mentioned that Becky had threatened to make them for lunch.) "Prince Charles? Back to the car and help me carry the bags inside. Then I want you to wash your hands.

160

Be quick about it or Becky and I–Hi, Becky–or Becky and I are going to eat these nice pancakes all by ourselves."

Bobby left the kitchen with considerably less speed than he had entered it. Roxanna let the screen door slam shut behind them. When they returned, arms full, Becky had four plates ready, and was heaping pancakes on each one. Roxanna sent Bobby off to wash his hands, and sat down to her plate full, saying, "I'm starved myself. How did you sleep?"

"Fine." Becky bent down a little and brushed her lips against Roxanna's cheek. Then she looked up. "Hey, where's Mel?"

"At the clinic...Bobby, you mean to tell me you washed your hands already?"

"At the—what's the matter with her?"

"Are you sure you didn't just look at the soap? Let me smell 'um. Okay, I'm sorry. Attack!"

But fingers clamped around Roxanna's upper-arm and she was held back. "What's Mel doing at the clinic?" Becky asked in a quiet tone of voice, "School hasn't started yet."

"She's there for a follow-up. You knew that."

"I did? You mean she went there for...treatment?"

Roxanna nodded, saying almost impatiently, "What I need is a pancake—will you let me go?" Roxanna jerked her arm, and together with Bobby, started in on the pancakes. Becky sat down opposite her, opening her mouth to speak and picking up a pancake simultaneously when the telephone rang. She stood up abruptly, went for the extension at the refrigerator, picked up the receiver, but let it drop back into its cradle just as fast.

"Roxy, how long is she going to be there?" Becky asked in a very polite voice.

Roxanna, too busy filling an empty, groaning stomach, managed to mumble, "Two weeks...." when it hit home. "Why did you hang up?"

"Why didn't you tell me she had to go today? I could've said 'see you later,'...'see you later, kid, break a leg.'"

Roxanna swallowed so she'd be able to speak, but Becky left the kitchen without another word, and Roxanna was left staring at empty space.

"Why didn't anybody have hair at that place. Are they all sick like Melissa?"

161

"Yes." She watched Bobby lick his fingers noisily. "Wanna go and find Freddie? Then come and play in the garden where I can keep an eye on you?"

"I'll go and ask him." Bobby slid off his chair with a pancake clutched in his greasy fingers as he slammed out of the kitchen. Roxanna was sure Bobby was going to tell Freddie all about them kids with no hair in that place.

Roxanna washed the dirty dishes, cleaned up the mess Becky had found necessary to make and leave behind, then busied herself unpacking what remained of the shopping, mostly Bobby's things. Melissa already had her supplies back at the clinic.

Her mind's eye recalled Melissa pulling on the long-sleeved flannel pullover—an extra Roxanna couldn't really afford—quickly, so her mother could see her in it, could see them cart her away in it. Hell, she'd probably be sick in it. Roxanna sat down heavily, and stubbornly continued picking pins out of the boy's lime and orange sweat shirt, until her sight blurred. She put her face into the plastic-smelling fabric, remembering.

When Melissa had realized they weren't going in the direction of the great big radiation machine, 'The Dinosaur,' but were going the other direction, to where she knew they were going to give her stuff that would make her sick, she had balked, and her going-away eyes spelled betrayal.

But I told her, I warned her. Chemotherapy. Radiation. In that order. But of course, she hadn't been listening....

"Are you all right?"

Roxanna jumped. She had neither heard nor seen Becky enter the kitchen, and sit down at the table. She lowered the shirt and looked at Becky who raised her left eyebrow in an 'okay, so I like to ask stupid questions.'

"Why didn't you tell me Melissa had to go in today?" Becky asked as she started to pick the pins from another shirt.

"You were..." Roxanna had to clear her throat, "...sleeping. There was no sense in waking you up."

"Yes, there was. There's something called moral support. You, of course, don't need it. You sit here and cry over some shirt...."

"Look, I'm not used to checking everything with someone—anybody—before I do it." Roxanna sounded down-right hostile.

162

Becky shrugged and nodded at the same time, noticing the bewilderment that shone clearly in her eyes. She asked quickly, "What did you get Bobby?"

"Zoe left a list of things. A lunch kit—there it is, some clothes. He's wearing the watch. Thank God she left money. Mel's growing so fast I had to get her a completely new wardrobe, so I'm broke."

"Don't worry, I'll feed you." Becky grinned, glancing at the clock above the fridge; it was one forty-five. "I have a rehearsal at two, I better be going. Will I see you tonight? Since I'm not at the club yet, you know, we could go to the movies—oh shit, what to do with Bobby?"

"I think you're baby-sitting tonight." Roxanna folded the shirt she had been working on, started to take another out of its plastic cover. "I'll be at the clinic with Melissa until she's sleeping. Or you could take him to a movie."

"Yeah, maybe I'll do that. I gotta go." Becky dumped a kiss on Roxanna's dark head and began to leave the kitchen. "When can I see her—I mean Melissa?"

"I don't know. Depends how sick she'll be...from the chemo. I'll let you know."

* * *

You shouldn't have yelled at her like that, Roxanna thought as she started up the car. She backed out of the driveway onto the street, swung the steering wheel around and pressed the accelerator down hard. The car shot forward. She drove to the clinic where she parked, locked the car, and jingle-jangled her keys all the way towards the West Wing. It was quiet all around her, not a child in sight. After the silence finally popped through her wary thoughts, she remembered it was because of nap time. And here she was jangling her keys, making enough noise to wake them all up.

Where was her head? With Melissa she was sure. The child was undergoing treatment right now. Roxanna wasn't only worried, she was feeling apprehensive, cold. God only knew how sick the child was feeling, but it still didn't make it right to yell at Becky like that. She did realize one thing—Becky knew when to lay off; she was a fast learner. Which didn't make it right.

Roxanna shook her head, entering the low-ceilinged building.

163

The receptionist, a skinny blond woman with bright blue eyes that spelled efficiency, broke off what she was saying to a dark-haired nurse drinking coffee behind her desk. She said say 'hi' to Roxanna, only to carry on talking to the nurse. Roxanna walked on into Melissa's ward. Her eyes zeroed in on Melissa's bed. All the other four beds in the room were occupied; only Melissa's bed was empty.

She sat with Melissa; her child's arm was held prisoner by a plastic tube (oh, how she wanted to rip that tube away) anchored in the hollow of her arm as it allowed fluid to rush into her body. She read fairy tales to Melissa to keep her occupied—to keep them both distracted.

Back in the recovery room where all the other beds were empty, they waited. They pretended they weren't, but they were. A nurse, knowing this procedure all too well, offered diet Coke. "It helps," she said, "we've got a special batch—or plain cola too—we leave the bottles open so they're flat. It helps stop the vomiting."

Nurses, Roxanna thought, were an under-estimated breed. Doctors had never given her any information about flat Coke. Did they know about it? Coca Cola and chemotherapy. What a laugh. Of course Coke didn't help all the kids, but it did work with Melissa. She didn't vomit if she drank a bit. Oh, maybe she allowed a tiny dribble to come up, spat it out, didn't care where. All through the episode her body balked. So Roxanna held her, held her as was her custom, singing to her, and after a while Melissa's body calmed down enough for them to start thinking of normality. Taking her child to her bed on the ward, Roxanna tucked her in, waiting for her to fall asleep, making sure she had, and then, went home. Home until the next day.

* * *

Switching off the engine and the car headlights, Roxanna was instantly wrapped in a shadowy darkness. The garage smells slowly drifted in through her open window, together with the odor of a hot engine. Behind her the garage door slid down; in her rear view mirror the gray mass seemed slowly to devour the driveway, the lights outside coming for her. But then the garage door came to rest, enveloping her, the car, the smells.

Darkness in its straight-jacket.

Roxanna let out a sigh and leaned her head on her hands which were still wrapped around the steering wheel. She was very, very tired. All afternoon and evening at the clinic and literally nothing to eat. She knew she should get out of the car, raid the fridge, and then she'd feel a lot better. But like Melissa, she had to get used to the happenings at the clinic all over again.

Suddenly, Roxanna was aware of clarity in the garage. There was no bulk of gray mass in her rear view mirror, instead she saw the driveway and the flood-light just off to the side. She turned in her seat to check what had happened when she heard a footstep beside the car; someone stood there. Roxanna jumped but it was only Becky. Swallowing her exclamation, Roxanna slumped backwards into the seat.

"Didn't you hear me come in?" Becky asked. "I scared you, huh? Give me a kiss."

"I stink. Vomit."

"Jeez, if that would kill me—come here." They pecked. Then Becky went on, "I missed you, but you can make amends. Let's go for a walk."

"I'm very tired, Becky. I'd like a bite to eat, then I'd like bed."

"We can stop at Casey's, have a foot-long crab-salad sandwich...."

Roxanna sighed. She wasn't really that hungry, but she'd like bed. "Casey's too far away...."

"Okay, no Casey's. Let's go for that walk. I'd like to talk to you." Becky stepped back to allow Roxanna out of the car. "The weather's great," Becky went on, slamming the door behind Roxanna. "There isn't a cloud in the sky, and the stars are shining like there's no tomorrow. Let's go." Becky tugged at Roxanna's arm, and reluctantly Roxanna followed.

"What about Bobby?"

"He's sleeping over at Freddie's. Come on."

"And when we come back we can have tea with the Straker Strangler, huh? Is the house locked?"

Becky was exasperated. "Yes, the house is locked. Come on. I want to talk with you."

Chapter 19

Van Buren was quiet, stretching out before them, street-lights with round light bulbs looming above them, their pools of light accentuating the ruler-straight character of the street. Some houses were dark, others alive with voices—a party somewhere. TVs blared, a couple was quarreling—their voices carrying. They didn't meet many people as they sauntered arm in arm along the street. A man walking his dog mumbled a greeting as they made way for him to pass. Two teenagers passed them, too engrossed in conversation to notice them. A car tore down the street in an obvious hurry or display of power.

As they strode along, Roxanna began to relax, made a mental note that she should take an evening stroll more often to clear the spider webs in her head—to relax.

"How was it growing up in a posh neighborhood like this?" Roxanna asked, breaking the easy, but somehow expectant silence between them.

"A horror."

"Sure." Roxanna laughed a little, thinking of her own meager childhood.

Becky said, "Eastern Straker isn't that posh. A couple of lawyers, surgeons, a King or two...." Becky snickered at her own joke, and rubbed her cheek against Roxanna's shoulder like a contented cat. "My folks entertained a lot and their snooty friends—especially my mother's—had snooty children. They were all a bunch of snoots, so I made very few friends on this block. One thing I remember well is how my mother used to dread my birthday parties—and Michael's, of course."

"Why?"

"We invited our weird friends. Weird because they were poor, you understand. Don't ask my mother where we found them. Certainly not at school. Then again, she never knew Michael and I were notorious with the crowd at the Waterfront, playing music. That's where those poor relatives came from." Becky's voice faded away, and looking at her, Roxanna noticed the frown on her face; that her gaze had turned inward, perhaps looking back on those days.

After a second or two, Becky continued, "I was probably snooty in my own right. The Snoot on the Waterfront. I'm still a snoot if I'm to believe Joan. Am I? Still a snoot?"

Roxanna squeezed Becky's arm, saying, "I'll have to study my Webster for the definition of 'snoot,' but if it means what I think it means, yes, you still are."

"Thank you." Becky looked surprisingly prim. "So I react like a runaway bulldozer sometimes. My ego probably has something to do with it."

"Or me," Roxanna said with a touch of arrogance. Then she sighed, "It wasn't your fault we couldn't get along at first...."

As they sauntered past yet another hedged in, brightly lit mansion, a dog barked its warning. Half the canine population of the neighborhood joined in, but the cacophony of alarmed dogs subsided quickly, as if they knew there really was no danger walking their streets.

Roxanna continued talking as though there had been no disturbance. "I didn't want you or anyone else to intrude in my life just then. I wanted to give it all to Melissa. I had it all planned and executed in my head. There was no place for a lover. Then you came along—well, you weren't exactly an earthquake...only...the ground shifted...a little.... Too much ground." Roxanna glanced at Becky who was pensively looking down, watching her booted feet walk. "Anything on your mind, Becky?"

"Well yes." Becky hesitated. "Melissa."

"What about Melissa?" Roxanna sighed at the starlit sky. Who mentioned shifting ground?

There was a short pause as they crossed the street for the return home, and then Becky rattled on as if making up her mind. "Ever since Bobby turned five, I've been hearing Joan and Zoe going on about a male model for him, and they fixed it, what with his father and everything. Hell, the man even obliged him further with a half brother. My brother, Michael, believe it or not, used to come over and take him to football games, played

167

basketball with him in the garden, shot hoops—you know, did things with him males are supposed to be doing, until...." Becky chuckled. "Until Zoe realized Michael wasn't doing it for the boy's benefit, but he was also coming over for...."

"Joan."

"Yup. After Zoe stopped feeling threatened by this, we sat down and...discussed it. Joan wasn't the least bit interested in him other than he was my brother, a human being—so what was the fuss? —and Zoe still wanted him for a male model but I realized Michael was going to get hurt in the end. So there we were, sitting with this great big problem...."

"How did you tell him?"

"The beauty of it is we didn't have to. Michael met Cathy and fell head over heels...." Becky chuckled again. "But all that aside, what I wanted to ask you—don't you want a male model for Melissa?"

"She has them," Roxanna answered dryly, "about ten doctors—seven males."

"Very funny." Becky sounded miffed.

Roxanna squeezed Becky's arm again in an apologizing manner. "I'm afraid I'm too busy saving her life right now. But I wasn't joking, you know. There are her doctors—not what I had in mind really—but they're central stage in her reality. We, as a household of women balance out the rest of her healing—her life. And I have a close relationship with her...and we talk when we have to. I believe in it all. Do you understand what I'm trying to tell you?"

"Yeah." Becky sighed, slowed her step even more, and, still looking at her feet, she said, "And her sex education?"

Roxanna looked at Becky. "You sure believe in sharing, don't you? Where did all this inquisitiveness come from?"

"How else am I going to know you?" Becky shrugged a little, smiled almost apologetically. "Joan and Zoe made this such an issue with Bobby, and I was just...wondering." Suddenly she sounded impatient. "I don't know my role in this. I don't even know if I can kiss you while she's watching!"

"I try to tell her what she asks, or when I believe the time is right. She will get the technicalities at school. Not that I'm going to leave it entirely in their hands. Right now it's important she reaches that certain age. What, eleven, twelve? But because both Bobby and Melissa are in a different kind of family, I think it's wise to enlighten them about their situation before school confuses the issue."

"Confuses?"

"Well, yes. Heterosexuality is the main assumption, remember? If school discusses homosexuality—and I think it will be mentioned—it will be a bit cruel to have it presented as a second-rate way of life. Because it isn't—and I want her to know that now."

"It's going to be tough on them, huh?"

"Growing up is tough on every child, isn't it? Just living is tough—walking around with a bald head is tough. I want her to have a happy, affectionate home life."

They reached the driveway, back from their loop, and started up towards the house. Becky detoured Roxanna from the front door to the back porch where it was darker, much darker. It was quiet, the silence bringing them closer.

Becky let herself into the house. A moment later the light on the back porch flashed on, and Roxanna felt safe to sit down in a garden chair.

"Want a drink?" Becky's voice came from the kitchen. Roxanna refused. Becky joined her a moment later, a long drink in her hand, and a plate full of apples and cheese for Roxanna. She placed the dish on the garden table, then sat on the ground, leaning backwards against Roxanna's knees. Roxanna put her hand gently on the crown of Becky's head, and for a while they looked silently into the darkness of the sleeping garden.

Until Becky spoke again. "You haven't answered my question, sweets. Zoe and Joan are two very affectionate people, especially with each other...."

"I've noticed." Roxanna began to munch. "Wow, I wonder if I've ever tasted anything so good—thanks, Becky."

"Oh, just a little something I whipped up....But see, they tone it down when Bobby is around. Too much. I mean, they do touch and they do kiss in front of him—a peck on the cheek. I must say they show love to the kid...."

"Isn't love the key word?"

"...and that's okay, you know?" Becky sipped her drink pen-

169

sively. "That's how we learn our worth, right? We learn to love that way—by what we see. How about us? I mean, when Melissa is around?"

"Do I really have to answer that? Melissa doesn't expect anything else, especially from me, and because she knows you're my friend. She saw our first kiss, for chrissake. I don't think she'll see anything wrong with you draped around my shoulders and kissing me." Roxanna sighed, a sigh for the future. "At least, not yet."

"Okay. Now, what about her health? You don't only underestimate me here, but you zip yourself up tighter than a zipper if anyone mentions the subject. What's the situation with her health? Aren't you supposed to talk about it?"

"It goes how it goes," Roxanna muttered, then louder, "I don't underestimate you, Becky. Thing is, you don't understand."

Becky let out a snort. "I don't understand?"

"No." It was but a mere whisper. She had unintentionally angered Becky, and because it had happened before, she knew Becky would not let it go. Right now she wished with all her heart that Becky would.

But Becky didn't this time. "Okay. Suppose I don't. So make me."

Roxanna looked up at the sky, and noticed in a detached sort of way that it was a beautiful black sky. The pinpoints of flickering stars seemed to ask her to be at peace. But nature wasn't the only thing asking.

"Don't I have the right to love her, Roxanna...the way she is? How is she, by the way? Will you have a little confidence in me? Don't I...."

Roxanna cut her off sharply. "You can love her all you want, Becky." She rose to her feet, and picked up the empty plate to take back to the kitchen. "There's one thing that bothers me though. Want to know what that is?"

"What am I doing here—waiting for the bus? Of course...."

"Lower your voice."

"I want to know what it is."

Changing her tone, Roxanna said too gently, "Please, let's talk about it some other time. I can't, I just...." She didn't wait for an answer, but went inside without looking back, and so did

170

not see Becky throw up her hands in exasperation before she, too, went inside the house.

* * *

The daylight hours have once again tiptoed into the night, and in the stillness of the room, I'll write it out for you, darling, Becky.

Roxanna bit the end of her pen, then wrote again:

I'm less vulnerable to changes these days, even the dark doesn't seem so frightening anymore. It finds me standing alone in the opened balcony doors where I hear hope chuckle, but I feel alone—alone because of the self-righteous, egotistical self-pity and guilt that I nourish like a putrid wound. Oh yes, I might as well write it.

I wanted to spare you the sore eye staring in the dark, searching for the future of a child who, if she sneezes today, could be dead tomorrow. I wanted to spare you wading the deep grim wells, sinking away into the relentless sucking mud, while reaching for the banks which aren't there. No, you don't know how bitter this stagnant water tastes, you can't know—you've never tasted my hopeless tears.

Yet sometimes when you look into my eyes, when you smile and kiss me, I think you do know, you've always known. Please know then that time was my enemy, that it blew up the bridge leading to my heart, not only to keep out the blundering tourists, but also lovers I did not plan to have. But you know that already.

And you're turning out to be so different from the carefree, live and let live character I fell in love with. Not a scatterbrain at all. It scares me. I thought I'd be safe. Whom do I love then? Did you want to try anger? Slap me in the face, waking me with insistent knocking—oh, why do you frighten me so?

Because you did underestimate her, Roxanna scolded herself, crumpling the paper, holding the ball of it in her hands. And because she wants you and you alone—no, here you cross no further; these are my boundaries....

Don't you know, Becky, in my pig-headed selfishness, I have squeezed my fears, my hopes and my helplessness all together into one big ball of sordid self-pity, not wanting to share? I don't even want to share it with a support group. Oh, it's so hard to let go. I know you want to take it all from me. I am beginning to feel

stronger though. Really. I find myself longing for your tender af-
fections, sometimes even your anger.

Roxanna tossed the crumpled paper back and forth from hand to hand. I long for laughter—mine, yours, Melissa's—ours. I long for less frustrated hope. But if I toss this to you, do you really, really want to catch it?

Chapter 20

A golden, tanned Zoe and a chocolate-brown Joan returned from Hawaii seemingly in love all over again. With their homecoming, life at 68 Van Buren Street settled down into its normal routine. Zoe and Roxanna returned to their desks, Bobby back to school, Joan to her shifts, and Becky to the final touches on her preparations for another season at the Blue Notes. Melissa, of course, was off at the clinic.

When Becky's absence from the old haunts where she had often been seen or expected to be seen became noticeable, curious friends launched a siege by telephone. Or they came by the house, only to be told that Becky couldn't come to the phone and was not to be disturbed in her sound-proof studio. The orders were hers, but rumors had a way of flying. So the cause of her sudden disappearance from her usual watering-holes became known almost before the week was through, and non-believers prayed for a speedy recovery from this brain damage, this damage of 'being in love.'

Roxanna kept finding scented lavender or oh, so tasteful cards lying about the living room with invitations for late summer parties, and not all included her, the cause of this celebrated damage. To lessen the blow Becky accepted an invitation or two, not always with Roxanna who didn't like being paraded around, not being much of a party person to begin with. Gradually things seemed to quiet down, and a few regular friends came around to visit—Cindy, of course, and Kenny, the tall brunette with bedroom eyes Roxanna had seen around before. And Roxanna noticed that Becky made a point to join Melissa and herself at the clinic's cafeteria for lunch, no matter how late she had gotten home the night before.

Becky also started to ask questions, persistently.

"Is it true that she has to give blood every day?" she asked one night after she had settled her head on her pillow, already looking asleep

Roxanna who was nearly half-way there, grumbled. "What?"

"Mel, your daughter, you know...."

Roxanna opened one eye to the darkness of the room, catching the numbers on her digital alarm-clock: ten forty-five. She felt Becky's arm heavily around her waist, one leg between hers as they lay, stomach to back warmly, cozily underneath the downy quilt required now that the nights were cooler.

"Uh-huh," Roxanna grumbled again, hoping her attitude would put Becky off and they could go to sleep—when the question sank in. Her other eye opened. "How do you know?"

"Norma Lewis told me."

"Norma...." Roxanna shifted. "Norma talks about her patients to just anybody?"

"Oh, thank you. I'm just anybody?"

But Roxanna's interest was suddenly awake. She turned into Becky's arms and frowned at the outline of her head on the pillow, but before she could think of anything to say, Becky offered softly, "How long have I been visiting Mel? Huh? I know Norma now and we were talking. I asked things, okay?"

"She has no right..."

"...To tell your very lover? People fight to have their lovers informed on medical procedures. You certainly don't tell me anything. And where does it say she can't talk about treatments?"

"Oh." Roxanna knew she sounded as lame as a deflated balloon, but hell, it was eleven and she wanted to go to sleep.

Becky wouldn't let her. "It's to check her white blood cells, right. See how they're doing?"

"Yes, oh night-person. I myself am a day-person and I'd like to—can we talk about this some other time?"

And Becky's voice was cool, sharp, cold even. "No, Roxanna. I want to talk about it now. No more later shit. You want to know why?" Becky didn't stop to take a breath. "Because I seldom get you this close up or we're making love, or you're asleep. I'm too tired or you're too tired...I get the feeling you shut me out of a lot of things in your life." Becky propped herself on one elbow. "Listen, don't you want to talk about Mel?"

"I'm not used to it," Roxanna said quietly.

"Okay, tell me. Is it true about her having to give blood every day?"

"Every single day."

"Why?"

Roxanna sighed, trying to rouse herself, and finding it surprisingly easy to answer, "It's sort of an inspection. For infection." Roxanna had to grin suddenly.

Becky laughed. "Don't start singing!"

"You hate musicals too?"

Becky pushed. "If there are too many blood cells, is this bad?"

"You ask me? Anyway, I thought you asked Norma."

Becky said, "We talked about general treatment, not patients. She was very professional in that regard, for your information. She did tell me that it's different with every child, even if the treatments are the same. So how about Mel?"

"If there aren't enough white blood cells, she has no protection. She gets an infection—the measles, a cold and pffft...." Roxanna's index finger made a slashing motion across her throat, and immediately she felt Becky's body stiffen.

"Jesus, how can you do that?" Becky swung the quilt away from her, jerked free from Roxanna's clinging, even apologizing, hands. Becky swung her legs out of bed, punched on the bedside lamp. In the yellow, shadowed light, Roxanna could see that Becky was angry; her face lacked signs of sleep. Becky started to talk rapidly, tersely, "You're so cold sometimes, you scare me! Or is that your intention, so I'll shut up and go to sleep? And never mention it again? Melissa cuts her little finger, and that's it? No protection? For chrissake, she's got cancer, not AIDS. What the fuck is going on?" Becky, in only her briefs, was pacing the floor like a madwoman. "I know I haven't...acted...as if I deserve your trust or anything—scratch that, I do! I like Melissa a lot, she's a beautiful child physically, emotionally, and I'd—am I good enough only for sex? No complications there, right?"

"You'd do anything for her?" The question came out of Roxanna, a low rumble, and out came what had simmered within her. She left the bed and approached Becky, repeating, "You'd do anything for her?"

"Yeah, yeah I would...." Becky put her hands on her hips and it was just like old times again.

175

"Well, you can't. I get this...this strange feeling you think you can buy her life. That your money—money, period—can buy her something. It can't, okay?"

"It can buy her all the treatments she needs, you hear me?"

"Yes, and so can the whole neighborhood!"

"No, we can yell as much as we want—sound-proof, remember? Is that what's bothering you—money? You've shut me out, kept me away from your feelings because of money? Oh, brother...." Becky threw up her hands in supplication. Roxanna grabbed her upper arms hard, nearly shook her.

"Becky, don't get me wrong. I'm grateful for what you've done...."

"You could have fooled me."

Roxanna hissed. "Shut up! No more. Did you hear me. No more."

"I haven't given any more." Becky tried to free herself, but Roxanna held fast. "Let me tell you something Roxanna. We O'Sheary's give to charities...." A sarcastic edge laced Becky's voice. "We sit around the table each year and...discuss it. Only this year, I didn't feel like discussing anything. I gave an order, I gave it before my turn, and the board is probably busting a gut trying to figure out why. I don't give a shit. I did it...." Becky's voice broke and she bent her head, shutting her eyes tight, "...because I'm not allowed to sit with her during the treatments, because you don't let me know what is really going on...."

"I'm sorry," Roxanna whispered, stroking Becky's bare arms, then dropping her own. "I'll get you some tissue and we'll go to bed. We'll talk. Now and in the morning, and in the afternoon, whenever we need to. You ask me what you want to know, I'll tell you. Peace?"

Becky sniffled, nodding, surprising Roxanna when she held out her hand, like a kid. And when Roxanna took that hand, Becky guided her back to the bed. Once again, they crawled under the cozy protection of the quilt, stomach to back, warmth against warmth, and the quiet, soft, regular breathing lulled them to sleep.

* * *

At her desk, Zoe took one look at her Avocado and Shrimp lunch package, and her mood dropped a notch. "Why do I always get discolored avocado? I hate black avocado. How's yours? See?"

"Have mine. No, I mean it." Roxanna, sitting close to the desk with her lunch opened up, made the switch. "I'm a sucker for avocado. As long as they're not hard as a rock, I'll eat them—you don't know what you're missing."

"I know. Thanks."

For a few second Roxanna let Zoe eat in silence. The office was quiet, abandoned, except for the sound of the air-conditioning turned up high.

"Did you talk with Philomena Lopez at the Alcohol Abuse Center?" Zoe asked around a full mouth.

"Yes."

"And?"

"I don't know," Roxanna said flatly.

"Oh? I'll put that in my monthly column, "I do not know anything about...."

"Well, Straker calls Nigel Sullivan a quack, but not Philomena Lopez and some other aides. They swear by him, that his methods work. Those who are against him say his methods are cruel and inhumane. I managed to get a hold of him when he was leaving the building, but he was in a hurry, couldn't really talk.

"He stresses a couple of points: he wants to see a healthy non-alcoholic gay community. Gays lean towards drink either because they haven't come to terms with their identity or they just find it so damn hard. He wants to break down what causes a patient's misery or blocks, and form support groups so that there is a constant positive place to express oneself. That 'deprogramming' technique is what some people say is brutal. As he puts it, 'I don't pamper.' It's all in there...cases, testimonials and also, harsh criticism—should make a good article. I hope you can read it through my sweat blobs—I don't believe this place. Is it going to be like this through what you natives call 'winter?' "

"Yes, but we call it Pneumonia Time." Zoe glanced at Roxanna's hastily scribbled notes. "I'll read this later." Zoe shut the folder, brought a shrimp to her mouth, and munched with a grimace. "I don't want to sound like a regular nag, but these shrimp have seen better days. Hey, I've been checking your hair. It's nice, long in the back like that."

"It's uncomfortable. Too long. Joan cuts hair, doesn't she?"

"Yup. But from tomorrow on she charges five bucks. She will also charge Bobby. I'll do anything to get my money back—you remember our trip to Hawaii? Cost me an arm and a leg, I tell you."

Roxanna grinned. "You're the one with the Latina lover. Tell me, is it true?"

"What?"

"That Latina women are hot-blooded, a hit in the sack...."

"You should know," Zoe countered. "Or how much Nordic blood do you have in there? It's a myth, isn't it? Just because she's Latina doesn't mean she automatically has hot blood, or that she's a hit in the sack, or...."

"All right, all right, I didn't know you'd get mad." Roxanna made as if to ward off Zoe. "Now, why did you want me here— just for the Center stuff?"

Zoe, picking her front teeth with the nail of her little finger, said, "Roxanna, the myth is correct."

After she finished straightening her face, Roxanna said, "I've got to get to the clinic. I'm having a talk with Melissa's teacher. You have fifteen minutes."

Zoe stuck her finger into a giant cup full of iced Crush, and stirred. "Okay. It's Bobby's birthday next week."

"Great. He'll be eight, right?" Roxanna restrained herself from tapping her fingers on Zoe's desk, but could not keep from glancing up at the clock hanging behind Zoe on the wall.

"Mel will be home...She's coming, when, Wednesday?"

"Yes, what about his birthday, Zoe?"

"We're giving him a party...."

"That's nice."

"And Joan and I are celebrating our anniversary. Thought we'd do it the same day, know what I mean?"

"Eight years. Who'd have figured? You!"

"Aw, come on...." But Zoe looked pleased. "What a catch I found, huh?"

"Your fifteen minutes are fast becoming ten."

Zoe took a deep breath. "It's about Melissa."

"What about...Melissa?" Roxanna looked genuinely mystified.

Zoe ploughed on. "I wanted to ask Joan to check it out but she doesn't work the West Wing any more, and she probably wouldn't have the time to go over and...check. Roxy, we're going to have kids running around the house, and it's not the noise I'm concerned about."

Their eyes met across the desk. Roxanna raised her left eyebrow, sure she was hearing things. "For God's sake, Zoe, you know Mel isn't contagious!"

"But the other kids are," Zoe said all in a rush, relieved that her reservations were out in the open. "I don't know enough about Melissa's condition and all, but can she...is she allowed to mingle this way? Some kids will have colds—they'll have every kind of germ...chicken pox, mumps, measles—what's so funny?" Because Roxanna was covering her eyes with a hand, bending her head, and her shoulders shook. "What's so funny?" Zoe said defensively. Here she was, probably making a fool of herself, and there Roxanna sat laughing at her.

"I'm trying not to cry." Roxanna catapulted out of the chair, paced to the window. "I guess it's my fault, keeping you all in the dark, not wanting to admit to things. I should be in one of Nigel Sullivan's groups! —except I don't drink, really. Not really. But I have been all blocked up, not sharing what I really have to face up to. I just didn't want to bother you people with this shit all the time, and it has slowly dawned on me that it was a big, big mistake." Roxanna turned away from the window, saying, "It was Becky who opened my eyes."

Zoe said nothing, only reached for her cigarettes.

"Don't look so smug." Roxanna grinned.

"Becky has a way with you. I don't know what she does, but she's not the only one who has found her match. Tell me. About Melissa. Do you still have some time?"

"You forget there are kids at the clinic, plenty of them. She would've been kept from them the first days of treatment, but the minute her white blood cells show a normal count, they let her out of isolation. And that's why she can come home Wednesday. Then she'll have to go back in another six weeks. And after that, if things are still okay...honey, that's why I have to go talk to her teacher. Maybe she can go to normal school now."

"Don't change the subject, Vaughan." Zoe exhaled forcefully

from her cigarette. "After that what?"

"After that, she'll have to go back for a check-up...say every three months. Then every year. Then if she comes through the next five years...she'll be...safe."

"Five years?" Zoe asked in a holy whisper. "That long?"

"Yes. That long. I do have to go now. Have the birthday party, Zoe. Everything has to go on as normal as ever. It's the best thing to do. For Mel, for us all. Ask Joan." Roxanna wriggled her fingers at Zoe. "See you later."

"Bye."

Zoe sat staring at the closed door long after Roxanna had closed it behind her. She let out a deep, weary sigh and crushed her cigarette into the ash-tray. She felt like crying—for her friend who coped emotionally, she knew not how, for Melissa, the skinny, bald kid who wasn't hers. But she could imagine what her stoic friend was going through, and then she smiled—for that friend who thawed if you knocked loud enough; smiled for Melissa who was going to make those five years, for sure.

Then Zoe started to plan parties.

Epilogue

The wind howled around the beach house. The shingles on the roof clapped in alarm, and sand splattered against the secured shutters. Inside, the children moved closer to the nearest adult, but even the adults faltered when nature's most powerful elements pushed at the house. Then the wind receded, almost reluctantly, leaving behind a charged stillness. They all huddled cozily under blankets in the living room, this after popcorn and a video on their rented VCR.

"Let me see it again," Becky demanded out of the blue; Joan knew what she meant—not the movie.

"Again?" Joan groped obediently at her throat, and came up with a small golden cross, its design gothic and embedded with diamonds. The chain was also gold, so thin you'd think it would snap at the slightest tug.

"Jeez," Becky commented, respect in her voice. She looked at Zoe. "It's beautiful. And its bribery, you know."

"Eh, well, I'm her cross to bear." Zoe grinned wickedly. "A mere trinket. I got it on sale. Fool's gold—twenty bucks."

"Ha ha. So now, let me see yours."

Joan countered quickly, "Hers? Nah, I got her a subscription to *Point of View*. A whole year!"

Joan guffawed at the idea; Zoe nodded, dead serious. "Just what I wanted. Wasn't that nice of her?" Still nodding.

Joan elbowed Zoe. "Okay, okay, show her, Zoe."

"When you're finished...?"

Finally, Zoe held out her right hand, and heads moved closer to inspect and admire the fourteen karat gold ring, the setting for a genuine Black Star sapphire.

"She likes stuff like that," Joan sighed resignedly.

"Blackmail," Becky insisted. "Your anniversary gifts are beautiful."

Joan cuddled against Zoe. "I like to invest in what I want to keep."

"Woah," Bobby commented a tad too loud. "That must've cost a lot of money." Not that he gave a hoot, but he wanted to be heard, just in case his mother, or anyone else forgot he was there. It didn't suffice that he was sandwiched in between Becky and Roxanna on one side, Zoe and Joan on the other, or that Super Heroes leaped at him from the pages of his comic book. No way. There was a mean wind blowing out there, and he didn't feel powerful himself at all.

Melissa lay stuffed under blankets on the couch, reading one of Bobby's comics. Becky rose up and threw more wood on the fire in the fire-place. Turbulent shadows thrown by the flames bounced across and off the walls around them. This didn't help Bobby in any way. Covert glances at a relaxed Melissa, made him suspicious that all wasn't lost. Even though he oh so wanted to crawl over and share the couch and read his comic book by the light of the end-table, his mother's side seemed more acceptable.

As if sensing his dilemma, Roxanna ruffled his hair, and broke the silence. "Listen to that noise out there."

Joan was shaking her head. "We should have our heads examined. Who on earth wants to come out here this late in the year?"

"I do," Zoe purred. "You know I love to be in the elements. I get all romantic."

"Can I have some more wine?" Joan stifled a yawn.

"God, how I excite her." Zoe looked at the others. "Are you going upstairs tonight?"

"Not if I have the choice," Roxanna replied promptly. "Do you really believe this measly little fire warmed up the second floor? Another thing—I don't want to be up there when the roof blows off."

"It's been up there for years, Vaughan. Oh, I know. Why don't you take Becky along? I bet the two of you can generate enough heat to warm up Mel's room too."

Joan elbowed Zoe to reproach her, but just like her partner, she wound up snickering. Roxanna looked at Becky. "I think we should just let 'em keep the fire going down here, don't you? Or should we have a competition—who can generate the highest

BTUs." And Becky fell into her arms laughing, until they were all laughing, silly with it.

After they recovered somewhat, Joan discovered something. "Hey, isn't it bed-time for the puppies?"

"No it isn't," Bobby said quickly. "Mom, can I sleep here?"

"No, you can't." Zoe consulted with Roxanna. "We can open Mel's cot in his room. They can keep each other company."

"That's a great idea. Mel?"

Melissa pretended she hadn't heard a thing, and read on as if her life depended on it. Roxanna, wise to her daughter as only she could be, winked at her cohorts. She reached out and passed her hand over the dark down which covered Melissa's head like a duckling's. "Have you seen what's growing up here? Feel it!"

All four adults did, oohing and aahing, getting up, throwing their blankets off. Shy all of a sudden, Melissa tried to shake off those thousand fingers. Then Becky growled deep down in her throat, and attacked Melissa. They struggled in play until Becky succeeded in rolling Melissa into a blanket. While she slid the rolled up, giggling child across the floor, Becky growled ferociously, "Where do you want her, Mommy?"

"Oh, leave her where I can find her in the morning."

Shortly the children were tucked in and asleep. The fire crackled with a fresh piece of cedar, and the bottle of wine was nearing its end.

"A toast," Zoe proposed solemnly. "To us. I love us all."

"Yes, a toast." Joan raised her chalice. "To our children. And don't sing it, Becky."

"To Melissa," Roxanna said. "To the future."

And Becky gulped dramatically, held her glass just as theatrically, and recited solemnly:

> *We are the music makers,*
> *the movers and shakers*
> *We are the dreamers of dreams.*

Dorothy Clarke was born in the Dutch Antilles, left for Holland at ninteen, has worked as a nurse, secretary and police officer while writing for obscure newspapers. She has travelled up and down a lot—Spain, South America and the States, always writing. She now resides in Spain.

Other Books from New Victoria

Mystery-Adventure

She Died Twice — Jessica Lauren—The remains of a child are unearthed and Emma is forced to relive the weeks leading up to Natalie's death as she searches for the murderer. ISBN 0-9-34678-34-0 ($8.95)

Woman with Red Hair—Brunel—The mystery of her mother's death takes Magalie into the swamps and the slums of France, her only clue the memory of a woman with red hair. ISBN 0-934678-30-8 ($8.95)

Death by the Riverside—Redmann—Detective Mickey Knight finds herself slugging through thugs and slogging through swamps to expose a dangerous drug ring. ISBN 0-934678-27-8 ($8.95)

Mysteries by Sarah Dreher

A Captive In Time—Stoner finds herself inexplicably transported to a small town in the Colorado Territory, time 1871. When, if ever, will she find a phone to call home? ISBN 0-934678-22-7 ($9.95)

Stoner McTavish —The first Stoner mystery—Dream lover Gwen, in danger in the Grand Tetons. *"Sensitive, funny and unabashedly sweet, Stoner McTavish is worth the read."* ($7.95) ISBN 0-934678-06-5

Something Shady— Stoner gets trapped in the clutches of the evil Dr. Millicent Tunes. *"The piece de resistance of the season...I think it's the funniest book I ever read."* ($8.95) ISBN 0-934678-07-3

Gray Magic— Stoner and Gwen head to Arizona, but a peaceful vacation turns frightening when Stoner becomes a combatant in the great struggle between the Hopi Spirits of good and evil. ($8.95) ISBN-0-934678-11-1

Adventure / Romance

Kite Maker— Van Auken—Melvina drives up to a women's bar in a spiffy new Cadillac convertible...and drives off with Sal , one of the mainstays of the community, in search of a long lost friend. ($8.95) ISBN 0-934678-32-4

Cody Angel—Whitfield—Dana looks for self-esteem and love through emotional entanglements—with her boss, with Frankie, a bike dyke, and Jerri, who enjoys sex as power. ISBN 0-934678-28-6 ($8.95)

In Unlikely Places—Béguin—Following a dream of exploring Africa, nineteenth century adventurer Lily Bascombe finds herself searching for the elusive Miss Margery Poole. ISBN 0-934578- 25-1 ($8.95)

Mari — Hilderley.—The story of the evolving relationship between Mari, an Argentinian political activist, and Judith, a New York City musician. ISBN-0-934678- 23-5 ($8.95)

Dark Horse— Lucas—Fed up with corruption in local politics, lesbian Sidney Garrett runs for mayor falling in love with a socialite campaign worker. ISBN-0-934678--21-9 ($8.95)

As The Road Curves—Dean—Ramsey, with a reputation for never having to sleep alone, takes off from a prestigious lesbian magazine on an adventure of a lifetime. ISBN 0-934678-17-0 ($8.95)

All Out—Alguire—Winning at the Olympics is Kay's all-consuming goal until a romance threatens her ability to go all out for the gold. ISBN-0-934678-16-2 ($8.95)

Look Under the Hawthorn—Frye—Stonedyke Edie Cafferty from Vermont searches for her long lost daughter and meets Anabelle, a jazz pianist looking for her birth mother. ISBN-0-934678-12-X ($7.95)

Runway at Eland Springs— Béguin—Flying supplies into the African bush, Anna gets herself into conflict with a game hunter, and finds love and support with Jilu, the woman at Eland Springs. ISBN-0-934678-10-3 ($7.95).

Promise of the Rose Stone—McKay—Mountain warrior Issa is banished to the women's compound in the living satellite where she and her lover Cleothe plan an escape with Cleothe's newborn baby. ISBN-0-934678-09-X ($7.95)

Humor

Cut Outs and Cut Ups A Fun'n Games Book for Lesbians—Dean, Wells, and Curran— Games, puzzles, astrology, paper dolls—an activity book for lesbians . ISBN-0-934678-20-0 ($8.95)

Found Goddesses: Asphalta to Viscera—Grey & Penelope—"*Found Goddesses is wonderful. I've had more fun reading it than any book in the last two years.*"—Joanna Russ. ISBN-0-934678-18-9 ($7.95)

Morgan Calabresé; The Movie—N. Dunlap- Wonderfully funny comic strips. Politics, relationships, and softball as seen through the eyes of Morgan Calabresé ISBN-0-934678-14-6 ($5.95)

Short Fiction/Plays

Secrets—Newman—The surfaces and secrets, the joys and sensuality and the conflicts of lesbian relationships are brought to life in these stories. ISBN 0-934678-24-3 ($8.95)

Lesbian Stages—"Sarah Dreher's plays are good yarns firmly centered in a Lesbian perspective with specific, complex, often contradictory (just like real people) characters." ($9.95)ISBN 0-934678-15-4   — Kate McDermott

The Names of the Moons of Mars— Schwartz—In these stories the author writes humorously as well as poignantly about our lives as women and as lesbians. ISBN-0-934678-19-7 ($8.95).

Audiotape read by author from **The Names of the Moons of Mars** ($9.95) ISBN 0-934678-26-X

History

Radical Feminists of Heterodoxy— Schwarz"—Numerous tantalizing photographs that accompany the warm lively narrative of the women and the times in which they lived." ISBN-0934678- 08-1   ($8.95)   —The Women's Studies Review

Available from your favorite bookstore or

Order directly from New Victoria Publishers, PO Box 27 Norwich, Vt. 05055